Compendium for Five

by
James Burlison

DORRANCE PUBLISHING CO., INC.
PITTSBURGH, PENNSYLVANIA 15222

ISBN # 0-8059-4724-8
Printed in the United States of America

First Printing

For information or to order additional books, please write:
Dorrance Publishing Co., Inc.
643 Smithfield Street
Pittsburgh, Pennsylvania 15222
U.S.A.

DEDICATION

This story is dedicated to my wife, Kathy. Her amazing persona is something to behold. She's like a shooting star, leaving her trail throughout our lives, demonstrating what courage, determination, and strength of heart is all about. Each day as I see her fighting her battle, I say thanks for this opportunity to acknowledge her spirit, not just as my special person but as the teacher, coach, and model to the many students and friends who she's helped over the years. My greatest hope is that she climbs her personal mountain, and her inner glow continues to shine for all of us forever, for I cannot envision life without her.

CHAPTER ONE

JB sat in the warm sun, thinking about Washington. The country would recover. *In fact,* he thought, w*e'll probably be better off, and it had been such a stroke of luck finding so many targets together in the two buildings, an opportunity too great to pass up.* He felt a twinge of sadness for the many talented, dedicated people who had been in the wrong place at the wrong time, innocently involved, but still paying the supreme price.

Susan stood looking through the window, watching JB, wondering who and what he was thinking or dreaming about. She was still reeling from the events of the past few days.

The warmth from the sun made JB drowsy. He nodded off and his mind drifted back. . . .

His early years flashed through his mind, and he was again twelve years old. *I must hurry to Mrs. Paulson's!* He pumped hard on the pedals of the old bicycle, fighting against a strong wind, panicked he would be late and miss his weekly chance to make half a dollar.

The two-lane road was lined with walnut and almond trees, overhanging limbs almost meeting. It took him ten minutes of hard pumping to reach the ranch house, and he breathed a sigh of relief when he saw the elderly woman working in the flower beds.

He called, "Hi, Mrs. Paulson; sorry I'm late!" and quickly jumped off the bicycle, leaning it against an out-building.

"Oh, hello Jimmy. It's cold today; I'm glad you're wearing the sweater I gave you." She beamed at him, pleased to see his youthful exuberance. She felt the lump rising in her throat as she thought about the long, uphill struggle he faced as an orphan, thinking, *I've taught many young people in my long lifetime. Oh how I hope someone will recognize your talents and help you along!*

1

He immediately went to work cutting grass and cleaning. She watched him struggle with the large bundle of rosebush cuttings, then went into the house to bake the chocolate cookies he loved so much.

JB was restless in his sleep as he flashed on to his job following high school when the Korean War was in full swing. The day following his eighteenth birthday he resigned and announced that he was volunteering to serve his country and would join the U.S. Navy.

CHAPTER TWO

JB was subjected to the usual battery of tests all military service volunteers endure, and at that juncture he came to the attention of a Special Section in Washington D.C. Hidden within the tests were special questions and mental exercises designed to pinpoint a certain special type of individual; it was so carefully designed that only a few of those tested had any chance to meet the criteria.

The Special Section was covertly connected with the Navy Department Computer Network and became aware of JB's existence before he reached the Recruit Training Center. The Special Section eagerly awaited the results of the additional tests to be performed upon JB's arrival in San Diego and thereafter throughout his basic training period.

The Special Section did not interfere with JB's recruit training, but his natural abilities to understand and adapt to any situation gradually drew him above his training mates. He became a recruit squad leader, learned his classroom lessons, and performed well in the physical training and sports. When the time came to select his company's Honorman, he was selected over older, more physical college types, and he proudly marched at the head of his troop during the recruit graduation exercise.

Afterwards he reported to Seattle and was immediately assigned to a troop transport ship. The Korean conflict was in full swing, and he commenced the first of many round trips, transporting military personnel between the United States and the Far East.

JB rotated from ship to ship within the Norpac group, thus serving under a variety of officers, many of whom were reservists called up for active duty. Some officers were specialists, assigned to continue Special Project's evaluation of JB and to report his progress. Their evaluation was a subtle program of mental interrogation and conditioning, designed to strengthen his already steadfast values. Their plan called for him to finish his tour of duty in San Francisco, separate from the navy at the Treasure Island Naval Station, return to civilian life, and then join the Special Project Team.

Six months after boarding his first ship, JB received orders for temporary additional duty. Upon his ship's return to Seattle, he would report to the Sand Point Naval Air Station for transportation to San Diego.

At North Island Naval Air Station in San Diego, he was met by a tough looking marine corps sergeant. JB followed the sergeant outside of the air terminal to the sergeant's car and was driven north and eastward to a military base somewhere in the desert. It was not a long drive, so he guessed it was in the vicinity of Camp Elliott where he had served his first six weeks of recruit training. They arrived at an unmarked military base, and JB delivered his orders to the officer of the day who instructed him to report to a nearby barracks. The tough-looking sergeant never left JB's side.

After checking into the barracks, the marine sergeant took JB into a private office. The sergeant stood ramrod erect, looking directly into JB's eyes for a few moments, then spoke: "You're here for special training. You're a class of one. I am just one of your instructors. You will be pushed to your limits. Do not ask any questions, pay attention to your training, and you'll be okay. My room is next door to yours, and I'm here to help you. Reveille is at 0500; good night." The sergeant left the room without another word, not offering an opportunity for JB to question him.

Still mystified, JB showered, turned off the light and lay down on his bed. He thoughtfully reviewed the day's activities, what the sergeant told him, and decided to accept whatever training was offered. He concentrated on relaxing and sleeping.

He set his mental alarm for 0430 and was up, bed made, clothes stowed, sitting quietly at his study table when the door opened just before 0500. The sergeant looked into the room, smiled to himself, and motioned for JB to follow him. They walked quietly to a small dressing room in the adjacent building and changed into warm-ups and running shoes.

They left the building, and JB jogged after the sergeant. During the next two hours, the sergeant determined JB's level of aerobic fitness. JB followed dutifully, running slowly, running fast, down the dark streets, through wooded areas, up and down steep trails, never saying a word.

As they approached their residence building, the sergeant slowed to a walk. He looked at JB and smiled. JB was soaked with perspiration; had scratches on his face and arms; and, though gasping for his breath, was walking straight and erect as was the sergeant. "Sergeant, will I be told what is going on here and what is the purpose of my training?"

A few moments passed. "Son, I am instructed to give you specific training which I am well qualified to do. I expect if whoever gave your orders wants you to know more, they will tell you. As for me, I intend to carry out my orders to the best of my ability, so my advice to you is do what you're told, learn as much as you can."

They walked along in thoughtful silence for awhile. Then the sergeant nodded to JB and said, "You'll do. Let's get a shower and some breakfast."

Following breakfast they went upstairs to the training rooms. The sergeant politely greeted the two Oriental men dressed in plain white frocks and introduced JB to his mentors. "Mr. Ikeda and Mr. Leong, may I present Jim Barrlo."

The two Oriental men politely nodded their heads toward JB, and he returned a nod to each of them.

The sergeant spoke, "I will conduct the physical training. Mr. Ikeda and Mr. Leong will teach you martial arts. Both have studied their country's martial arts since their childhoods and both have taught for more than thirty years. It is an oversimplification to say that you will learn to protect yourself, to disable your opponents, or to destroy whomever you attack. To put it bluntly, you will learn to kill."

Although JB's subconscious was prepared to accept and follow the training orders, he nevertheless felt shaken by the sergeant's stark words. He spoke, "Sergeant, Mr. Ikeda, Mr. Leong, I cannot help but feel the unanswered questions in my mind but I assure you that I will accept the training and try my best to make my training period 100 percent successful."

Neither the sergeant nor the other instructors showed any emotions or replied other than to nod their heads.

The sergeant turned and left the room with JB following.

For the next ninety days, the routine never varied. The sergeant was at his door just before 0500 each day, and his teachers worked him relentlessly, often until late evening. The sergeant taught him body conditioning and the wizened old Oriental gentlemen turned him into a silent, deadly offensive weapon.

He did not graduate, and there had never been much conversation between he and the sergeant. Today was no different but he saw respect in the sergeant's eyes when they shook hands in parting.

Soon JB was back aboard ship and told his shipmates that he had attended an advanced clerical school in San Diego. Outwardly he resumed his old shipboard routine, but secretly he continued his new mental and physical routines.

JB routinely received temporary additional duty assignments during the next thirty-six months. Each time he was met and accompanied by the sergeant. The training was expanded, each session including rigorous physical conditioning and the use of firearms and explosives. Each session added a new dimension to his overall being and new talents, combining his newly learned techniques with those learned in prior sessions. JB became more than highly expert at demolition, firearms, making and using homemade weapons—he became a deadly killing machine. Throughout his training periods JB had a nagging mental reservation about using the learned techniques, and at times during each training session he would find himself looking into the sergeant's eyes, silently begging for an explanation for the deadly weapons training. He could see and feel the compassion in the sergeant's eyes and the desire for JB to accept the training, without question. He respected the sergeant's position and refrained from asking, but the doubt remained in his mind.

JB's final temporary duty orders directed him to report to Bethesda Medical Center. Placed in isolation, he waited patiently for whatever was going to take place, thinking, *Will I finally learn the purpose of my training? Who's responsible and what's in store for me?* Shortly following his evening meal, darkness closed in on his mind and he slept.

JB awoke in a bright, sunny room. As he began sorting out his confusion, the door opened and a doctor entered JB's room. "Good morning. Looks like we'll be releasing you today. Your new orders will be here shortly. Now, let me look you over one last time." The doctor hurried through a cursory examination, looking into JB's eyes, checking his pulse and blood pressure, and listening to his heartbeat.

Soon after the doctor left the room, an orderly delivered JB's uniform, extra clothing and personal effects, and a large envelope containing his orders. The orders directed JB to proceed to Treasure Island Naval Station in San Francisco.

JB arrived at Treasure Island late on a Wednesday and reported to work at 0800 the following morning. Soon after a young officer approached him. "Good morning, Mr. Barrlo, please come with me."

He responded, "Good morning, Sir," and followed the officer. They walked briskly down the hallway, stopped at an unmarked door, and the officer knocked. JB heard the door lock release. The door opened and he followed the officer into the office. The ensign closed and locked the door and turned to JB. "Please sit at the end of the table." There were four other officers present. His eyes grew wide as he recognized them and recalled they had served aboard ships with him. Dr. Johnson sat at the other end of the table, staring at JB. JB was totally in control of himself and sat comfortably, waiting for someone to speak.

The doctor spoke, "Gentlemen, will you please leave the room. I need to speak to JB alone."

The others left the room, and after an endless wait the doctor sighed deeply, then asked, "Do you know why you're here?"

JB sat calmly, looking directly at the doctor, then replied, "I cannot imagine how or why I should know, but yes I feel I know, and of course the answer is yes." JB continued, "Perhaps I should condition my yes upon your telling me what is happening. Why have you chosen me for your project?"

JB sat quietly, waiting for answers to his questions.

"JB, my name is Johnson. I'm a medical doctor. You already know the names of the other men you saw in this room. Suffice it to say, they're also medical doctors, each specializing in a different field. We've been working with you for the past four years, training you and preparing you to be an important member of our group. Our project that you refer to is unique in that it is totally apart from any governmental or political support and direction. We are loyal United States citizens devoted to protecting our president and our country. You have been selected to become a part of our group because you have the exact qualities and talents to fill a specific position within our group. We spent several years putting together the profile, with information and requirements, and another year sifting through test results of voluntary recruits to our armed forces to find what we were looking for. You're a perfect fit."

JB sat expectantly, staring at the doctor, waiting for him to continue.

The doctor smiled and said, "Our final confirmation of success is your agreeing to join us, and I can't tell you how relieved I am to finally hear your words."

A smile crept across JB's face and he said, "This whole thing is frightening, incredible, absolutely unbelievable, but I can tell you that I'm honored to have been chosen. But I also realize that I was destined for this role. There's no yes or no, there's just the future to look forward to."

The doctor sat quietly for awhile, sighed deeply, and spoke, "JB, you are well trained and qualified to join our group. This is a long-term project, so be patient. You will be instructed how to proceed. I'm a medical doctor, specializing in memory functions of the conscious and subconscious minds. I am a loyal and dedicated servant to our president. In fact, I have known the president since we were in grammar school together, and we were together at school through college. Then I went into medicine and he went into public service and, ultimately, higher politics. We have always been close friends, so when he finally determined he could win the presidency, he asked me to join him on a special project. Our president is wealthy, so he has funded the entire project from the beginning. We named the project Compendium. As it turned out, the president's Special Project was perfect for me. I centered my career on medicine, neurosurgery, and psychiatry. I will explain Compendium to you, but first I feel that I owe you an explanation of your involvement." The doctor paused, waiting for a response.

JB sat silently, waiting for the doctor to continue.

The doctor gave a small nod and continued, "The key to the special project was finding the right individuals. Secrecy was all important, so our recruiting had to be handled very carefully. When we started our project, our president was still a senator, and our project staff consisted of three people, the president, his brother, and myself. I devised the parameters for the operatives we were seeking for the project. His brother was the Undersecretary of the Navy and arranged for me to work with the Navy Department; this enabled me to work my testing parameters into the battery of general tests given to all naval and marine corps recruits. I devised the test questions to furnish names of all potential officer candidates. Hidden within these were additional test results that pinpointed the personnel with the qualifications to become a member of our special project. I assembled a team of experts, both military and higher education, to train and condition you. You were the last of the five candidates to be selected and conditioned. Each of you were periodically sent to our special project center for temporary duty, and during your final temporary duty at Bethesda, I placed you into a new electro-hypnotic state that I've developed and opened up your subconscious mind.

"For a full day, we literally poured information into your mind. To set your mind at ease, let me give you an example. Rather than teach you a foreign language, we simply *told* your subconscious mind a complete vocabulary, proper accents, dialects, and how to use them. As a result, you *knew* the language as if you were born with it. The same thing was done with a multitude of subjects, including self-defense and a complement of military warfare information.

"When I brought you out of your hypnotic state, all of the information stored in your subconscious mind was there, ready for your use as needed. Your subconscious knowledge of literature, philosophy, arts, science, and many more subjects will be far beyond that of the instructors you will encounter when you enter college and will make your subjects easy for you to master.

"The only thing I could not implant into your mind was the actual conditioning of your body. I selected a dedicated American hero from the Marine Corps to handle that part of your training. You're well acquainted with the sergeant.

"The entire project has progressed nicely so far. All five agents are selected and at last trained and our plans called for you to bury yourself into the general population, lead a normal life and as the need arises, we will ask for your help in certain projects. The manner in which we request your help will instruct your subconscious mind in what must be done. Until then you will continue to live your life as a young man after graduating from college."

Everything the doctor said made sense. They sat silently for a few moments. Then JB asked, "May I ask you a few questions?"

"A few. . . ."

"You mentioned Compendium. What did you mean?"

"A compendium gathers together and presents the essential facts and details of a subject. It is also an abstract of a field of knowledge or of a field of work. I call the five of you my compendium. President O'Sullivan is our subject. Your field of work is to protect him and help accomplish his goal— freedom and a decent life for everyone, regardless of race, color or religion.

"Each of you is different from the others. I labeled the other four Digest, Survey, Sketch, and Precis, but you, JB, I call Apercu. You do not get bogged down in details. You go right to the heart of the matter and quickly grasp your impression of the whole situation or problem. The five of you didn't just happen. Our plan is to harness five who will think, plan, and react in all dimensions and still be able to work together as a team. I am thankful our plan is working, and I'm grateful to have found you because a team needs a leader, someone to rapidly understand the ramifications of the problem and react with speed and keen sensitivity. You are that person, and I pray that by working together we can prevent the sinister forces from taking over our country."

"Our country has the CIA, FBI, and other professional law enforcement agencies. Why did you feel the need to set up your Compendium?"

"The president determined a long time ago that our CIA and FBI cannot be trusted to handle certain sensitive matters. Further, both he and I are suspicious that not only the CIA and FBI but all of our law enforcement agencies are infiltrated."

"By whom?"

"Foreign powers, the underworld, private interest groups, you name it."

"What happens when you and the others directing the Special Project die, leave the Project, or get found out?"

"Of course we'll die, sooner or later. Even when the president completes his term or terms, the project will continue, and if any of us get found out, we're trained to resist until death. As for the Compendium, there are no written or recorded records of your names or whereabouts. If the president and myself are eliminated, the five of you will remain hidden within our country's population. I programmed your subconscious to respond to certain instances of injustice, and if any of those instances occur, you will seek out the perpetrators.

"Of course assassination plots are always contemplated against our president as well as any leader of any country in the world. I will tell you two things that you should never forget. First, the president and I do not trust the CIA, FBI, law enforcement agencies, or any political leaders. There's too much greed for money and political power. Second, one of the few automatic responses programmed into your subconscious is the threat of death to our president. If our president dies, you will not rest until you are satisfied his death was by natural cause. If our president is threatened, you will respond, and if he is assassinated, you will pursue the matter until the plot is exposed to the world and the perpetrators caught and punished. I will tell you the others have been counseled in a similar way."

They sat together quietly, not talking. Finally the doctor stood.

JB started to rise, but the doctor spoke, "Please, stay seated. It is time for me to go. I will leave you with these final words. You have an inherent goodness. That was the basis for your selection. I could not, nor have I tried to place any instructions within your subconscious that would have you do anything evil or against your basic goodness. At times you will question your actions but will always understand the ultimate need outweighs the pain and suffering inflicted upon innocents. Your mind is quite critical and it will tell you that I am telling you the truth. That is why you are calm and relaxed with me. Our president is a good and decent man. He has many faults, as does any mortal, but he sincerely believes in freedom and a better world for all people. This Special Project is his personal contribution to our country. Your participation within this Special Project is your contribution to mankind. I hope that no one ever learns of this Project, so that our only reward will be self-satisfaction in knowing that we've helped ordinary people have a better life."

JB closed his eyes and leaned back, trying to relax. His mind raced, *The sergeant, knowing how to fight, making bombs, speaking foreign languages, now, I see why the master plan the . . . .* He wondered about the other four. *Who are they? How could I recognize them?* There was no question in his mind, the doctor had been completely truthful to him. He truly felt a part of the Special Project.

He began wondering, *How can I describe myself? Should I be called programmed, conditioned, or what? I have not been changed, merely added to.* His inherent honesty and basic concept of fair play was the core they had used to build upon, and build they had done! Although his subconscious was aware of their efforts, he hadn't realized the extent of their intrusion into his inner being. It was the combination of their efforts and his innate qualities that made him a living cybernetic weapon of immeasurable limits. He was now ready.

CHAPTER THREE

JB was separated from active duty, and the days passed swiftly until it was time to enroll in college. He chose a liberal arts curriculum and looked forward to immersing himself in his studies.

He visited the college gym regularly, working hard at body conditioning. The college boxing coach had watched JB work on the heavy punching bag and asked, "JB, looks like you can use your hands, how about putting on the gloves with Cosmo?"

JB knew Cosmo was a top-rated college middleweight and thought, *Should sharpen me up and give me a good workout.* He replied, "I'm not a trained boxer, but I'd like to try. Sure, let's do it."

The coach brought Cosmo to the ring. "JB, meet Cosmo. Cosmo, meet JB." When they touched gloves, JB noticed Cosmo confidently sizing him up.

The coach said, "Cosmo, go easy on JB, and JB, try to move fast, give Cosmo something to chase. This is not a championship match, so don't try to kill each other."

Cosmo was quick with his hands and feet, but thanks to his martial arts training, JB seemed to know exactly what moves to make to avoid being hit. They boxed for two rounds before the coach stepped into the ring, stopping the fighters. "JB, thanks. You gave Cosmo the best workout he's had for a long time. You've got good speed. If you want to learn how to hit, come around for our workouts."

Cosmo eyed JB and held out his glove to shake hands. "JB, you're quick, glad I don't have to face you in our regular matches. Stay in touch and let's do this again sometime."

JB shook gloves with Cosmo, "Thanks, Cosmo. I'm afraid you're out of my class, but it's been good to meet you."

As JB walked away from Cosmo, he heard Cosmo mutter, "Out of your class, my ass!"

Even with his school studies and his extra-curricular activities, he found time to escape to the nearby ocean coast and often would take a seaside cottage down on the Monterey Peninsula to be alone.

It was during those alone times that he would ask himself, *What is my destiny, where am I headed, what is the purpose of my being? Think man, think! What exactly should I be doing with my life?* Over time, his subconscious pushed his conscious mind to an understanding of his designated purpose. At first he felt overwhelmed by the enormity of his goal, but he also felt a soothing calmness. Not understanding why, he calmly accepted the task and felt at ease with his innermost feelings of being a part of something bigger than he could see or explain. He realized all of this would take time.

JB continued frequenting the boxing gym for workouts and often sparred with Cosmo. One day he overheard the coach pleading, "Cosmo, I've been notified you are failing Literature and near failing several others. I need you on the boxing team, but if you fail any of your classes, you'll be ineligible."

"I'm trying, Coach. I go to the study lab and the library every day. I just don't understand much of what's being taught. I won't give up, I promise."

"I understand, Cosmo, but you've got to be as tough outside the ring as in it. If there's anything I can do, tell me."

After the workout, JB followed Cosmo to the library and watched while Cosmo tried to locate research materials needed for class work. JB watched Cosmo go into the stacks to retrieve books and then followed. "Hi, Cosmo, how's it going?"

"Ah, JB, this is awful. I spend so much time looking for information to help with my studies, and then many times I've selected the wrong stuff. I'm having a bitch of a time getting by."

"Look, Cosmo, I'm taking these same classes. Let me help you. You know, show you where to find your answers and help you complete your projects."

"Boy, I could sure use some help. If I don't get my grades up, I'm out of here! I'll appreciate anything you can do for me."

JB beckoned, "Let's go to the study lab and see where you need help."

In the study lab, JB discovered Cosmo's main problem was understanding what his literature professor expected in written projects. Cosmo wasted so much time on his literature projects, he didn't have enough time left to prepare for his other classes.

JB and Cosmo worked together for the next week, often until late at night, and, with JB's help, Cosmo's classroom results began to improve. In the meantime, they developed a close friendship.

By the end of the semester, all of Cosmo's grades were safely above average and when the grades were handed down, Cosmo was jubilant, "Hey, JB, let's celebrate!" During the course of the evening, Cosmo asked JB, "What are you planning to do this summer?"

"Don't know, guess I'll look for a job or maybe go to summer school."

"JB, my friend, I owe you, come to San Francisco with me! I guarantee you a job."

With Cosmo's help, JB ended up working at Anastacio's Fish Company, handling the fish and seafood and making deliveries to local markets and restaurants.

Many small fish companies operated in the wharf area, and it soon became obvious all, including Anastacio's, were in the same business–using the fish business as a front for other activities.

The hours were long, and JB worked hard sorting, packing, and delivering tons of fish to the customers.

The salmon arrived late from Eureka one day and pushed JB's deliveries into the early evening. While parking his truck, he noticed a light in the manager's office. *How unusual,* he thought. *The manager is always gone when I finish.* The area was deserted. He moved back into the darkness and waited to see if anyone had heard his arrival and might be investigating. He waited patiently for about five minutes. He heard nothing but noticed shadows and silhouettes moving about in the manager's office. He felt the hair on his neck standing, and his heart pounded as he crept silently along the side of the building, edged up to the manager's window, and listened. He heard voices cursing in a foreign language and the sound of someone being slapped and beaten. He was familiar with the building layout so he scurried quietly across the loading dock to the main entry hall, then silently down to the manager's office door. The sounds and the curses were louder, and it hit him suddenly. He understood every word! "You guinea son of a bitch, where's the money? I'm going to rip your balls off if you don't tell me!" He heard the pommeling and knew he must react quickly.

He turned the door handle, opened the door, and walked in. As a diversion, he spoke loudly, "You gave me too damn many deliveries today. There's no way I could finish before midnight!" He quickly surveyed the scene and saw a man tied to a chair in the center of the room, surrounded by five Oriental men. Three of the Orientals were big, and all looked tough and nasty. His entrance took them by surprise, and for just a moment they stood staring at him. He sprung across the room and immediately took out two of the men, one with a strong kick to his ribcage, the other with a hand chop across the throat. JB continued moving around the room and slammed his elbow into the solar plexus of a third man, crushing the man's chest as if it were a soft melon being hit by a sledge hammer. The next few seconds were a blur. The two remaining men threw whirling wire weapons toward JB, and both attempted martial arts moves. He dodged away from the whirling wire weapons, moved quickly from one to the other, and in turn dealt each a death blow.

13

The fight had lasted less than ten seconds. He turned quickly and found the man slumped against the ropes holding him in the chair. "Jesus, I hope he's alive!" The man's face was a bloody mess, his nose smashed, teeth broken, eyes swollen closed, and ears almost torn from his head. JB pressed his fingertips to the manager's throat and was relieved to find a pulse. "He's alive!" he whispered. The pulse was weak so he quickly untied the ropes and gently lowered the man to the floor. He knew he must hurry. As JB lowered the body to the floor, he knew the heart must be stimulated and the breathing passage cleared. He remembered several of the workers used narcotics regularly so he ran into the other offices searching for drugs. He found some packages of unlabeled white powder. He broke one, tasted it, sensed it was procaine, and fleetingly thought, *How could I know it's procaine, not heroin?* JB ran back to the boss's office with the package of white powder, checked the boss's breathing passage, then squeezed closed the breathing passage. When the man gasped and snorted for air, JB released his hold, and the man inhaled the white powder from JB's palm. JB checked the manager's pulse and found it strengthening. He ran to the telephone and dialed Cosmo's number. Cosmo answered and JB quickly explained what had happened.

Cosmo told him, "Stay put, someone will come immediately!"

Within minutes, four emergency ambulances, several doctors, and two car loads of big, menacing men arrived. The gunmen spread out around the area to ensure security, and the doctors prepared the manager for transport to a private hospital. The remaining three ambulance vans hauled away the dead Orientals. The entire operation took about fifteen minutes. Then they turned to him. JB thought, *Oh shit, how can I convince them I single-handedly took out the five professional hoods with my bare hands?*

Cosmo was there, and when the gunmen began pressing for an explanation, Cosmo came to JB's rescue, commanding them, "Put JB in a car and let's get to the hospital!"

The men pushed JB into the rear seat of a waiting car.

Cosmo rode in another car and reached the hospital ahead of them. He waited at the emergency entrance and motioned them to remain in the car. Cosmo walked over and spoke to JB through the open window, "He's going to be okay. They beat him pretty good, but he's a tough bastard. He couldn't see when you walked into the room because his eyes were swollen, but he prayed you were there to help. He heard the action. He said it sounded like you were using a meat ax. You know that you saved his life, don't you?"

JB shrugged.

Cosmo continued, "He knows."

"It was really nothing, you would've done the same."

"Are you kidding?" Cosmo said. "There's no way I could've taken on five pros and come out alive. Come to think of it, how did you manage?"

"I don't know," JB said. "Instinct, I guess. I'm glad he's okay."

"Look," Cosmo said, "you may not understand family ties, but you've just saved the life of my grandfather's oldest and favorite son. My grandfather will be indebted to you beyond your wildest dreams. You name it, you'll have it."

JB thought for a few moments, then offered, "I would be honored if I could meet your grandfather. Nothing more, just to be able to meet him, pay him my respects."

Cosmo gave instructions to several of the guards, got into the car, and signaled the driver to leave. The long black limousine sped away.

As Cosmo explained that JB's car was being taken care of, JB was wondering, *How and why is Cosmo suddenly the person in charge?*

Cosmo saw the wonder in JB's eyes and smiled, "You didn't save my uncle, you saved my father. I'll go with you to visit my grandfather, and I want you to know, for the rest of our lives, I'll be indebted to you for saving my papa's life."

They rode in silence the rest of the way home. When he got out of the car, Cosmo said, "I'm going back to be with my father. Don't be alarmed by the men stationed up and down the street. They're here to make sure you're okay."

JB noticed men about half a block down the street in each direction and another man across the street, hidden in a doorway. He looked back at Cosmo who said, "There's been someone watching all summer long. Now a few more. Get some rest, I'll see you soon. If you need anything, call this number." Cosmo handed him a plain white card with a telephone number.

JB sat in the darkness thinking, *The evening's events have been a stroke of luck. Walking in on those local Chinese tong bastards while they robbed a mafia kingpin. How could I have been so unobservant not to have seen Cosmo's connections?* He mused, *Cosmo is a good friend. He arranged for my job, he stood by me, and he's been open and honest with me.* His last conscious thought before sleep was, *I must be careful not to unnecessarily harm Cosmo.*

Next morning the fish company had the same hustle and bustle but most of the faces were new.

The dispatcher called JB over, "JB, you've got a new route, our regular downtown delivery. It's worth more money for you and you won't need to work late. Just so you'll know, Mr. Anastacio made the change."

The following Friday, his pay envelope was bulkier than usual. He opened the envelope to find a passport in his name with a proper photo. JB recognized the photograph. . . . *Great,* he thought, *they must have connections to be able to extract a photo from my inactive navy personnel file.* There was also a round-trip ticket to Palermo, first class.

JB's flight to Palermo was to leave at nine o'clock that evening. He hurried home to shower and pack. When he arrived, Cosmo was waiting. "Your bag is packed. Get rid of that fish smell and let's head for the airport. My grandfather will entertain us at dinner tomorrow night, and we'll leave early Sunday morning for our return trip."

JB was pleased Cosmo was going along.

They made it to the airport just after flight time, but the flight was held. They boarded the plane and settled down for the long non-stop trip to Rome with connection to Palermo.

CHAPTER FOUR

JB looked around the first class cabin, noting the only other passengers were four tough looking characters seated in the rear, two on each aisle, adjacent the entrance. He looked over at Cosmo and arched his eyebrows inquisitively.

Cosmo smiled and answered the questioning look, "My grandfather is a big stockholder in the airline. We have the main cabin and the observation deck to ourselves. He wants you to sleep well and travel undisturbed."

JB was covered by a blanket and alone when he awoke. He looked around the cabin and saw bright sunlight coming through the small round windows. He dressed quickly and went downstairs to the main cabin. He met Cosmo and Cosmo spoke, "It's almost four in the afternoon in Rome and we'll be landing soon."

No sooner did they depart Rome than it seemed they were descending into Palermo. A car and driver awaited them. They left the air terminal immediately and sped out of town, up a mountainous road. The winding road led up and up, until they were almost to the top of the mountain range. They traveled along the ridge road for a few minutes, then turned onto an unmarked side road and immediately encountered a large metal gate. Even though not a soul could be seen, the gate swung slowly inward. JB felt as though he was being watched.

At length, they stopped in front of a big white stuccoed villa. JB had seen beautiful homes before, but he thought, *Never anything like this!* It was a massive Mediterranean structure, two high stories tall with balconies at every window on the second level. The turret roofs were round and steep, while the connecting sections were square peaks. As beautiful as it was, it gave JB pause . . . *It looks like a fortress in disguise.* The roofs were too steep to allow footing, the balconies and iron work covered all the entries, and the turrets

17

at each end covered every possible direction of attack. The large circular driveway was completely open, and nearly all trees and shrubbery were more than a hundred yards from the house. The grounds were lighted in all directions, and the landscaping was beautiful, but then again he noted that the open space was covered by a manicured lawn and section after section of blooming flowers, none more than a foot high and certainly not enough to conceal an intruder. Lights were on, and a tall, gray-haired man held the front door open. They got out of the car, and Cosmo walked quickly across the front porch. Cosmo embraced the Old Man and the Old Man said, "Hello, my grandson." The Old Man kissed Cosmo in the traditional way.

Placing his arm around JB's shoulder, Cosmo orchestrated an introduction. "Grandfather, may I please present my good friend, JB."

The Old Man greeted JB with a strong embrace and as JB looked into the bearded face, he thought he saw tears welling up in the Old Man's eyes. "You have my eternal gratitude for saving the life of my son. Please, please, come into my home."

JB gauged the Old Man's age at seventy to eighty years. He was about six feet tall; trim around the middle; and, JB thought, *Probably a tough, muscular man in earlier years.* The Old Man had a chalky pallor, and with a stab of compassion, JB realized, *The Old Man is not in good health.* JB was not awed by the Old Man but he felt certain respect or, he thought, *Is it a combination of fear and respect?* His feelings were puzzling inasmuch as he suspected the Old Man had been a leader in the underworld. JB wondered, *How many men have died at his mere nod?*

The Old Man led them across the main entry hall and into a large room looking out over the valley and city below. The Old Man invited them to sit and asked his manservant to bring them wine. They did not speak for a few moments, then the Old Man asked JB to tell about the attempted extortion and the beating of Cosmo's father.

JB told the story and the Old Man sat quietly, nodding, then shaking his head.

When JB finished, the Old Man asked Cosmo to leave the room for a few minutes. "I must be alone with this fine man."

Cosmo left the room, and the Old Man turned his dark eyes upon JB and said, "I need to repay you. Please tell me what I can do for you. There's no limit."

JB sat looking at the old Man. Then in a calm, strong but quiet voice belying his young age, JB told the Old Man, "I am thankful I was able to save Cosmo's father. My reward was in helping a friend. Nothing more is needed."

The Old Man smiled, sat thinking for awhile, then replied, "I adopt you as part of my family and I'll be honored if you forever more call me grandfather."

"That will be my pleasure!"

The Old Man sat, pondering JB's reply and thinking about the reports received from his people in San Francisco. Then the Old Man said, "You did an incredible thing in killing those five Oriental hoods in such a short time, without a weapon. I am intrigued by your talents and I want to know more about you."

JB smiled knowingly at the Old Man and said, "I suspect that you have already investigated me completely. I stay fit with regular workouts and I spend some time practicing boxing with Cosmo. There's nothing more that I can say."

After some silence, the Old Man replied, "That's true."

The Old Man arose from his chair and walked to the window. Turning around, facing JB, the Old Man smiled and said, "It worries me to owe you such a favor as I am no longer a young man but we shall see. Now, let's have dinner together and honor our meeting!"

They joined Cosmo in the dining room and enjoyed a sumptuous feast of marinated calamari, grilled fish, pastas, roasted lamb, and desserts, all accompanied by vintage wines.

After much laughter and story telling, it grew late, and knowing they must leave early the next morning, the younger men retired to their rooms to sleep.

They made the early morning trip across to Rome under bright, clear, beautiful skies. They hardly had time to stop at the gift shops before their flight was announced. JB soon slept, not awakening until the plane was ready to land at San Francisco.

JB and Cosmo were met by their Friday evening driver, and they rode on in silence until they arrived at JB's apartment. "Cosmo, how can I ever repay you. This has been an incredible weekend. I feel I've been looking through stained glass and I've seen a miracle! Your grandfather is a magnificent person, and if I never see him again, it's been the greatest weekend of my life."

"It has been my pleasure, JB, you earned every moment. I'll see you soon."

CHAPTER FIVE

While sitting in the theater with Isabel one Friday evening, JB felt a hand slip into his coat pocket. He turned to look at the person, but in the darkness of the theater, he could only make out general details. The stranger left the theater, and JB waited a few minutes before excusing himself.

JB quickly looked around the lobby–it was empty. He went into the men's room, but it was also empty. He pulled the note out of his coat pocket. The note read, "Sometime before eight tomorrow morning, go to a public telephone and call 482-3590."

JB memorized the telephone number and then flushed the paper down the toilet. He returned to his seat and watched the rest of the feature.

Afterwards they stopped by the local drive-in restaurant for a snack, and then he dropped Isabel at her home. On his way home, he stopped at the all night convenience market, found a public telephone, and dialed the number. It was answered after the first ring. A man's voice said, "Hello."

JB spoke, "You asked me to call?"

"Yes. I need to speak to you secretly. Wait twenty minutes and then come to room 112 at the Capri Motel on South Main Street. Do you know the place?"

"Yes," replied JB.

The voice continued, "Do not be alarmed. I will be waiting. It is a small suite, so when you enter turn on the sitting room lamp, turn up the television set, and stand by the bedroom door. I will be in the bedroom and we can talk through the doorway."

The telephone line went dead.

How strange, JB thought, and yet it felt like a telephone call he had been waiting for. *How strange*, he thought again.

He drove around for awhile, satisfied himself he wasn't being followed, reached the motel twenty minutes later, and did as instructed.

He waited inside, unafraid but not knowing what to expect.

The door was ajar, and JB could see the man standing just inside. The man said, "My name is unimportant. I work for a special branch of our government, and we need your help. I don't know anything about you, other than an ultra top secret instruction came down from the White House that we should ask for your help. Dr. Johnson immediately dispatched me to see you. We have a situation in Europe that must be handled. I am instructed to tell you the man's name is Kay Ubu. We will deposit one hundred thousand U.S. dollars into your special account in Zurich. I will leave a new passport with a French visa, airline tickets, photographs, and information about Ubu on the bedside table. Do not bother to ask any questions. I do not know anything further." The man stepped back into the darkness of the room and then slipped out the back door.

JB made no effort to catch him or to follow; his mind was already planning how he would handle the assignment.

JB concocted an excuse to Isabel that he would need to be away for a few days and obtained permission from his professors to make up missed class work and then caught a plane to Paris.

It was midmorning when he arrived. He first visited a barber shop, then a men's clothing store, and when he walked out of the men's store, his total appearance was that of a young Frenchman. He hailed a taxi and directed the taxi driver to the Hotel Potet. There was no problem checking in, and for all the world to see, he was just another young Frenchman.

He was tired from the trip, so he slept for a few hours and then went out to find a local newspaper. He found the morning newspaper and settled down at a street cafe to enjoy an espresso and brioche.

He scoured the paper and found the item he was looking for.

Making note of the hotel where Ubu was staying, he left the cafe and hailed a taxi. He directed the taxi to a street corner near his destination, paid the driver, and got out to walk the remaining distance.

JB found the address he was looking for and rang the bell. An elderly lady opened the door slightly and asked, "Who do you want?"

"*Bon jour,* Madam, I need to see Cabal. Please tell him that JB is here."

She closed the door and he waited the short time it took her to return. She directed him down the hall to Cabal's apartment.

JB went down the hallway and knocked lightly on the door. The door opened and he entered. Inside the room, JB faced a small, wrinkled old man who stood wordlessly, looking at him.

JB said, "I need a large caliber pistol with a long barrel and a silencer. I also need six rounds of ammunition for the gun. I need it now."

The old Frenchman looked at him, then, without saying a word, went to the desk, opened the top drawer, and took out a box. He walked over to JB, handed him the box, and said, "I've been expecting you. It's sighted and loaded. It is already paid for. Please go, *mon ami*."

JB went directly back to his rented room. He opened the box and found a long barrel .44-caliber magnum equipped with a Waukesha silencer. The gun was loaded with six rounds of extra load titanium tipped bullets. The silencer was the best available, and the bullets would explode soft tissue or almost anything for that matter.

He lay down on his bed for a short nap and to wait for darkness.

In early evening, JB began walking the streets looking for an unattended, unlocked motor scooter or bicycle.

He spotted a Vespa scooter parked in an alleyway next to a restaurant, locked with the front wheel turned. He checked to make sure no one was around or watching as he quickly picked the lock and then pushed the scooter to the other end of the alley.

Without a key, it took him a few seconds to bypass the ignition. Then he started the scooter and leisurely drove away.

He drove toward the center of the city until he approached L'Hotel Cinc. He drove on up the street adjacent the hotel, looking for an alley.

In the second block from the hotel, he turned into an alley, made certain it was not a cul-de-sac, then parked alongside several other scooters. He locked the front wheel with the cable lock he had purchased earlier in the day.

It was a warm evening, and he joined the strollers heading up the street toward the hotel.

He looked at the row of waiting limousines, and he spotted the official flag he was looking for. It was the third limousine back, so it would be picking up its passengers soon.

JB waited in the shadows of the marble columns in front of the bank next door to the hotel, about one hundred feet from the passenger loading zone in front of the hotel. He slipped out the pistol and silencer, coupled them together, and stood waiting, the gun hanging down by his side.

His target appeared at the front door of the hotel, and as he descended the front steps toward the waiting limousine, JB calmly raised the gun and shot his target through the right temple. He had fired three shots in about half a second. The first two shots had hit the target but the third bullet, having nothing left to hit, traveled on and ricocheted off the front wall of the hotel. The target was dead before he slumped to the sidewalk and blood and brains were splattered all around.

Suddenly there was much confusion around the front of the hotel. There had been no pistol shot noise, just the slap, slap of the first two bullets striking the head of the target, and there the whining ricochet of the third bullet.

By the time the doorman looked around and the escorts from the limousine had jumped out to see what was happening, JB slipped around the marble columns and reentered the flow of pedestrians.

JB heard the shouting followed by screaming. He and the other pedestrians stopped and looked back. Not seeing what was happening, several people continued walking away from the hotel. He joined them, thinking, *Requiescat in pace. May he rest in peace.*

JB entered the alley where his scooter was parked, unlocked the scooter, started up the motor, and drove down the alley, away from the hotel. He moved out of the alley in less than one minute after the assassination and was several blocks down the adjacent street before he heard the police sirens.

JB drove back to the outskirts of town; broke down the pistol into its many parts; and disposed of those parts into the dirty, slow moving Noir River. The pistol itself was untraceable, but he felt compelled to dispose of it piece by piece.

JB motored back toward the nightlife section of the city, parked the scooter among many others, and went back to his hotel. All the time he wore flesh colored latex gloves which he now tossed into a refuse can.

The president looked up as his aide entered the office.

"Good morning, Mr. President, here is your morning report." The aide placed the printed report on the president's desk, next to the coffee tray, then turned and left the office.

The president waited until the door closed, then picked up the report and began scanning the first page. His eye caught the headline, "Assassin Strikes," and the president focused on the item. "Kay Ubu, leader of the South Africa Revolutionary Congress, was shot and killed early last evening by an unidentified gunman. Police say the slaying appears to be a political assassination and the work of a professional. The SARC claims it was the work of the white South African government. A government spokesman in Pretoria has denied the responsibility . . . ."

The president slammed the report down and let his head drop down, his forehead resting on his hand, supported by his elbow on the desk. He sat motionless for several minutes, then picked up his telephone and punched the number one redial button.

The telephone rang only once before it was picked up.

"Good morning, Mr. President."

The president asked, "Have you confirmed the results?"

"It is confirmed, sir. We had an agent present. He witnessed the event but saw no sign of the participant."

The president dropped the telephone back into its cradle, turned his chair so that he sat looking out over the White House rose garden. He thought, *Life can be so brutal, but it was something that had to be done. It will set the revolution back a least a year and will stall the communist takeover of South Africa.* His mind raced ahead to the problem in Central America and a solution he had been thinking about for some time.

JB left Paris early the next morning. The flight to San Francisco was routine, and he was able to relax and drowse, catching up on his rest. While en route, his thoughts turned to Isabel. They had been dating, and he yearned to see her and be with her again. Their relationship was moving slowly, and he thought, with despair, *Why, why don't her parents like me? Why do they go out of their way to keep us apart?* It was true. He spent many weekends alone because Isabel was compelled to spend time with her parents or in helping at home. JB could see her anguish when she explained away her parents' possessiveness and their opposition to her social life. He accepted her thoughts that it wasn't him but that her parents would object to her dating any young man. Invariably he would end up meeting her downtown for a movie date or a school dance date. They had kissed many times, and he now longed to feel her lips again, even the quick little smooches she offered as they met around the school campus. He dozed and dreamed of her.

He arrived in San Francisco before noon and was back home by late afternoon.

He had a tentative movie date with Isabel, so he called her from San Francisco and told her he would meet her at half past six.

They spent a comfortable evening and he resumed college classes the following day.

Several days later, a plain white envelope slipped under his front door. Inside he found a small square piece of white paper which read, "Deposit made in Union Bank of Switzerland; access is by fingerprint."

CHAPTER SIX

JB was falling more and more in love with Isabel, and by now she was crazy for him. She attended college but only to be near him. Her one and only wish was for her and JB to be married. They spent many hours together, and invariably he would want to make love to her. They petted passionately, and he told her again and again that he loved her, wanted to marry her, but could not until he finished his schooling. She steadfastly held her ground that their lovemaking should wait until marriage.

The school year was drawing to a close and JB started thinking about the upcoming summer vacation time. He looked forward to seeing his good pal Cosmo but wasn't sure he wanted to spend the summer handling fish. A plan was developing in his mind. He had been thinking that he should try to visit the Old Man, so he would call Cosmo and suggest they take a trip to Italy. For years he read and heard about the Amalfi Coast area, south of Naples, and was drawn to the area by those stories.

He called Cosmo that evening and told him the plan.

"Sounds like a great idea," Cosmo said, "but I'm sorry, I can't make it. I'm running the fish company and I can't leave during the heavy fishing season."

JB said, "You've helped me lots, Cosmo, so I'm not about to bail out on you. I'm coming to San Francisco to help you work the fish, and we can have some good times this summer."

Cosmo immediately and emphatically said, "No way! You're going to Italy, and while you're there you'll see my grandfather. It will make him very happy."

"Look Cosmo, maybe we can work together this summer and then both go to Italy next year."

"I told you, no way! It's settled," stormed Cosmo. They made plans to get together when JB returned from Italy.

JB saw Isabel that evening and told her his plans, "I've wanted to visit Italy, and since you'll be away with your family for most of the summer, I've got to get away too or I'll lose my mind over missing you."

She was saddened by the idea of not seeing him for such a long time, but she understood his need for diversion. They parked in a darkened off road spot outside of town, and they spent the rest of their time together that evening embracing, kissing, and gently exploring their love for each other. They breathlessly whispered undying love to one another and talked about marriage at the end of the following school year, and although another year seemed like an eternity, the thought of marriage contented her.

Soon the school year was over, and after saying some passionate good-byes to Isabel, he was on his way to Zurich.

It was tourist season, and the plane was fully loaded with passengers. He splurged his last few dollars for a first class ticket, so he traveled comfortably.

He slept most of the way to Zurich.

The plane landed at noon and he immediately went to the Union Bank. There he arranged a withdrawal of twenty-five thousand dollars, some in U.S. travelers cheques and the balance in lira.

JB checked into the Hotel Limmat and placed a telephone call to the Old Man in Palermo.

The Old Man was delighted with the telephone call and said, "I am pleased that you called me. It would make me very happy if you would come to visit me. Please, excuse my short invitation, but I just learned of your visit yesterday."

JB said, "I am honored with your invitation and I'll come tomorrow. I'll call the airport immediately and book my passage."

The Old Man laughed and said, "That won't be necessary. My trusted driver is in Zurich waiting for you. You can leave whenever you choose."

JB hung up the telephone and walked to the window. He looked down; saw the limousine parked in front of the hotel; and saw the Old Man's driver, Josef, patiently sitting slightly slouched over in the driver's seat.

JB called the desk and asked them to ready his checkout. He quickly repacked his few belongings and went downstairs.

He left the hotel and found Josef parked adjacent the entrance, standing on the sidewalk, holding open the rear passenger door. He walked over to the car.

Josef smiled and said, "I'm glad you won't keep him waiting. Your visit will make him very happy."

JB got into the car.

The car pulled smoothly into the street and headed for the mountainous road to Italy.

"Please, relax and rest. If you need anything, press the button on the console by your side. I have arranged for meals along the way. We will be aboard the ferry to Palermo by tomorrow morning." The dark glass curtain slid up between the driver and JB.

JB settled back, closed his eyes, and before he dropped off to sleep, he thought, *He probably found out about my visit from Cosmo, but I wonder, is he having me watched constantly? They must be watching because I didn't have a hotel reservation! Does he really trust me? Does he still wonder about my feelings toward him?*

The rocking motion of the big and powerful limousine quickly put him to sleep.

Josef nudged him awake. He looked around sleepily and noted it was twilight. The car was stopped at a small country house, just off the highway. He got out of the car and followed Josef into the house. Josef introduced them, "JB, may I present Signor and Signóra Anastacio. They have gracefully invited us to eat in their home."

The aged couple greeted them warmly and invited them into the large country kitchen. It was an old but sparkling clean kitchen and the delicious odor of cooking food awakened his appetite.

The old woman went to the stove and prepared to serve their meal. The old man poured each of them a glass of dark red wine and told them to sit at the kitchen table and taste the special antipasto. The cold meats and pickled vegetables were strange to JB, but they were delectable.

The old woman brought them a delicious homemade soup, and as they finished it she served the main dish. It was browned and precooked polenta, shaped into round cakes about one-inch thick with marinated, braised, then sautéed pieces of rabbit. She served the polenta and rabbit covered with a small amount of her homemade sauce, and after taking his first sampling bite, JB thought, *This is a meal that gourmets would die for.*

The old man and the old woman silently watched JB and Josef devour the meal. She brought second helpings, and JB could see the pleasure in her eyes as she served yet a third helping.

When the men had finished eating, the old woman quickly cleared the table and brought steaming cups of chocolate flavored coffee.

They enjoyed the coffee, and then Josef signaled it was time to go. As they arose to leave, JB motioned to Josef, "Wait here." He returned from the car and held out a small silver statuette of the Madonna. It was a beautiful artistic representation of the Virgin Mary he had purchased in Zurich, intending it for Isabel.

The old man shook his head no, smiled and said, "It is our pleasure to welcome you into our home. When you reach Palermo, please give our greeting to my brother. Tell him that we miss him and look forward to his next visit."

JB glanced at Josef.

Josef smiled and said, "They're part of the family, and the old man told them about your saving the life of his son, their nephew. They feel forever indebted to you and are thankful that you came to their home. Now it is time for us to go." JB spoke to the old woman, "You would do me great honor by accepting this small gift. I bought it with love, and it would make me happy for you to have it. I feel that one day I will be back to visit you and until then the Madonna will watch over you."

Signora Anastacio accepted the Madonna and JB could see the glistening in her eyes as she spoke, "Bless you young man. We will pray for your happiness and good fortune. You are forever welcome in our home." The old man nodded his agreement.

JB felt their warmth and sincerity, so he kissed the old woman's hand, shook hands with the old man, turned, and went outside to the car.

Underway again, JB sat looking out of the car window, thinking about the Old Man, wondering how far his network of influence reached. He also thought, *How did he know I was in Zurich?* He answered himself, *Cosmo probably told his grandfather about my plans or I could've been tailed from San Francisco. In any event, I need to be more vigilant.*

He settled down to relax during their drive through Italy to the South Coast and he thought about his upcoming visit with the Old Man. *This will be the time to forever cement our relationship.* He mused, *Why do I need this so much? Is it because I can't recall my real father?*

JB dozed and the miles flew by as the powerful car raced down the highways at high speed. The constant motions caused JB to sleep fitfully throughout the night.

He awakened to a rocking motion of the car. Opening his eyes, he saw that Josef had driven the car up onto a loading ramp and was preparing to drive aboard a large gleaming white ferry boat.

They were aboard soon, and Josef blocked the wheels of the car and opened the door for JB.

JB got out of the car. He noticed the large doors were closing, and yet their car was the only car aboard. He looked doubtfully at Josef.

Josef said, "This is not a regularly scheduled ferry. The Old Man is anxious for your visit, and after all, the shipping line is his." Josef shrugged his shoulders and continued, "He loves you like his son, so he wants to make sure your trip is swift and safe. Relax, go up onto the deck for some fresh air, tell the stewards if you want anything. I'll see you when we dock. Now I'm going to sleep."

JB wandered about the ship, enjoying the fresh sea air. The sun was up. The warmth of the early morning sun, along with the smooth blue water and gentle breeze made him feel great. He settled down on the aft deck and asked the steward for morning espresso. He sat, looking back toward Italy, sipping the warm drink, and wondered, *I have so much to look forward to with*

Isabel, but what about my agreement with the special Project Team? Will my life mission permit happiness with Isabel?

He dozed in the warm sun, dreaming of Isabel and her warm loving touch.

The crossing lasted a little over four hours.

Josef awakened him. "We are almost there. Let's get into the car and be ready to disembark as soon as we dock."

They went below and got into the limousine.

The ship docked, and the huge door swung open for them and in minutes they were speeding up the now familiar mountain road toward the Old Man's estate.

JB leaned forward from the back seat and said, "Tell me, Josef, how can the Old Man always feel safe in his home?"

Josef smiled and asked in return, "During your other visit and during this visit, have you ever seen another car or person on the road leading to the Old Man's home?"

JB suspected the road was well guarded but he hadn't realized the road was private.

They soon arrived at the Old Man's house. As before, JB was met by the personal valet and immediately ushered into the study.

The Old Man greeted JB warmly, in the traditional way, embracing him and kissing him.

JB had grown fond of the Old Man, so he warmly returned the embrace.

They sat down by the large windows overlooking the valley and city. Wine was served, and the valet left the room.

When they were finally alone, the Old Man started talking.

The Old Man spoke fluent English, but he switched to his native language and JB was momentarily distracted, listening to the Sicilian dialect. Then he noticed something was wrong with the Old Man's speech. He sat silently, listening.

The Old Man smiled and said, "Do you notice the problem with my speech?"

JB nodded yes and waited for the Old Man to continue.

"My doctor tells me that I've had a series of small strokes. He also tells me the strokes will continue, and sooner or later a large stroke will kill me. It could happen at any time. On the other hand, I may live for years."

They both sat quietly for awhile.

JB broke the silence, "It makes me sad to hear of your problem. I wish there was something that I could do for you."

The Old Man waited for a few moments, then replied, "There is." The Old Man continued, "It is strange how our two lives have come together, you so young, me so old, from such different backgrounds. It must have been meant to be." The Old Man closed his eyes, rested for a few moments, opened his eyes, then said, "I have something that I want to tell you about.

I don't know a great deal about it, but I've been picking up bits and pieces of information from my people in New York."

JB sat silently, waiting for the Old Man to continue.

Sighing deeply, the Old Man continued, "Someone is planning to kill your president. I don't know who, but it is impossible to keep a plan totally secret when a number of people are involved. The fact that I've been getting bits and pieces of information from different sources points toward a large group."

JB was totally surprised. He continued to sit quietly for a few moments, trying to organize his thoughts. Then he asked, "What is the information that you're referring to?"

The Old Man replied, "Little things, such as . . . a prostitute in Boston told by one of her regular patrons that he couldn't wait for that Boston asshole snob to be blown away. When she asked who he was talking about, the man drunkenly told her, 'Don't worry, honey, you'll read about it in all the newspapers and your television will be full of it.' Then a longtime White House domestic employee overheard the president's wife threatening the president if he didn't stop his philandering. You may be surprised to learn that we control a large number of your congressmen, some through drugs, some through sex, and many through their greed for money. We have a constant flow of information from each of them and a common thread has emerged . . . intense disagreement between your president and the political combine that got him elected. They are unable to control him since he got elected, and apparently he reneged on major commitments to them in return for their political support. But most of all, your CIA discovered your president set up his private intelligence group some years ago when he was a senator. He uses his personal wealth to cover the costs, and the private group has been in existence for years. As is usually the case, sooner or later a weak spot develops due to greed or some other weakness, and the CIA penetrated the group. They weren't able to learn much because their man was eliminated but they know a special intelligence group exists. Try as they might, they have not been able to penetrate again. They questioned a naval officer fingered by their man but couldn't get any information from him. They used mind drugs to no avail, and he was physically tortured to death without revealing a single bit of information. The CIA is frantically trying to break into the special group without success.

"The general consensus among my Council is that your president will be eliminated by his political enemies if they cannot bring him under control. What no one knows is that we've had the president's father, his brothers, and now the president himself under our control, and we do not want to lose him. We know nothing about a special intelligence group, and the president has never reneged on a commitment to me. I do not expect to live long. When I die, my eldest son will lead the Council, and I would like for you to help him. Nothing may ever come of this, but if it does, at least you'll know that it may be a plot from high within your own government."

The Old man looked drawn and said, "I need to rest now, my son. Please join me later for dinner and then you can be on your way tomorrow."

They dined together that evening and when the Old Man wished him *bona sera,* hugged him, and left the room, JB sensed that it was probably the last moment he would see the Old Man alive.

CHAPTER SEVEN

Josef awakened him early the next morning and drove him down to the airport at Palermo.

He shook hands with Josef and saw the sadness in his eyes. He told Josef, "I'm headed for the Amalfi Coast, south of Naples."

Josef smiled sadly and said, "We will know your whereabouts, and if you're needed, I will contact you."

They said their last good-bye, and JB went into the air terminal to purchase his ticket to Naples.

It was a short flight across to Naples, and he was soon driving south in his small rented car.

It felt good to be alone, and he looked forward to relaxing in the small fishing villages along the coast. There would be plenty of tourists, but mostly the tourists would be going to Capri and the flashy tourist resorts. He planned to visit the quiet little fishing villages and to disappear into the local population.

He skirted the Pompeii area and drove down the winding road out into the mountainsides, high above the sea. It was a beautiful drive but a dangerous one. The local buses and cars all drove too fast, and if he tried driving slowly, the other cars drove close behind him, honking their horns, passing him dangerously and shaking their fists at him in frustration.

JB soon gave up all thoughts of a leisurely drive and settled down to serious road racing. He quickly came to realize that he was an expert driver, and the small Alfa flew around the turns. The other drivers were no longer pushing him. He became the aggressor, and soon he passed drivers who had irately cursed at him a short while before.

The twisting drive down the coast lasted until after noon, and he was tense and exhausted when he finally arrived in Positano. It was a beautiful town, made up of many small whitewashed buildings and houses, perched on a steep hillside that led down to the fishing docks at the seaside.

JB had little hope of finding a room this late in the day. He pulled off the main road and began winding his way down the steep streets, looking for a hotel or inn.

Near the sea, he turned and drove slowly up the narrow seaside street and spotted the market section of town. Boats were beached, and the fish stalls were selling today's catch to the many people crowded around. He was unable to get past the area in his car, so he pulled into a side street and parked between two buildings. He got out and walked down towards the activity. He spotted a small bistro, and just realizing his hunger, stepped inside.

JB sat at a small table near the front window so he could watch the waterfront activity. A pretty waitress came to his table and asked for his order. He selected his meal and was delighted with the freshly baked bread, a delicious fish stew, followed by fresh fruit and cheese. When he finished, the proprietor came to the table and sat.

"You are a stranger in our village. May I ask why are you here?"

JB replied, "Driving down the high, mountainous highway, I saw Positano gleaming in the afternoon sun. It was exactly the way I've dreamed it would be, and at that moment I fell in love with your village. I need serenity, and this looks like the perfect place. You're correct, I am a stranger but I look forward to being your friend."

The proprietor looked at him and said, "I am looking for a young man traveling from Palermo. You match the description of the young man. Are you from Palermo?"

JB smiled to himself and thought, *The Old Man has quite a pipeline.* He spoke to the proprietor, "Yes, I'm traveling from Palermo. I visited a very dear friend there, and I am saddened by his illness. I need some peace and quiet."

The proprietor smiled and said, "I've got just the place for you. There's a small house down the street. It overlooks the sea, and you will be alone as much as you wish. If you would like to see it, I will take you."

JB said, "Thank you, this is a pleasant surprise, and I appreciate your courtesy."

The proprietor replied, "It is my honor to help you. I also love the Old Man, and he asked that you be treated good and with respect."

JB paid for his meal, and they walked together down to the small whitewashed house. It was sparsely furnished but comfortable looking, so he accepted. The proprietor insisted that JB should not pay a rental, but after much wrangling he agreed to accept a token payment and arranged to have the house cleaned daily. The proprietor also arranged to turn in the rented car at a nearby resort hotel. JB retrieved his baggage from the rental car and walked back to the house.

JB settled in, and the next few days passed quickly. He spent his days walking around the hillside, exploring the town, and each day he was invited into a different home for his meals. The town knew about him and he was treated kindly.

It was a quiet little village and had seemed sparsely populated when he first arrived. As the days passed, he came to realize the town had a large population, mostly fishermen and their families. The more he explored the town, the more he realized the daily hustle bustle taking place. The high spot of each day was just before noon when the local fishing dories returned with their morning catch. The resorts and restaurants for miles around had representatives at the fish market, and they cajoled, pleaded, and bargained for the choice fish from the daily catch. Local families from miles around also came to the markets to shop for fresh fish. It was a gala affair, and he timed his daily walks so he was in the market area for the daily festivities.

The fishermen would land their boats, pulling their small dories up onto the beach and deliver their catch to the fish stalls. There, family members would take over and handle the cleaning and selling of the catch. The fishermen would clean, check, and repair their fishing gear and then go to the local bistros. They ate, drank, and often fought throughout the afternoon before withdrawing to their homes in early evening for their dinner and early retirement. Their boats were away before sunrise the next morning, and the following day was a repeat of the day before. Occasionally a fisherman would be lost or injured at sea, but ordinarily it was a regular and predictable lifestyle. During the first few days, JB was away when the house cleaner came by. Each day when he returned, he found a clean house and a freshly baked bread or dessert in the kitchen. During the next several days, he made a point of staying within eyeshot of his house to learn who was cleaning and baking for him.

He watched her leave the house, walk down to the fishing beach, and enter a fish stall. He was not near enough to see her face clearly, but obviously she was young, buxom, and curvaceous. The following day, he again saw the house cleaner leave, and as before, she was young, buxom, and curvaceous, but not the same lady from the previous day. He watched for the next two days and satisfied himself that two young ladies were alternating the cleaning of his house and both worked in the same fish stall afterward.

As the days passed, he learned his way around the town and became acquainted with many of the local families. He also started waking up during the night, becoming more and more restless. Late one morning, he wandered among the fish stalls, mingling with the customers. Again he watched the young lady coming from his house, walking toward the fish stalls. He tried not to stare but she noticed him watching her and as she walked past, straightened noticeably, thrusting her breasts forward and higher. He could feel his color redden and a stirring in his loins. She smiled demurely as his stirring became a yearning. He watched her enter the stall, joining the other young lady and some older woman handling the fish. He was almost in a state of shock as he wandered closer to their stall, and he tried to think of a convenient way to meet the ladies. During this time, both young ladies secretly watched him with longing in their eyes. JB wandered in and out among the fish stalls until he noticed some stalls closing. He saw the older woman and one of the young ladies leave, walking across the street, then on up the hill. The other young woman continued tidying up. JB wandered by, swallowed hard and looked at her, "*Buon giorno, Signorina,* my name's JB. Thank you for taking care of my housecleaning."

She looked directly into his eyes, smiled and spoke, almost in a whisper, "I'm Ruby." She dropped her eyes, turned, picked up some fish wrapped in paper, and walked away from him heading across the street and up the hill.

He slept until the bright sunlight awakened him. He smiled, stretched his arms, then he showered, dressed, and hurried to the fish market area.

The day's festivities were almost over, so he walked to Papa John's Bistro.

Several fishermen were there, and although half drunk, they were quiet and subdued.

JB settled down at a table nearest the front window and ordered his lunch. He looked out the window, toward the beach, and saw a small crowd of people milling about near one of the boats.

It was quiet in the restaurant. As JB sat waiting for his food, he heard sobbing. The noise came from the beach area. The waitress brought his food, and he asked her, "What is going on down on the beach?"

She replied sadly, "Signor Boronio drowned while fishing this morning."

He asked, "What happened?"

"They were seining for the small fish. It was windy and rough out on the water. He must have stumbled and fallen overboard. He got entangled in the nets and drowned before they got him out of the water." She continued, "The family is poor and Signor Boronio did not have a son to fish with him, so he was alone at the time of the accident. I feel so sorry for the family."

She walked away, and he sat looking out of the window, not touching his food.

Shortly he got up and went over to the proprietor. "Papa John," he said, "do you know the Boronio family?"

"Yes, they live up by the church. They have several daughters but only one son. He is in the Naples Prison, but his crime was not serious. They are very poor so I have been paying the family the small stipend to clean your house." Papa John continued, "It is a shame for the family to have such hardship. They will have a struggle until the son gets out of the prison and comes home to fish."

JB went back to his table, finished his lunch, and left the restaurant. He walked up the hill to the town and went into the hotel frequented by tourists. He found a public call box and telephoned the Old Man in Palermo.

JB told the Old Man, "Signor Boronio drowned this morning. His son Salvatore is in the Naples Prison and Signora Boronio needs Salvatore to fish and support the family. Will you get him released?"

The Old Man replied, "Salvatore will be released in about thirty days. If needed it can be arranged sooner. I will handle it."

JB spoke, "Thirty days will do. I will use Signor Boronio's boat and fish for the family until Salvatore is home. Thank you for helping." JB left the hotel and walked down the hill to the Boronio house.

JB knocked on the door, and when the door opened he said, "*Buon giorno,* Signora Boronio, my name is JB. Please, may I come in and talk with you? I am an acquaintance of Papa John."

She opened the door for him and from her dress and manner she was obviously in mourning.

They had not met, but she knew who he was. She motioned for him to sit at the kitchen table and brought him a glass of wine.

"Thank you, Signora Boronio. I have word that your son will be released from the prison in about thirty days so he can return home and help you. Until that time, with your permission I will use your dory to fish each day, and you can continue to sell the fish as before. When your son returns, he will take my place."

The tears spilled down the wrinkled, sunburned cheeks, and she tried to smile through her tears. She came to him, pulled him to his feet, and embraced him. She sobbed quietly as she said, "Please, come to my husband's rosary tonight, and we will be honored by your presence at his funeral tomorrow. The fishing fleet will not sail tomorrow because of the funeral, but it will sail again the following day."

JB assured her that he would come to the rosary that evening, and then he left the house and walked down the hill. He went directly to the beach and located the Boronio boat. He stood staring at the dory, thinking, *I hope I'm able to handle the boat and use the fishing gear!*

He walked back to his house and lay down on the bed to think about what was taking place.

JB awakened late in the afternoon, dressed, and went down to the bistro. Most of the fishermen had gone home by then, and the bistro was nearly empty. He ordered a light snack of cheese and bread with a bottle of wine.

As he sat eating, a grizzled old fisherman came over and said, "You have done a very kind thing for Signora Boronio. All of the village knows what you are doing. You shall have whatever help you need." Then he turned and walked away.

JB finished eating and went out of the bistro. He walked up the hill to the church, went inside the old church, and sat down in a rear pew. The light was dim inside the church, but he made out Signõra Boronio and her four daughters kneeling in the front pew.

The church filled with villagers. The rosary soon started and must have lasted for an hour.

JB left the church after the rosary while the villagers greeted him with quiet "*Buon giornos,*" nodding their heads.

He walked down to the bistro, and then, deciding not to go inside, continued on up the street, not wanting to talk with anyone. He went to his house and spent the rest of the evening sitting on the small front porch, looking out over the sea, thinking about the day's events. The Old Man had sounded tired, and JB thought, *He is more than tired, he's fighting for his life and there's nothing I can do to help. He's new in my life but I'll miss him.*

The village was bustling as he left his house, walked down toward the cafe, turned, and headed up the hill towards the church.

The Mass was scheduled for eight that morning, and the church was almost full when JB entered. Soon the church was overflowing. He sat in the rear pew and was aware of the many glances in his direction.

When he arose to leave, the man sitting next to him lightly touched his arm and whispered, "You should come to the wake."

JB nodded and followed the people out of the church and up the hill to the cemetery. It was a short walk, and the burial casket was carried on the shoulders of six men. The mourners stood around the grave site, and although JB couldn't see the Boronios, he heard the mourning and praying.

JB followed the crowd to the church hall. It was noisy, and he saw tables laden with food lined against the wall. The music started–spirited sounds of accordions, guitars, and mandolins, and some of the people were beginning their village dances.

Soon, the hall was alive with the dance, and the music raged non-stop.

JB turned toward the food tables and caught sight of Signõra Boronio. She motioned him over.

JB went over, and she embraced him, "Thank you for coming." She introduced him to her daughters, Ruby, Lucia, Maria, and Josea, and he felt tongue-tied. Ruby smiled demurely as she greeted him. Her eyes twinkled, and his eyes kept going back to her as he moved around the hall with Signõra Boronio, meeting the other villagers. All of the people were friendly and welcomed him.

He sat eating some food, drinking wine, and when he saw Ruby sauntering toward him, he thought, "*Que arrivano guay . . . here comes trouble . . . !*

Ruby took his arm and led him onto the dance floor and she whispered, "Just relax and follow what the other young men are doing. The man's part is simple, the women do all of the dancing!" Her eyes twinkled as she spoke.

The dancing was fun, and soon JB was caught up in the lively dancing. Ruby and Lucia took turns dancing with him, not allowing him to sit down.

While dancing with Ruby, he asked, "Do you take walks around town?"

She casually brushed her hand against the nape of his neck. He was electrified! Outwardly she appeared calm, but as he looked into her eyes, he saw and felt the volcanic storm smoldering. He saw a bead of sweat trickle down from her hairline, and he whispered, "You need a man to taste that drop of sweat on your face!"

"Well?"

He brushed her hair away, wiping the sweat with his thumb. Her eyes smoldered as he licked and kissed his thumb. His loins felt heavy, he felt himself growing, and he knew he must get away from her.

"This afternoon I am walking to my friend's house in Amalfi. The whole town knows when I come to your house, but there's a private beach about half a mile south which I must pass on my way. I shall have many drops of sweat that I would love to wash off in the ocean."

With his heart in his throat, JB replied, "It's not safe to swim alone. You should have a young man to watch over you."

"Perhaps," she coyly replied.

The hall was warm and all perspired freely from the active dancing. Her womanly scents kept him in a constant state of arousal. Ruby tried not to show it, but she was also excited and took delight in his arousal as well.

By mid-afternoon, the heat of the day along with the food and wine had taken its toll. The gathering thinned as people began leaving, some staggering and weaving. He told the girls that he must leave, and although they protested and wailed disagreement, he read anticipation and eagerness in Ruby's eyes.

He found Signora Boronio by the door, said his thanks and good-bye, then went out of the hall and down the hill. He had drunk enough wine to set his head spinning, so he made use of the iron railings in his descent to the waterfront and home.

After entering his house, JB stripped his clothes off and lay down on the bed. Though not completely drunk, he passed out into a deep sleep.

In what seemed like the next moment, JB was shaken awake. Ruby said to him, "It is time for you to go to the boat. Your food for breakfast is in the pail on your kitchen table. Go now and I'll see you later this morning," and, with spirit and a touch of anger, she said, "I waited and waited for you at the beach yesterday!"

It was still dark, but JB could see the lanterns around the boats and heard the men talking as he approached the beach. He walked down to his boat and found the fishing gear cleanly stowed aboard the boat. Several of the men walked over and greeted him "*Buon giorno, mille grazie por pescadore*," and started pulling and pushing his boat toward the water.

JB tossed his bag into the boat and helped the men.

JB saw other boats already in the water with men at their oars, sculling away from the beach. It was new for him, but he watched the others, copying them, and he slipped toward the open sea.

A man in a nearby boat called to JB, "Pull your oars slowly, together, and follow my boat."

JB nodded yes and followed.

It was hard work, but it felt good.

They rowed for about an hour, and JB was surprised at how far they traveled. The boats were spread over a large area, and some fishermen had stopped, putting their nets out into the water.

He continued following the other boat until it came to a stop.

The other fisherman called to him, "Put your oars into your boat, same as I'm doing."

He laid the oars against the gunwale.

Then, the other fisherman called, "Take the four large floats that are laying on the top of your nets and place them into the water. Let them float away. As they float away, carefully feed your net over the side of your boat. The net will spread out and the weights on the bottom will position your net. Watch me."

JB watched through the mist. When the net was out, the fisherman smiled across to JB and said, "Nothing to it. Let's see you try it."

He did exactly as instructed and the net spread out and dropped down into position.

Then the man called again, "To retrieve your net, do the same thing, in reverse. Be patient, I will tell you when to draw your net. We must do it at the right time because we will not have a second chance. Now eat your breakfast and relax."

He felt chilled, sitting in the early morning mist and breeze. He ate his breakfast and thought about Ruby. She had been magnificent, and he became aroused just thinking about her. Just for an instant he thought of Isabel and felt guilt. *Perhaps if she would make love with me I wouldn't think of straying?*

The sun rose and he dozed in the warmth. He was awakened by the fisherman calling to him, "It is time to draw our nets in. Good luck, you are on you own. As the net comes into your boat, leave the fish in the net. We'll head back as soon as the nets are in." With that the fisherman turned away and started hauling in his net.

JB did the same. By now the sun was high in the sky and it was blazing hot. The sun's glare bounced off the water and he felt the heat on his face. Ocean swells moved through the area making it hard work retrieving the net. The net filled the bottom of his dory and he was surprised at the weight. He hauled on the net lines until the large floats came up alongside. The net was filled with what looked like bluefish and a plentiful number of silvery shad and other herrings. JB carefully lifted the floats into the dory and set them on top of his net. Then he set his oars and started rowing, following the other fisherman back toward the village. The smell of the salt air was exhilarating, and he was soon covered with sweat from the strenuous rowing.

They were around the point and about two kilometers from the village. The tide was flowing out and the ocean swell resisted his rowing. He concentrated on pulling the oars, carefully following the other fisherman. After what seemed like an eon, the other fisherman stopped pulling. JB didn't wait to be told and looking over his shoulder, he saw that he was about fifty yards from shore.

The other fisherman called, "Watch me land and then you do the same."

The other fisherman pulled hard and fast on his oars and kept his boat moving perpendicular to the wave line toward the beach. He rode the small waves up onto the beach, jumped out, and, with help from the other men standing by, pulled the dory up onto the sand.

Without hesitation JB pulled hard on the oars, heading directly for the same beach area. The incoming waves lifted the boat. Suddenly men appeared on both sides, and, with the boat's incoming momentum, lifted it up onto the beach.

JB sat, exhausted but not wanting to show his state in front of the other fishermen. The men left his boat and went back to the water's edge to help the others.

JB stood up slowly, and on rubbery legs stepped out of the dory. Signora Boronio hurried toward him followed by her daughters. When they saw the catch inside the net they let out squeals of delight. They crowded around JB, all excitedly talking at once. Signora Boronio hushed her daughters and said to JB, "You have caught bushels of beautiful fish. You must be very tired. We will take care of the fish and the nets. You should go to the bistro with the other men."

JB turned and bumped into Ruby. With a twinkle in her eyes, she tossed her hair and turned away.

The two girls went past him and helped their mother remove the fish from the net. It was indeed a good catch and the Boronio family would do well today.

JB joined the other fishermen and walked down to the cafe.

When JB entered the cafe, a young fisherman sitting at a table with a few others waved him over to their table.

The young man stood and said, "I am Guido. I was in the boat next to you. You did fine, much better that we expected. All of the villagers appreciate what you are doing for Signora Boronio. Please, join us."

The men stood, and JB walked around the table introducing himself and shaking hands. JB sat and the men resumed their talking of the day's fishing, boasting in a friendly fashion about who caught the most and largest fish.

Other men drifted by the table, introducing themselves and toasting JB's success in handling the dory.

By mid-afternoon, JB was well oiled. He excused himself and walked home in as straight a line as his legs would allow. His arms, back, and shoulders ached from the morning's work, and he wondered if he would be able to go out the following day. JB knew for certain that he must get some rest . . . .

He was awakened by a noise in the kitchen. Signõra Boronio and Ruby were busy setting out his supper on the small kitchen table. He slipped on his trousers and a shirt, then walked into the kitchen. *"Bona sera, Signõra, bona sera,* Ruby," he said.

Signõra said, "It is important that you eat a hearty dinner. We brought your meal tonight. Starting tomorrow night, you will come to our home and eat with us." As she turned to leave, she said, "Ruby will stay and clean the dishes and prepare your food for tomorrow morning. Now, sit down and eat."

Ruby stood watching her mother walk away from the house, then turned to face him. He sat at the table but hadn't touched the food. Her eyes blazed with passion, and she started to unbutton the buttons on her blouse. She said, "We do not have much time. Please, make love to me now!" He stood and resolutely held her away. "I cannot make love with you now because my heart's with Isabel. Please, go home before I lose control." She insisted on reaching out and grasping him with her hands, so he pulled her close to him and held her tightly. It was awkward–Ruby was passionately strong in her demands, almost out of control. He kissed her, exploring her mouth and tongue with his, and he felt her body shudder. He moved his hands down her body, and using his strength, he slowed her body motion. He felt her movement smooth to an erotic rhythm before he stepped away.

His face was covered with perspiration, and between her gasps for breath, she continued kissing him. "Oh, JB, we will be good together, but you must not call me Isabel or even think of her!"

He felt sadness as he whispered, "Isabel is my first love. I think of her constantly and I've missed her tenderness. You almost had me until you calmed. I'm telling you of Isabel because I tasted your tears while you kissed me, and your tears tasted the same as my Isabel's."

She stared deeply into his eyes and he saw the tears on her face. Then she dropped her arms and stepped away and whispered to him, "It is time for me to go." As she turned to go, she spoke softly to him, "Whenever you ever make love to Isabel again, I hope you think of me as you thought of her. I will be sad until I can be with you."

He ate the cold dinner, set aside some food for the morning, then fell into bed.

JB set his mental alarm to awaken at 0400, and he had just awakened when he heard the knocking on his front door.

"Good morning," Guido said, "it is time to go."

"Come in, Guido, it will only take me a few moments to get ready." Despite his aching and sore muscles, JB dressed quickly, picked up his bag of food from the kitchen, and hurried back. "Thanks for waiting, Guido, let's go."

They walked down the street to the boats, and, as the day before, some boats were already in the water. JB went to his boat, stowed his food inside, and waited for the men to help him launch the dory.

They launched JB's dory and he rowed toward the fishing area. This morning there were many shouts of greeting as he followed Guido to the open sea.

All went well, and, after dozing for awhile, he was ready to haul in his net. The rowing and the net handling were hard work but he was catching the rhythm. Of course, he realized, the sea was calm, and no large waves tested his seamanship.

The trip back was uneventful, and the ladies squealed gleefully when they saw the catch. JB put the boat and fishing gear in order, then joined the other fishermen hurrying to the bistro.

JB walked along with Guido. "Guido, tell me about yourself."

"Not much to tell. I'm twenty-three. My papa drowned in a fishing accident when I was thirteen, and I've fished our boat since. I have no brothers or sisters, and I live with my mama, further down the beach, couple streets past your place."

"I didn't see you at Siñor Boronio's wake. Do you know the Boronio family?"

Guido said, "I went to school with Salvatore and I see the family at church. The Boronio daughters are beautiful, but I am not handsome enough for them."

JB looked at Guido, then said, "That's nonsense! You're a handsome and strong-looking young man."

Guido replied, "You're very kind. I'm also shy and I don't know what to do. I didn't go to the wake because I don't know the dances, and I have no one to teach me." Guido lowered his head, obviously embarrassed.

They walked on in silence for awhile, and then JB changed the subject, asking Guido questions about boats and fishing.

They went into the bistro, found a table, ordered some wine, and continued talking about boats and fishing.

JB began to formulate a plan. The fishermen worked every day except Sunday. He had seen posters announcing a community dance on the second Saturday night of each month, at the church hall. He would convince Guido to go with him to the next dance and he would convince Ruby and Lucia to teach Guido the dances, just as they had taught him.

A couple of hours later JB and Guido left the bistro to go home for their afternoon nap. As they walked past the fish market area, JB noticed the Boronios were almost finished selling their fish. They stopped at the Boronio fish stall and JB said, "Good afternoon, Siñora Boronio. May I please introduce my good friend Guido. He has helped me work the dory and catch the fish. Without his instruction I could not have caught so many."

Guido was embarrassed but pleased with the introduction, and JB could see Guido sneaking a glance, past Siñora Boronio, at the daughters. They were giggling and looking appreciatively at the two young men.

Siñora Boronio thanked Guido for helping them and invited both of them to come to her house for Sunday dinner.

Guido declined and replied, "Thank you for inviting me Signora Boronio, but I must decline. Each Sunday I take my mama to visit her sister, and it's too late now for me to arrange for someone else to take her. Her Sunday visits are important because they like to go to church together. Please, do me the honor of inviting me another time."

"I am pleased with you, Guido. Give my regards and good wishes to your mama. Of course there will be another time, soon. JB, we'll expect you at one o'clock."

They said good-bye to the signora, waved to the giggling girls, and headed on up the street to their house.

After walking a short distance, JB looked at Guido and said, "Did you notice Signora Boronio's daughters?"

Guido laughed and said, "Are you kidding? I felt like grabbing them both and taking them away to my secret beach. I don't think I'll be able to sleep so well tonight, thinking of them."

The time was right, so JB said, "Guido, let's go to the Saturday night dance. I have met the Boronio girls and I'm sure they will be at the dance. I will introduce you to them."

Guido looked at him and said, "I would really like to go, but I don't know the dances. They will laugh at me."

"No, Guido," JB replied, "no one will laugh at you. I will not allow anyone to embarrass you. If anyone should laugh at you, we will leave together, and if it is a man who laughs, I will kick his ass!"

Guido smiled and said, "You are the best real friend that I've ever had. If you think we should go, then we'll go!"

JB noticed more spring in Guido's walk. Obviously Guido was excited about going to the dance. They reached JB's house, Guido clapped him on the back, and said, "I'll be by for you tomorrow morning. Get a good night's sleep."

JB dined that evening with Signora Boronio and her daughters.

During the meal the signora told JB, "I received a letter today from the Naples Policia. They will release my son at his next parole hearing in three weeks time." Tears began to trickle down her face. She dabbed at her nose and told her daughters to clear the table. "Come," she said, "we will have a glass out on the porch while the girls clean the dishes."

JB got up and followed her out onto the front porch.

They sat on a settee and Lucia brought them each a glass.

"*Grappa*," the Signora said, "it is made by my brother-in-law in the next village. We use it to celebrate special occasions." She lifted her glass, toasting him.

JB acknowledged her toast and sipped from his glass. His eyes watered from the fiery liquid, and he felt it reach his stomach.

They sat quietly, watching the twilight turn to darkness. Finally the signora looked at JB and said, "I cannot describe to you how grateful I am for what you have done, but I have still another request."

JB replied, "If I am able, I will help. what do you want?"

"My twin daughters are nearing eighteen years, and it is time for them to have husbands. Their father would've arranged marriages for them, but he is gone. I have no brother and although my son will be home soon, I cannot trust him to do the proper thing. Will you help me select two fine young men for my daughters?"

"Signora, I will be honored to help you." He sat silently for a few moments, then, "As a matter of fact, I have become acquainted with a fine young fisherman and I am sure there are other genuine young men available. You met Guido at your fish stall this afternoon. Please make certain your daughters attend the village dance next Saturday night. He will be there."

JB finished his drink and got up to leave. "Thank you for supper. I must go now. The morning will come too soon."

The signora also got up and asked him to wait for a moment. She went inside, then returned with a paper bag. Handing it to him, she said, "Lucia prepared your morning meal. We hope you are safe tomorrow morning and catch many fish."

JB took the bag and looked past the signora. Both girls were standing behind their mother, Lucia smiling, Ruby pouting. "Thank you Signora, for your kindness, and please tell Lucia that I will think of her when I eat my breakfast."

The girls giggled and Ruby's pouting disappeared.

As JB walked away, he turned to see they were still standing on the porch watching him. He waved once and hurried an down the hill. He felt good tonight but wistful. The signora had asked him to step in and perform an important family task and he had agreed. He thought, *I cannot take this chore lightly. It affects the lives of Lucia, Ruby, their mother, my friend Guido, and whoever else comes into the picture.*" The task was sobering and he thought further, *Thank God I didn't take advantage of Ruby.* A smile creased his lips as he thought, *Guido, my friend, whichever one you end up with, and you will, you're in for a grand awakening. Both girls are marvelous!*

The next few days passed with no surprises. On Saturday, he went home from the bistro soon after noon.

Although Guido was very anxious about going to the dance, he showed up at JB's house right on time. Together they walked up the hill to the church hall.

The hall was already crowded. Mothers and fathers sat along the walls, talking to one another, pretending not to watch their daughters. The young girls clustered at one end of the room, the young men at the other, and an older couple stood in the center of the dance floor.

The music started, and the older couple signaled for the young ladies and young men to come onto the dance floor. The girls giggled, and one by one, started walking toward the older couple. JB and Guido joined the other young men, and there was much pushing and shoving, as none of them wanted to be the first to move onto the floor. Finally one young man took the lead and the others started walking toward the center of the floor.

Guido seemed ready to bolt. His face was pale; the sheen of perspiration covered his upper lip. JB grabbed Guido's arm and whispered, "Take a deep breath and do exactly as I told you! Keep looking at me, do what I do, and everything will be okay."

The older couple matched the ladies and young men into partners. JB saw Ruby and Lucia join the procession and prodded Guido into the line of young men.

JB had calculated correctly. Guido matched with Lucia and he matched with Ruby.

Soon the dancers were matched, and the older couple started to waltz. One by one, the young couples followed. JB led Ruby onto the dance floor. She placed her left hand upon his shoulder, and they swung smoothly among the other dancers.

JB watched Guido. Guido looked frozen. Then JB saw Lucia place her hand on Guido's shoulder, take Guido's other hand in hers, and gently nudge him to start moving. She looked directly into Guido's eyes and almost as if hypnotized, he started moving. She guided him around the floor, the rhythm from her body flowing through their hands, and Guido began to relax.

JB concentrated on dancing with Ruby. Her smoothness and her womanly odor intoxicated him. JB searched the crowd for Guido. Guido's pallor was gone, and Lucia smiled brightly. He maneuvered near Lucia and Guido. When the music stopped, they exchanged partners. The music started again and they resumed dancing.

JB noticed Lucia let her eyes follow Guido. JB teased, "How do you think Guido and Ruby look together?"

She looked at him, smiled, and rolled her eyes, "You're unkind! I think I'm in love with him. My sister . . . he is so manly and strong!" Her eyes looked for Guido and a worried look crossed her face. "Look!" she cried. "Now Ruby is smiling at him!"

Sure enough, Ruby and Guido smiled and talked as they danced around the room. Guido's steps were awkward, but he was obviously well coordinated and athletic.

More young people moved onto the dance floor, so now it was crowded. When the music stopped again, JB saw another young man take Ruby as a partner, leaving Guido alone. JB walked Lucia over to Guido and excused himself. They danced away as the music started and JB looked for the refreshments.

He sighted Signora Boronio and walked over to where she was seated. "Good evening, Signora."

"*Bono sera,* JB," she replied.

He lifted his eyebrows toward Guido and Lucia, questioning the signora. She smiled and nodded her head, "*Cierto que dura!*"

He smiled back, leaned down and whispered, "*Piacere,* one down, one to go."

He danced with several young ladies that night but most often with Ruby and Lucia. Guido danced with a few others but kept going back to Lucia whenever he could grab her before the other young men.

Walking home, Guido bubbled with excitement. "JB, all the dances I've missed because I couldn't dance, and the signorinas, they're beauties to behold–and Lucia. Ah, Lucia!"

They sat on JB's front porch, sharing a glass of whiskey. After a few drinks JB asked, "Guido, what do you think of the Boronio girls? Do you think you are worthy?" he chided.

Guido looked at him, then bashfully answered in an agonizing voice, "I think I'm in love with Lucia, but what do I do?" Guido's eyes were wet with tears, and his shoulders shook as he kept himself from crying in frustration.

JB put his hand firmly on Guido's shoulder, gripped him tightly, and gently shook him. He said, "Guido, you are a normal young man. No one ever knows exactly what to do or say. All you can do is to be honest with her and with yourself. You are *Italiano,* you must let her know how you feel. If she loves you, she will let you know." The liquor was taking hold, and JB could feel sadness creeping into his mind. "Guido, along with life comes lost love and missed love. You've missed love because you couldn't or wouldn't hold yourself out to the young ladies in your village. Now you see what is there, and you want it but you're not sure what to do. Accept the risk! When you get the opportunity, and you will get your chance, be open and honest with her. She will know and she will let you know. There can be nothing greater in this world than finding the one you love and having her love you in return." He paused, then continued, "I will speak to Signora Boronio and arrange for you to call on Lucia."

It was dark on the porch, but Guido saw the glistening in JB's eyes. With concern and puzzlement, he asked, "JB, you've been down this road, haven't you?"

The silence roared in their ears, and finally JB spoke, "Guido, I have a lady who loves me with all of her heart, and I love her, but her family drives a stake between us, and I don't know what will happen. I've been able to put her out of my mind since I've been here, but she's out there, where I must return, and I guess I'm afraid of losing her."

Again they sat for long moments. Then Guido spoke, "JB, you've told me what I must do and now, I'll turn your words back to you. Be honest with her and with yourself, let her know how you feel, and if she loves you enough to want to be with you, she will let you know." He shook his head

46

and continued, "It is hard for me to believe that I have even a small chance to be with her. Please, please, help me."

JB spoke in a choked voice. "I will talk to the signora. I think Lucia likes you, let's see what happens." With that JB sent Guido home. "Don't worry, Guido, go on home and dream about your new love."

Guido left smiling. "Good night, my friend. Someday I shall find a way to repay you."

Later that night, Ruby crept into JB's dreaming as he lay half awake, wanting her badly. They began making love frantically, then slowed, prolonging their passion and ecstasy. His dreaming flowed into the afterglow. "Ruby," he dreamed, "your mother also wants me to find a husband for you. Please tell me if there's a young man in the village that catches your eye."

"JB, I may be young but I'm not a fool. I know that you are leaving soon, and you will break my heart. My heart may someday mend, but the scar will always remind me that you were my first love."

He looked into her tear-filled eyes and continued, "Guido has a friend. His name is Carmine Luca. He was always the little fat boy when he was young, but he has grown to be a handsome young man, and I'm sure you've noticed him at church. He and his father each have a dory, and I see him at the fishing area each day. I know he adores you, but he is too shy to talk. I see him sneaking looks at you and I think he would make you a good husband."

"I will try!" she sobbed.

Wistfully she kissed him and slipped quietly out of his dreams.

Sunrise was soon over but JB slept soundly until late morning and then headed up the hill to Signora Boronio's house for Sunday dinner, with a plan for each of her daughters.

After dinner, JB and the signora sat on the front porch. It was a hot day, but a cooling breeze came up during the afternoon.

JB told her about Guido.

She replied, "I know of his family. It is a good family and I have seen Guido working. He works hard and is obedient to his mother. I think you have made a good choice. You should tell Guido he is welcome to visit our house. Bring him with you tomorrow night when you come for supper. After supper I will allow them to sit together on this porch."

He asked her, "Do you know a young fisherman named Carmine Luca?"

She looked at him surprised. "The Lucas are a fine family. I would expect that Carmine's father has already arranged a marriage for his son."

"Would you consider him for Ruby?"

"Of course, providing Ruby accepts him. You have been a very busy young man," she said, eyeing him curiously.

"I'll find out tomorrow about Carmine. Perhaps this porch will be a busy place during the next few weeks."

She continued eyeing him curiously and openly. Finally she said, "You are an unusual young man. Obviously you are still young. On the other hand, you are so mature in your thoughts and actions. You come here as a tourist, and yet, within a few days, you are like one of us. You work in the dory like it is your own, and when my husband dies, you assume the responsibility for my family's welfare. Then, out of the blue, we receive word my son will be released to come home and take care of us. I have a strange feeling you're responsible for his release."

JB sat quietly for a while, not taking his eyes from hers. Then he smiled, shrugged his shoulders, and said, "Let's just call it good fortune I happened to be here, and I've been able to help you with your problems. I can't stay much longer but it looks like everything will work out for you and your family. Now I must go. Tomorrow morning will be here much too soon and I need to rest."

JB arose from the old wooden chair and called good-bye to the girls in the kitchen.

Walking down the hill, JB turned and waved to Signora Boronio. She waved back, with the perplexed look still on her face.

Next day Guido carefully positioned his boat near JB's boat so they could talk while they ate their morning meal while waiting for their nets to fill.

As they ate, JB said to Guido, "I talked to Signora Boronio yesterday. She told me to bring you to their house for supper tonight. She approves of you, but you must follow your village's custom. You must present yourself to the family for their approval and Signora Boronio wants to be certain Lucia approves of you. How can you miss? You smell like a fish, look like a fish, kiss like a fish!" JB laughed. "Everything should go fine unless she prefers older men!"

Guido moaned, "JB, how can you make fun of me at a time like this?" Then cried loudly, "What if Lucia doesn't accept me?"

JB sat, watching Guido, seeing his distress, then said, "Guido, you are my friend. I will not lie to you. I feel she cares for you. In fact I think she is crazy for you. All you can do is to go to her home and find out for yourself. Please remember, she was raised to be quiet and demure when she's around strangers, and she has never been courted before. So you should be calm, and allow her time to show you how she feels, in her own way. I will venture to say that I think you and Lucia will be man and wife within two or three months, at the latest. But then again, I may be wrong. Above all, Guido, you must realize it's not the end of the world if she rejects you."

Guido sat speechless for awhile, then told his friend, "I will follow your advice, and I am grateful for what you have done."

They sat quietly in the hot morning sun, boats rocking gently in the ocean swell. JB watched Guido and could see that Guido was now relaxed. He called across the water, "Guido, now I need your help."

Guido looked at him and said, "Anything for you, my friend."

48

"Lucia's sister Ruby needs to be courted also and I think Carmine Luca would be a good match. Will you introduce me to Carmine so I can learn if he would like to meet Ruby?"

Guido sat up excitedly and replied, "Of course! Carmine and I are good friends. We have fished together since we were small boys. I like him very much, and you could never pick a better young man. But I will tell you, we must move fast! I heard his father is planning to arrange a marriage for Carmine with a family in the next village." Guido continued, "Today we will sit with Carmine in the bistro and you can talk to him."

Later, after bringing in their boats and catch, they found themselves in the bistro with Carmine.

"Carmine," Guido said, "tonight I am going to eat supper at Signora Boronio's home and I will court her daughter Lucia."

"Oh you lucky man," said Carmine. "How did you arrange that? She's a pretty woman."

"My friend here arranged it for me." Guido motioned toward JB. "Otherwise it would never have happened. What do you think of her?"

Carmine replied, "I have seen her and her sisters helping their mother with selling their fish. Both of the older daughters are beyond my wildest dreams. You are a very lucky fellow."

"Carmine, as you know, JB is fishing for Signora Boronio until her son comes home. He spends much time with the Boronio's. Listen to what he has to say."

The two young men looked at JB, waiting for him to speak.

"I eat my supper at Signora Boronio's home each evening. They took me in as one of their family. I hear the girls talking as they clean the dishes after supper, and I heard Ruby say to her sister Lucia she watches you every day and thinks you're the perfect young man."

Carmine blanched and sat speechless.

Guido looked at Carmine, then laughed loudly. "Now I know what I looked like when you first talked to me about Lucia." Then, Guido turned to Carmine, "Carmine, you have this one chance in your lifetime to pick your own wife, forever. If you don't move quickly, your father will arrange a marriage for you. Let JB help you meet Ruby and you can decide for yourself what you want."

Carmine drained his half-full glass of wine in one gulp, then asked, "How can you help me to meet her?"

"You should tell your father that you are going to call on Signora Boronio, and ask her permission to court her daughter Ruby. Then you will come with me to Signora Boronio's home the day after tomorrow to eat supper and to meet the signora and Ruby. I will arrange permission from Signora Boronio."

Guido told Carmine, "Don't worry about a thing. JB will tell you exactly what to do and I will learn tonight when I see Lucia. We are two very lucky young men, so let's toast our good fortune."

The three of them proceeded to toast everything that came to mind, and by early afternoon, JB dragged them out of the restaurant. "Guido, we must go home and rest before tonight, and Carmine, you need to clear your head and talk with your father."

They staggered toward their homes, and when Guido left JB in front of JB's house, Guido promised to be bathed, clean shaven, and ready to go, at JB's house, half an hour before their supper time. With that Guido and Carmine swaggered off up the street, and JB went inside for his afternoon nap.

It was a warm afternoon and JB was drowsy from the many toasts at the restaurant. He relaxed, closed his eyes, and immediately fell into a deep slumber and started dreaming. . . . He heard the creaking noise, opened his eyes quickly, looking around, and saw his closet door swing slowly open. A naked Ruby tiptoed from the closet, across to his bed. He watched her, marveling at her beauty.

She smiled knowingly as she watched him growing, and her eyes glittered as she watched his manhood unfold. She sat on the side of the bed, took him with both hands, and began stroking, "*Con amore, con amore*, my mind is full of you today! Waiting for you this past hour was the longest hour of my life!" Her harsh breathing echoed in the room, and her eyes flared; she would wait no longer. She stretched out beside him, and they turned, kissing deeply. She breathlessly whispered, "Now, you are mine!"

When he told her that he was arranging for Carmine to court her, she sobbed, "Why can't I stay with you? I'll die if you leave me!"

JB held her tightly for awhile, and, as her sobbing slowed, began talking quietly, "It is important that you have a good husband. You've told me that you like Carmine, and I know he will be crazy for you. It is time to arrange your marriage, so I will talk to your mother tonight."

Her sobbing stopped. She nestled her head into his shoulder. Her voice was muffled as she said, "I know you mean well, but why can't I stay with you forever."

JB gently pushed her face away from his shoulder, and looking into her eyes, said, "I will be leaving soon. I must return to my own life and you must remain a part of your village. I will never forget you, and I want you to have a happy life. Carmine is a good young man, and he will give his life to please you. You can be happy with him if you devote yourself to your marriage."

She started sobbing again and he thought, *What more can I say?*

Looking at her, JB was surprised to see her smiling and sobbing at the same time.

"You're right, I will do all that I can to make Carmine want me. I will not come to you again, although I know that I will spend many sleepless nights thinking of our togetherness."

His eyes jerked open from his dreaming, his head ached, and he was soaking wet . . . .

That evening Guido nervously forced down his supper. Afterwards Guido and Lucia left the house for a stroll around the neighborhood.

The other daughters cleaned the supper dishes while JB and Signora Boronio sat on the front porch.

They watched the young couple strolling up and down the street while they discussed Carmine and Ruby.

The signora's eyes were bright with curiosity as she listened to him and she marveled at his efficiency in resolving the problem with her daughters.

They agreed Carmine could come for supper the next night, and Guido would be allowed to call on Lucia three times weekly. She cautioned him, "Guido should not press for marriage until courting Lucia for awhile."

There was much activity at the Boronio home during the weekday evenings, and the neighborhood was buzzing with excitement. The curious neighbors could tell that two weddings were not far off.

The next two weeks passed quickly.

Each evening as JB left Signora Boronio's home, she would hand him a bag containing his morning meal for the following day. Each evening they sat on the front porch and talked.

JB was surprised to learn that Signora Boronio was thirty-eight years old. She looked older, and as he looked closer, he saw the beauty hidden beneath her sunburned, wrinkled face. The harshness of the hot sun had taken its toll on her face, hands, and arms.

She subtly probed about his past life and what JB planned for his future, but she was unable to learn anything substantive. She was enthralled with their verbal jousting and was strongly attracted to him. She did not betray her attraction, keeping her inner feelings to herself.

One evening, overflowing with gratitude, she burst out, "My son will be home Saturday! His father taught him well so he will have no problem handling the dory. I cannot find words to thank you enough for the help you have given us."

She trembled with excitement, and he felt relieved and thankful he had helped the family.

"That makes me happy, signora, your son can start the boat next Monday morning. The weather will continue good for awhile longer; he should do fine."

JB talked to Guido and Carmine about Signora Boronio's son. Both agreed to help their future brother-in-law with his fishing chores. They also told JB about the son's past. Salvatore was an arrogant, unmindful son, often in trouble, sent to prison for drug trafficking around the resort areas. The son's past bothered JB, and he worried Salvatore would not accept his family responsibilities.

On Saturday JB fished as usual and went to the bistro afterwards with Guido and Carmine. It was mid-afternoon when a tall, husky young man entered. The young man paused, looked slowly around the room, and focused on their table. He swaggered slowly over to their table and sneered at Guido and Carmine, "So, my future brother-in-laws are comparing notes about my sisters. Perhaps I will not approve of you for my sisters."

Guido's face turned crimson as he slowly stood. Guido was smaller and six inches shorter but obviously ready to stand up against Salvatore. Guido started to reply but before he spoke, Salvatore smashed him squarely in the face, knocking him backward over his chair. Carmine stood, and the son caught him with a roundhouse to the side of the head, sending him sliding across the floor. Both Guido and Carmine were cold-cocked, unable to rise.

JB saw the action coming and quickly slid from his chair and stood to one side.

Salvatore turned to JB and said, "So, you must be the great savior to my family. You don't look like much to me. You're finished. I'm home now, so you're not needed any longer. You have fucked up my family enough. I'll decide what's best for them so get your ass out of town!"

JB watched Salvatore while helping Guido and Carmine to their feet. Both were groggy. He led them out of the bistro and heard the son loudly proclaiming, "How about those three yellow bellies!"

JB led the duo up the street to his house, revived them, and cared for their wounds. Guido's lip was badly split, his nose was bloody, and his cheek was turning blue from the punch. Carmine's left eye was swollen shut and turning blue. Their wounds were superficial but would look rather embarrassing for a few days.

By now both were alert and angry, wanting to return to the bistro. JB calmed them down and talked them into going home.

JB stood watching them walk away and decided to handle the matter now, rather than wait for the confrontation that was sure to happen at tonight's dance.

He walked to the bistro, entered the front door quietly, and walked up to the bar. As he entered, conversation ceased and all eyes turned toward him.

Salvatore held court at a large table and looked amazed when he saw JB. His amazement turned into a sneer, and he jumped up, striding quickly toward JB. "I told you to get your ass out of town," the son yelled and grabbed JB's arm.

JB was a blur of motion as he turned and landed six hard blows to the son before another word was spoken. The first blow to the solar plexus finished the fight. The other five blows were for show, and he was careful not to damage the son.

Salvatore stood, gasping his breath. JB spun him around and almost carried him out of the front door. JB continued pushing and half-carrying Salvatore up the street to the wharf. Some of the other fishermen started to follow but stopped when JB yelled loudly, "This is a family matter, stay away!"

JB took the son among the empty fish stalls and slammed him against a wooden wall. By now the son regained his breath and started swinging his fists toward JB. JB parried the attack easily and proceeded to hit the son with painful blows to the shoulders, elbows, ribs, and chest. He was careful not to strike so hard as to cause permanent damage.

In no time, Salvatore was unable to raise his arms to attack or even defend himself. The son stood shakily, moaning from the pain.

JB shoved him down into a sitting position, stood over him, and began to talk. "I'm the one who arranged for your release from prison, and you were released so you can care for your fatherless family. Marriages are arranged for your two oldest sisters. Once they are married, their husbands will make sure that your mother and your other sisters are properly cared for. Until that time, you will fish with the dory fleet. You will do exactly as your mother says, and you will not interfere with the marriages of your sisters. If you decide to leave, you will be returned to prison for a long stay. I have arranged for several villagers to keep me informed about your conduct. If I hear even a single bad report, you will immediately be returned to prison. If you try to leave before your sisters are married, I will find you and take you back to prison after I punish you."

The son tried to stand. JB slapped him a dozen times, so fast that all of the blows landed as the son's head snapped back.

JB continued, "Tonight, at the dance, you will go to Guido and Carmine, apologize for your actions today, ask for their forgiveness, and you will welcome them into your family. I am going now. You will go directly home and apologize to your family for your vulgarity."

JB went early to the dance that evening and stood waiting against the wall behind the kiosk. JB watched the Boronios enter. The mother was followed by her son, Ruby, and Lucia. The Boronios sat down together, the son politely waiting until his mother and sisters were seated. He was in obvious pain.

The signora sat demurely, the sisters chatted gaily, and the son was quiet, looking at the floor.

A few minutes later, Guido and Carmine entered the hall. They looked around, spotted the Boronios, and resolutely walked toward them. Guido, followed by Carmine, walked directly up to the son and announced, "I'm here to dance with your sister, Lucia. If you object, let's go outside now!"

The son looked at Guido, looked at his mother, looked at his sisters, then stood up. "Guido, I want to apologize for what I did today. My mother told me what a fine man you are. Please accept my apology and my blessings for you and Lucia." The son held out his hand.

JB saw the surprise, then relief, on Guido's face.

Guido looked down at the son's outstretched hand, back to his face, then shook hands. "I appreciate your apology and I accept."

The son turned to Carmine and repeated the scene.

The mother sat watching, her face dispassionate.

The son excused himself and left the dance hall.

The music began.

Guido and Carmine invited Lucia and Ruby to dance, leaving the signora sitting alone.

All was well, so JB slipped away from the dance hall and headed down the hill. He went to the bistro, had a glass of wine, said good-bye to Papa John, then left and walked home.

Most of the villagers were at the dance, so it was quiet along the waterfront.

JB walked past the deserted fish stalls and the beach where the dories were lined up on the sand. He felt a stab of sorrow as he walked up the street. He had grown to appreciate and love the hard-working, dedicated fishermen and their families.

After arriving home, JB packed his few belongings and lay down to sleep. He was certain Guido and Carmine would make sure all went well with the Boronios so there was no reason to stay around longer. He planned to catch the early bus to Naples tomorrow morning.

As he lay in the darkness, thinking about the past few weeks, he heard the front door open and close. He quickly and silently moved off the bed and stood against the wall beside the doorway to his bedroom.

JB heard someone walking quietly through his house, toward the bedroom. He saw the shadowy figure walk through the bedroom door and caught the familiar scent of Signora Boronio.

JB watched her walk to his bed, lean over, and search for him.

She sighed with disappointment and turned to leave. She saw him standing naked against the wall. She walked over to him, "You will have to pardon me, I couldn't let you go without saying good-bye."

JB looked into her sad eyes and unsmiling face, leaned toward her and gently kissed her lips. He felt her body shudder, and her lower lip began to tremble.

She stepped back, reached up and untied her hair, letting it fall down about her shoulders.

JB reached and started unbuttoning her blouse. He heard her heavy breathing and his hands trembled as he undid her buttons, one by one.

Her blouse unbuttoned, she moved her arms back and let her blouse slip off her shoulders. She was not wearing a bra or slip.

JB gasped at her beauty. Her breasts were large and her nipples were erect.

He reached for her waistband, and slowly pulled her skirt from around her hips, dropping it to the floor. She was not wearing panties, so she now stood completely naked. He stepped back and looked at her loveliness. Her heavy thighs blended into her large rounded hips. Her belly was rounded and flowed to her narrow waistline. Her thick, dark pubic hair stood out against the whiteness of her body. He had seen naked girls and women but never any quite like the signora.

Her eyes were partly closed and she stood naked, waiting for him.

He moved close to her and she felt his hardness. He was strongly erect and she placed a hand on him.

She traced her fingers up and down his turgidity and moaned with pleasure as his hands moved down her body. They kissed deeply, and as she opened up to his exploring touch, she moved backwards toward the bed, and he followed.

She grasped his head and pulled his lips to hers. They kissed deeply, and he felt her body trembling.

They lay entwined, and he became aware of her quiet sobbing. He lifted his head; looked at her; and saw the smiling, sad, tearful-eyed face. He whispered, "Oh, Signora, you are so beautiful and so full of love. I have never before been loved so completely."

Now she smiled, "*Mille grazie*, now, love me again!" she continued holding him within her, and she could feel him growing hard. "Maybe this time it will be heaven." And they made love again.

It was late when she left his bed. She kissed him hard, saying, "I have died a thousand deaths watching you these past few weeks, each day wanting you more and more, knowing that nothing could ever come of it. I could wait no longer and even now I'm saddened that our time is gone. Promise me that you will stop at my home before you leave tomorrow."

Perplexed, JB looked at her, "How did you know that I am leaving tomorrow?"

She smiled down at him, "When you love someone, they will tell you the important things with their actions. You have handled my family's immediate problems, so now I feel you will leave us to our lives. You are a strange and private young man, but except for our age difference, I could make you very happy. I will think of you often, and I will dream of what could have been. Now, promise me you will see me tomorrow before you leave!"

"I am leaving on the morning bus to Naples. I promise that I will come to your house. It will make me both happy and sad because I feel a closeness with you that I've never felt for anyone before."

She dressed quickly, kissed him again, and disappeared out of the house.

He awoke early on Sunday morning, wrapped in the bed covers. The bus would leave at ten o'clock.

It was eight o'clock when he left his house and went up the hill toward town.

The Positano that tourists saw when passing through and when visiting the local hotels was far up the side of the mountain. It consisted of one lone winding street that was the main road passing through. There was one large, modern hotel, frequented by tourists and another smaller, older hotel, used mainly by businessmen and locals. Many small shops lined both sides of the street, selling souvenirs and mementos. There were several sidewalk cafes, a couple of discotheques, and a few bistros. The local streets were steep, narrow, and cobblestoned. Few cars traveled these steep streets, and the houses were almost hung from the hillside. Each day JB fished, he marveled at the beauty of the town, the many whitewashed, red tiled houses perched on the mountainside, and the winding stoned streets. The views from the main street and the tourist hotel were magnificent but couldn't compare to looking up at the village from the sea.

It was already warm, and JB sweated as he climbed the hill towards Signora Boronio's house.

It was noticeably quiet as he knocked on her door. The door opened immediately, and she stood there, dressed in a long housecoat, her hair wound into a bundle. She had dark circles below her eyes, and she looked tired. She beckoned JB to enter, and she stood back, holding the door. She closed the door, and as he turned to face her, cried out and threw her arms around his neck.

JB broke away from her kiss and looked searchingly around the room.

The signora spoke, "They're all at church. We will be alone for at least a few minutes."

JB turned back to her and kissed her, pushing her gently back against the door.

"No," she cried. "I want you to stay!" She pulled away from him and rushed out of the room.

He followed her into the kitchen.

JB had marveled at her beauty in the darkness of his bedroom. Her room was bright with the morning sun. He could see time's disfavors in her face and hands, but the full picture was a breathtakingly beautiful one.

"I give you my heart and my love," she told him. "No one could ever make love to me the way you did last night. I am yours forever. I will dream of you every night, and every time I see the boats come home, I'll be wishing you were in the boat, so I could watch you walk across the beach."

JB kissed away the tears streaming down her cheeks and buried his face into her bosom.

She lifted his head and saw his tears. "I know that you cannot stay. I only hope you will someday soon come back, even if for only a day. Now we must calm down; my children will be home soon."

They were in the kitchen, and she was serving him coffee when her children came into the house.

The girls crowded around JB, all chattering at once, wishing him goodbyes.

JB stood to leave, and Salvatore beckoned him into another room and spoke, "Sometimes it takes a good man to bring another to understanding. You awakened me, and I promise you I will devote my life to caring for my family. If ever you need me for anything, let me know and I'll be there."

They shook hands and embraced strongly.

"Salvatore, stay with your mother. I will go alone."

The signora stood by the door.

JB turned to go, put his arms around her, placed his cheek against hers, and whispered, "Good-bye, my love. We shall meet again, *con amore.*"

JB left the house and walked away, up the hill toward town. When he turned and waved his last good-bye, his vision was blurred, and they could see his tear-filled eyes glistening in the morning sun.

The lump in his throat was almost gone by the time he reached Giovanni Street. JB walked to the old hotel to wait for the morning bus.

He had forgotten about the tortuous, steep, and winding road cut into the mountainsides.

The bus traveled slowly, and he sat looking, longingly, back at the beautiful village. Looking up and down the coastline, he saw the areas where he fished and saw the boats now in a line on the sand at the bottom of the hillside village. He thought, *How could I have been so fortunate to have befriended these exquisite people?*

The bus rounded a curve, and the village disappeared from view. JB turned in his seat, put his head back, and closed his eyes.

It was late in the afternoon when the bus arrived in Naples. JB looked forward to a long, hot shower, but first he would find a telephone and call the Old Man in Palermo.

JB alighted from the bus and joined the throng of people heading into the station building. He felt a hand on his shoulder, turned, and there was Josef.

"Hello, Josef, what brings you here?"

"Please come with me. The Old Man needs to see you."

JB followed Josef out of the station and got into the waiting taxi.

They sat silently for awhile as the taxi drove through Naples. "Where are we going?" JB asked.

"I have a plane waiting for us. The Old Man did not ask me to come. He is seriously ill, and I'm afraid he will die soon. You mean very much to him, so I thought a visit from you would help."

"I was looking for a telephone to call the Old Man. I wanted to visit him before I return to America. What's the matter?"

"Two weeks ago he suffered a stroke of some magnitude. His sons came home and brought medical specialists. So far it looks like a losing battle."

They rode on in silence for awhile. Then JB asked, "How did you know where to find me?"

"I knew your whereabouts at all times. The Old Man was pleased with the way you handled yourself and the help you brought to the Boronio family. They were in need, and you responded without hesitation."

They arrived at the airport, and Josef directed the taxi driver to a small building several hundred yards from the main terminal. The taxi stopped alongside a helicopter. The helicopter's blades were slowly turning; its running lights were on and the door was open, awaiting their arrival.

Once airborne, they headed west, out over the Mediterranean Sea.

They skimmed along over the sea at an altitude of thirty meters.

"Why are we flying without lights?" he asked Josef.

"This is an unscheduled flight. Don't worry, it's a short flight, and our pilot is experienced."

JB sat, looking out the side window, watching the dark sea flash by. The pilot smoothly maneuvered the helicopter away from the boats in the area, and soon JB could see the Sicilian coastline.

They came in low over the coastline, flew up the valley for about ten minutes, then veered sharply left, up and over a mountain range. The helicopter slowed, then turned, gently settling toward the landing pad.

The door opened, and strong hands helped them to the ground. JB followed Josef, ducking his head as he walked from under the whispering blades.

A long, black limousine waited. They got into the back seat and the car pulled away. It was a short ride to the villa.

The same old gentleman waited at the front door. He opened the door and beckoned JB to follow. The butler led him up the stairs and to the Old Man's private quarters. Two men stood beside the bed, watching a doctor at work. All turned, and he was surprised to see Cosmo.

Cosmo came over to JB, and they embraced. JB saw the sadness in Cosmo's face as Cosmo motioned to go outside the room.

In the hallway, Cosmo whispered, "My grandfather is dying. The doctor says he will probably die within a week's time. He was awake a little while ago, and he asked for you. Let's go to his bedside and hope he will awaken again and know that you're here."

They went back into the room. Cosmo's father embraced JB and thanked him for coming.

They stood in silence for awhile. The Old Man stirred, opened his eyes, and looked up at them. His eyes widened when he saw JB, and he nodded his head, moving his lips whisperingly, "Come close, my son, and listen to me."

JB bent down and listened carefully.

"I know I am dying. This will be our final good-bye. You will not attend my funeral. Agents and police from all over the world will be there, taking pictures. You must remain anonymous. I have not found who is plotting against your president but it is happening. It will be up to you to discover what is planned and take steps to prevent it. None of my family knows what we talked about. If you tell anyone, your life will always be in danger. You can depend upon my son and my grandson, but you should never tell them about the plot. You will not need to worry about the Boronio family. Each day their fish will be purchased by the hotels at prices to allow the Boronios a comfortable life. Now, give me our final embrace, and then be on your way."

JB looked into the Old Man's eyes, put his arms gently around him, and whispered, "May God bless you for your many good deeds, and may God forgive you for your mistakes. I love you, and I will miss you. *Arivederci,* my grandfather."

JB stood, and the Old Man waved a feeble good-bye and whispered, "Now go."

JB shook hands with Cosmo and Cosmo's father, embraced them, then turned and left the room. Josef was waiting for JB and led him back outside to the waiting car.

They returned to Naples on the same helicopter that brought them to the villa.

At the Rome airport, he browsed the shops, buying gifts for Isabel.

JB boarded the late evening flight to San Francisco and spent most of the return trip concerning himself about what the Old Man had told him and daydreaming about his time in Positano.

CHAPTER EIGHT

JB was busy during the next few days, catching up on lost moments with Isabel and completing his arrangements for his final college year.

One morning JB picked up a newspaper and read, "Underworld King Is Dead." With a lump in his throat, JB read the news item about the Old Man. JB was saddened the Old Man had asked that he not attend the funeral. JB explained to Isabel he would be away a few days with the Naval Reserve. She bought it and he flew to San Diego.

JB spent the next week with the sergeant and for the first time saw the sergeant in fatigues which bore the name patch, "Browning." He thought, *So the sergeant has a name!*

The sergeant was impressed with JB's physical condition and spent hours refreshing his skills in martial arts, demolition, and firearms. The intense physical training part of the week was welcomed, since it helped him to forget about the passing of the Old Man. JB had retained his expertise in self-defense and all kinds of weaponry. The sergeant was especially impressed with the way he handled handguns. JB was quick, accurate, and deadly, hitting multiple moving targets dead center at 150 feet. The sergeant mused, *When the time for action comes, he'll be ready.*

On a weekend evening after his return, JB and Isabel sat in the local movie theater. He felt a slight tug on his coat pocket and looked at the man sitting in the next seat. It was dark, and all he could discern was the man looked similar to the one the one who delivered the Paris note.

A few minutes later the man left.

He excused himself and went up the aisle.

JB reached the lobby and looked around without seeing anyone other than the snack bar attendants, then disappeared into the empty restroom.

He took the note from his coat pocket and read, "Come to the Capri Motel tonight, same room. Don't be alarmed." The note was unsigned, same as the prior note. That same feeling he had experienced before suffused his body . . . *my destiny.*

JB bought some popcorn and returned to his seat. He didn't see the remainder of the movie.

JB turned on the room lights as he entered the door. He felt the déjà vu when he saw the door ajar. He walked toward the door and heard a voice. "Please, don't come into the room. I'm the same one as before. I have been instructed to ask for your help. The name is Enrique's Place in San Salvador, December 27, at noon. I know nothing more, I have no further information nor can I answer any questions. As before, I have been instructed to tell you one hundred thousand American dollars will be deposited to your special account in Zurich. I am going now. Please don't try to follow me."

JB allowed the man to slip away, then left the motel. At home he turned out the light, undressed, and lay down. He felt strangely receptive to the information furnished by the unknown man and lay thinking about the message.

The school year passed quickly. Soon the school would close for the Christmas holidays. Obviously the special Section had selected JB's target for a time when he could be away without attracting attention.

JB booked round trip seating on a flight from Los Angeles to San Salvador under an assumed name and the following weekend drove to San Francisco to visit Cosmo.

They dined out and while awaiting service, Cosmo spoke. "Before my grandfather died he told us he sent you away and told you not to attend the funeral." He watched JB carefully and saw the sadness.

"Cosmo, you know I would've been there. Thanks for telling me you know why I missed the funeral. I was heartbroken, and I still find it hard to accept that he's gone." He paused, then raised his glass, "Here's to the Old Man, your grandfather. May he rest in peace."

Cosmo raised his glass, and they toasted the Old Man they loved, each in their own special ways.

They sat quietly for a few moments before JB spoke. "Cosmo, I need some special identification. Can you tell me who to see?"

At that moment their meals arrived. During dinner several of Cosmo's friends stopped by the table. They finished eating and were sipping an espresso when Cosmo spoke. "Go to 2791 Irving Street."

JB nodded, smiled, and replied, "Cosmo, thank you for not asking. This is something personal."

"No need to explain. I know you wouldn't ask if it wasn't important."

They said good-bye, promised to meet again soon, then he drove to the Irving Street address.

The man was expecting him and proceeded to photograph and prepare the identification documents under the assumed name furnished by JB. The entire process took about two hours.

He was now ready to travel as a bank courier with a United States passport and numerous additional identification.

He spent Christmas Eve and Christmas Day with Isabel at her parents' home. She and her family were leaving late on Christmas Day for a ski vacation. This time JB was thankful no invitation was offered.

Early the next morning, he drove to the San Francisco airport and took a flight to Los Angeles. He made connection and settled down for the five-hour flight to San Salvador.

JB passed through immigration without a hitch despite intense scrutiny from the military guards examining the papers of all passengers.

He checked into the Hilton, went to his room, unpacked his small bag, and took out the package of cigarettes. He planned to use a device furnished to him by the sergeant.

JB checked the address of Enrique's Place and found it to be on Calle de la Humberto, an area of nightclubs and restaurants.

JB left the hotel and took a taxi to Calle de la Humberto and found a restaurant, not far from Enrique's. He dined alone then walked up the street. He spotted his target, noting that it was a sidewalk café, and looked it over carefully but inconspicuously, deciding to place the explosive device near the glass doors separating the inside portion of the restaurant from the sidewalk section.

Next morning JB spent several hours assembling the bomb and disguising his appearance. He added gray fringes to his hair color which was now combed straight back in the latest Central American style. He changed his facial appearance by placing small rolls of cotton between his gums and cheeks and changed his skin color with a light covering of dark-tinted cream makeup. He worked carefully and painstakingly, making certain he looked natural. The transformation made, he packed his bag and checked out of the hotel.

To maintain anonymity, he took a taxi downtown and directed the driver to let him out two blocks from Enrique's Place. JB walked to Enrique's and entered. He tipped the maître d'hotel generously, was seated at the table of his choice, and ordered a light lunch. While waiting for lunch, JB inconspicuously placed the explosive device to the underside of the chair.

JB was eating when a Mercedes sedan pulled up in front of the restaurant. Three men got out of the sedan and entered the restaurant. They were greeted profusely by the maître d' and seated at a large corner table located against the back wall. Two large, rugged looking men entered and took positions on each side of the table, watching the crowd.

JB finished his lunch and left the restaurant. He walked down the street one block, crossed over to the other side of the street, and doubled back toward the restaurant. While window shopping, he timed his walk so he was about half a block away from the restaurant when the large street clock struck noon.

JB triggered the device with the electronic switch in his wristwatch.

There was a thunderous explosion, and the restaurant disappeared into a fireball. Heat from the explosion blistered the paint of the black Mercedes sedan parked in front, and the car burst into flames as well. The concussion from the explosion smashed windows up and down the street and knocked pedestrians to the ground. People poured out of other buildings up and down the street, trying to help the ones caught by the flying debris, glass, and the force of the blast. The restaurant and the buildings on each side were destroyed. The street was in chaos, people running in all directions. JB pulled the earplugs from his ears and dropped them into the debris on the street. Then turned and walked away from the disaster scene.

Several blocks away, he hailed a taxi for the airport.

His plane departed at 1400 and was in Los Angeles by late afternoon; San Francisco shortly after dark.

Walking through the air terminal, JB picked up a late edition of the Chronicle. A front page headline read, "Drug Kings Assassinated." He read on: "Three reputed drug kings from Central America are among the dead in an explosion at a local restaurant. . . ." He sighed deeply and read on: "Fifteen are known dead and more than twenty others are hospitalized with varying injuries." A twinge of remorse hit him, and he agonized, *Why did it need to be today? Why couldn't they assign me to kill those three and give me time to plan and execute them without involving innocents? What have I become to be able to do this to strangers?* JB tossed the paper into a waste receptacle.

Back in school, the weeks passed quickly. JB and Isabel announced their summer wedding plans. Her father was displeased with Isabel dating JB, and now he was incensed. Still determined to break up the relationship, her father planned a family vacation during the Easter break, excluding JB. JB didn't mind because he was expecting to have other business.

He decided to spend his spring school break in San Diego.

Immediately after finishing his classes, he packed a few things, got into his car, and headed south. He drove straight through, stopping only for gas.

He arrived in San Diego at 0200 and called the sergeant's telephone number. He heard a gruff "Hello" after the first ring. "I've been expecting you," the sergeant said. "I'll meet you at the east gate in two hours." The telephone line went dead.

At 0400 JB drove up to the east gate and was waved through by the marine guard. JB parked in his usual spot, and spotted the sergeant.

"Good morning, son," said the tough old sergeant. "Let's go to work."

JB followed the sergeant into the windowless building, and the training began.

JB was expert at all phases covered by his training. The next week was spent in learning more advanced techniques in demolition, checking out the latest weapons, and most of all physical conditioning.

The latest automatic machine gun was miniaturized and weighed less that twelve pounds. Only a foot long, the ammunition chamber was longer than the gun barrel and could fire the full sixty rounds in five seconds. New compact night vision goggles allowed unrestrained movement in the dark. The latest explosives were powerful enough in small quantities to make them easy to disguise and hide from detection.

The days were long and the physical conditioning was grueling. By the end of the week, he was again fine-tuned and ready.

The sergeant did not talk much, so, as before, JB was unable to find out who the sergeant was working for. He voiced some concerns to the sergeant and felt certain those concerns would be relayed up the ladder.

At the end of the week, he said good-bye to the sergeant and drove home.

As with all major universities, the large corporations visited the campus during the months prior to graduation to interview graduating seniors for choice job positions. Each interviewer talked to the professors and department heads to learn the names of the best students. JB was at the top of each professor's list, so he was targeted by the interviewers. Among the industrial management and consulting companies, Deesco was considered to be elite. JB talked to several different firms but there was never a doubt in his mind. He should do his internship at Deesco, and when they offered him a position, he immediately accepted. They were generous in their offer, a good starting salary and travel during internship. They also offered time off with pay to allow him time for his upcoming marriage and honeymoon. Soon after JB graduated with honors.

CHAPTER NINE

JB started work the next week, and the wedding was set for August. He moved to San Francisco immediately following graduation, and, together with Isabel, selected an apartment in the Marina on Scott Street, just off Lombard. He buried himself in his work and was surprised when he discovered how much he enjoyed it. The doctor certainly understood his basic personality and ambitions. JB was well suited for industrial management and consulting, and experience with Deesco would help him immensely when he started his own company.

He renewed his friendship with Cosmo and they met frequently for lunch or dinner. He asked Cosmo to be his best man, and Cosmo arranged a honeymoon for JB and Isabel at the Mauna Kea Hotel on the big island of Hawaii.

Isabel's family was polite but still unreceptive toward him. The wedding rehearsal went smoothly, and the prenuptial dinner was as JB expected. Isabel's family was well known in the community, and the wedding was an occasion to invite all of their friends. JB had no family, so he invited a few new acquaintances from Deesco.

Several hundred people attended the wedding and reception. It was the social affair of the year. JB relaxed and let Isabel's family have their glory.

Her father cried as JB and Isabel drove away from the reception. JB smiled grimly and thought, *Probably from frustration.*

All went excitingly, and they spent the next week acclimating themselves. Once the dam had burst, Isabel found a big appetite for making love.

They spent their days lazing in the warm sunshine, swimming in the ocean, and making love whenever they could find a private place. They found their private places on secluded beaches, among the palm trees and bushes, in their bungalow, and once on a catamaran while sailing. They rejuvenated themselves by dining out and dancing away the early evenings. They slept as one after long sessions of making love.

The week passed quickly, and they found themselves on the plane headed back to San Francisco.

He spent the next three years at Deesco, working hard to learn the many small nuances of the consulting business. During this time, the president was reelected.

They bought a home in the East Bay suburb of Lafayette and settled into a comfortable marriage. During the first and second years, Isabel presented them with two lovely daughters.

Using Cosmo's connections, JB bought the house in Positano from Papa John, and upon learning the house next door was available, bought the second. He planned to surprise his new family with a *real* Italian vacation when the moment was right.

JB traveled extensively on company business, mostly to southern California. Twice each year, he managed to visit the sergeant for his updates on the latest weapons. JB worked hard throughout the year to keep himself in good physical condition, so his visits to the sergeant were short and could be worked into his business schedule.

During his latest visit to San Diego, the sergeant told him, "I've been instructed to tell you no leads have developed. I assume you know the meaning of the message. I've also been instructed to tell you you will be needed again soon."

A few days after the sergeant's message, JB received an unannounced caller at his office. He was interrupted by his secretary's announcement. "A Mr. Jones is here to see you. He said you made the appointment last week. The appointment is not scheduled in my appointment book. Perhaps you failed to inform me?"

"I'm sorry Phyllis, it slipped my mind. Please show Mr. Jones in."

She left his office and returned with the visitor.

JB stood, walked around his desk, and greeted his visitor. "Good morning, Mr. Jones."

They shook hands, and JB told his secretary, "Phyllis, please hold my telephone calls. I need a few minutes alone with Mr. Jones."

She left the office and closed the door.

JB turned to the stranger. "Well, Mr. Jones, or whoever you are, what can I do for you?"

"May I speak freely?"

"Yes, surely."

"Thank you for receiving me. This will only take a moment. I have been instructed to give you a message. The president will visit San Francisco in two weeks, on June 22. His visit will be announced next week. He will stay at the Palace Hotel. The Palace Hotel received an unsigned threatening letter, ordering them not to receive the president. His travel plans were leaked by someone."

JB looked at *Jones* and asked, "Are you the one who called on me before?"

The man smiled, nodded yes and said, "We've seen a couple of movies together." The man continued, "I don't understand the significance of the message, but whatever the reason, I wish you good luck and success. Our president needs all of the protection and help he can get."

Without another word, they shook hands, and the visitor left JB's office.

JB sat down and pondered the message. The president had been told about the threatening letter. The president knew a leak had occurred. Security would surely be increased. *What can I do? What is my mission here . . . ?*

JB spent the next two weeks thinking about the message. He imagined what he would do if he were planning to assassinate the president. JB played the various scenarios over and over in his mind. He needed to be present when the president arrived at the hotel. He would discipline himself against watching the president. He would observe the crowd and surroundings. If something happened that security could not handle, perhaps he could be ready to help.

In due course, the president's visit was announced. There was much excitement in the city, and many people would turn out to greet the president.

JB worked through lunchtime on the day of the president's visit. The president was scheduled to arrive at the hotel in mid-afternoon.

At 1400 JB left his office and walked up Market Street to the Palace Hotel. The sidewalk was jammed with people, and the police had sealed off the streets, prohibiting any cars or buses from entering the area.

He slowly worked his way through the crowd, and by three o'clock was directly in front of the hotel entrance. He carried a small modified Baretta, limiting his effectiveness. He was concerned a larger weapon would be difficult to conceal from the many prying eyes of the policemen and Secret Service men. The president's car would stop about twenty feet from the spot where JB stood.

His back was against the hotel wall adjacent the main entrance, giving him a good vantage point to observe the crowd around the hotel entrance. Uniformed policemen were everywhere and numerous Secret Service stood facing the crowd, alertly scanning the throng.

He heard the roar of the crowd on Market Street as the motorcade approached. The motorcycles and marked police cars leading the procession moved past the hotel entrance to allow the president's car to park directly in front of the entrance. The other limousines stopped, and no less than twenty Secret Service jumped from their cars and encircled the president's limousine as it stopped. The rear door opened, and the president stepped out onto the sidewalk, smiling and waving at the crowd, squinting into the sun.

Suddenly there was a scuffle near the president. Shots were fired. It was a slow blur in JB's mind. . . . A middle-aged woman, standing at the front of the crowd, a few feet from the president, pulled a pistol from her purse and was firing. The Secret Servicemen wrestled with her. The president staggered to his left. Her fire had hit the president in his side and another man in the side of his head.

There was screaming and confusion. All attention focused on the shooting. He knew at once the lady was a diversion. The main attempt would follow.

He watched the nearby crowd for the unusual. A man in a business suit next to the hotel entrance took something from his coat pocket. He pressed it to the bottom of his right forearm. As he raised his right arm, JB gave a mighty shove sending a woman reeling across into him. Automatic pistol fire sprayed erratically into the crowd. JB heard bullets hitting flesh and the president's limousine. Policemen and Secret Servicemen leaped upon the gunman, wrestling him to the sidewalk, finally shooting him.

The security officers quickly controlled the scene and moved the crowd away from the hotel entrance. JB moved back with the crowd. He counted ten bodies on the sidewalk and was sure more were wounded.

The president was up, thrown into the back seat. The limousine sped away, surrounded by motorcycles and police cars. The president had been wounded. But he was alive!

JB melted back into the crowd and continued back down Market Street. He took his car from the parking garage and drove down the Embarcadero, looking for an exit out of town.

The newscaster on the car radio was recounting what had just occurred at the Palace Hotel. "An attempt was made on the president's life. The president was first shot at by an unidentified woman. The president was hit in the side and has been rushed to a local hospital. A security officer standing next to the president was hit in the head and died instantly. The first attack was followed by a second attempt. According to witnesses, an unidentified woman grabbed the attacker's arm, forcing the gunman to fire wildly into the crowd. In the ensuing struggle, both the security officer and the unidentified woman were shot and killed by Secret Servicemen. There appears to be no question the unidentified woman saved the president from being shot by the security officer. Twelve are known dead, with an estimated ten seriously wounded."

JB drove east across the Bay Bridge. He switched to another radio station and heard essentially the same information. None of the witnesses said anything about the unidentified woman having been pushed from behind. There was no doubt in his mind—the first woman's attempt was a diversion. The security officer had intended to kill the president and create mass confusion by spraying the president and the surrounding crowd with the automatic pistol fire.

CHAPTER TEN

Over the years, JB had become good friends with his neighbor, David Protect. David attended local schools, the state university, and medical school at the University of California in San Francisco. He was recognized as the top gastroenterologist in the San Francisco Bay Area, regularly receiving referrals from all hospital medical centers in northern California and was frequently called in for consultation at the major medical centers at Stanford and U.C.L.A. David was an internist and a brilliant surgeon, but his expertise and main interests were the development of new, innovative surgical techniques and in particular, non-invasive surgery. He expanded upon endoscopy and developed techniques to reach vital organs with surgical wires or tubes, allowing surgical repairs by guiding surgical instruments through the tubes to the proper place within the damaged or diseased organ. He was often able to delay and redirect the advancement of fatal conditions in the vital organs of many patients, allowing them to live their final days in reasonable comfort.

JB marveled at David's innovative thinking.

David was unpretentious, and many people in the neighborhood were unaware that David was a medical doctor of considerable stature.

JB and David were together often—David constantly asking JB questions about the consulting business, his background and plans for the future. He responded by probing David for information about his new surgical techniques and medical experiences. Their families enjoyed spending time together, so as time passed David and JB became close friends.

David was intrigued with JB's enormous range of knowledge and became more and more interested in the human brain. A medical school classmate was a neurosurgeon of some renown in the Bay Area, so David revived their acquaintance. His friend allowed him to observe brain surgeries and soon

David was assisting on many surgical cases. It became obvious to David that by using his noninvasive techniques he could reach areas of the brain that were considered inaccessible through modern surgery. David discussed his ideas with JB and become more and more obsessed with putting his ideas into practice.

JB realized that David needed a mentor, and Dr. Johnson immediately came to mind. JB placed his call.

The following day, the same man who had delivered Dr. Johnson's messages to JB came to JB's office. JB explained his idea. "David is a brilliant young surgeon. He wants and needs help in better understanding neurosurgery. Dr. Johnson is an expert, so I would like him to spend some time with David."

The man left JB's office without saying a word.

Three days later JB received a confidential, special delivery envelope. Inside was a short note, "Bethesda arranged for David. Have him contact Dolly Peters in the Neurology Research Dept." He reread the note and then pitched it into his electronic waste basket where it was immediately shredded and burned.

That evening he waited until David started his evening jog. He joined David and together they ran through the neighborhood. David excitedly explained a new technique he was working on. JB waited for a break in the conversation, then said, "David, I've heard about a neurology research department that is working on some new and radical ideas in treating human brain disorders. I've obtained the name of a doctor involved in that research. I think you should call her and ask if you can visit their research center."

David looked at him and replied, "JB, I know you well enough by now to know you've probably already arranged my visit. I wouldn't miss this opportunity for the world. Give me the doctor's name and number; I'll call him first thing tomorrow."

JB smiled and said, "He's a her! Dolly Peters, Bethesda Medical Center." They jogged on in silence; and when they reached David's house, David turned and said, "I'll let you know what happens, and thanks again."

JB maintained a close friendship with Cosmo. They were eating lunch at their favorite out-of-the-way Italian restaurant hidden among the wholesale fish houses adjacent Fisherman's Wharf. Cosmo was toying with his coffee, not looking at JB.

Cosmo's eyes flicked up and saw JB watching him. Cosmo smiled fleetingly, shrugged his shoulders, and said, "Before my grandfather died, he called me to his bedside and spoke privately to me. He told me that if I ever hear anything about a presidential assassination, I should pass that information to you, without question."

JB sat quietly and waited for Cosmo to continue.

"Something strange is going on. I have a U.S. senator named Conway on my payroll and he has a weakness for young girls. The young girls who I send to him keep me informed about all of the senator's business and, of course, he's told how to vote on any issues that come before the senate. A young girl that spends much time with the senator told me the senator has been telling her that a plot is forming to kill our president. The plot is designed to look like a Cuban assassination attempt. The senator rambled on and on about Satan."

JB watched Cosmo for a few moments. Realizing that Cosmo was finished with his story, JB said, "Thanks, Cosmo. I appreciate the information. Thanks also for not asking me to explain why your grandfather told you to keep me informed. If you hear anything more, please let me know."

They sat silently for awhile. Finally Cosmo spoke. "You should never forget, I have the connections. If you need help for any reason, you must call on me. I believe in you, I trust you, and I will never ask you why."

JB smiled at Cosmo and replied, "Thanks, my friend, and I hope you realize I feel the same toward you."

JB felt certain the plot to assassinate the president now demanded his action. He decided to learn about the vice president, then work his way down through the presidential staff and key congressmen.

His business was functioning smoothly, so he cleared his schedule book, explaining to his secretary that he needed at least a month off and arranged to call her once weekly for messages. JB maintained active reserve status as a cover for his trips to San Diego, and that evening following dinner, alone with Isabel, he explained, "Isabel, you know that I'm in the naval reserve and have been since I was released from active duty over eight years ago. I've worked my way into an important position, and I'm now involved in a vital project relating to our president. It's something that I shouldn't be discussing with you, but I'll have to be away much of the time during the next few weeks and I don't want you thinking that something's not right between us."

She reached across the table, placing her hand over his. "JB, I think I know you well enough by now to sense if something were amiss. I often detect a tenseness in your demeanor but never toward me or the children. I'm curious about what you're doing but I'll never press you for information beyond what you feel that you can share with me."

He moved his head slightly from side to side. "Honey, I've done some things in my lifetime that I'm not too proud of, but I can tell you, since our marriage I've loved only you, and I love you now, more than ever before. I can tell you I'm involved in a serious investigation that causes me some concern about the safety of you and the girls. I promise you I'll do everything possible to protect all of you, and I won't jeopardize your safety. Thank you for your trust."

He made the final arrangements at his office and then set about planning his investigation.

JB sat in his study, thinking and planning. He realized that his best source of information was Dr. Johnson, so he reached over, picked up the receiver, and dialed a number that came into his mind. JB heard the telephone ring one time, and a voice answered, "Good evening, Bethesda."

Not knowing what to say, he replied, "This is Apercu. I need to talk to my doctor."

The voice on the other end of the line hesitated for just a moment, then responded. "Thank you, sir. I'll see that he gets your message." The line went dead.

He replaced the receiver and sat back, wondering how could he have known a number to reach the doctor.

He arrived in San Diego on a Saturday and was met at the airport by Sergeant Browning.

He waited at curbside in front of Lindberg Field.

The sergeant stopped his car alongside the curb, not far from JB; got out; and opened the trunk for JB's luggage.

JB spotted him, waved, and walked quickly over to the car. The sergeant smiled at JB, and they shook hands. The handshake was as firm as before, but JB noted the yellowish coloring in the eyes and skin of the old sergeant.

They got into the car and drove away. There had never been much conversation between them, so silence was not uncomfortable.

The sergeant broke the silence. "Obviously you've noticed the color of my eyes and skin." The Sergeant paused, then said, "They think I may have cirrhosis. Apparently my liver function is stopping and when it stops, I die. They told me I'll have much pain and discomfort, and of course they've scheduled me for more tests, but the doctor seemed to know what he's talking about. This may be our last time together."

They rode on in silence for awhile. Then JB replied, "I can honestly tell you, I wish it were me rather than you. But that will not change your situation. I've grown to respect you as a person and I love you and care about you." He paused, inhaled deeply, and continued, "I've got a doctor friend that never, ever accepts initial diagnosis. He has an inventive mind and often finds a way to help patients who other doctors have either misdiagnosed or have done all the normal and accepted treatments and procedures without success. I hope that you will let me help you."

The sergeant looked over. "I'd be very grateful for your help. Now let's get on with the job at hand. Dr. Johnson is at my home now waiting to see you. He's scheduled to leave at midnight. You'll spend this afternoon and evening with him. We'll begin our training tomorrow morning."

JB broached the topic again. "Sergeant, like I said, I know someone who may be able to help you. He's a brilliant medical doctor and a close friend of mine. It might help you to get a second opinion, so, with your permission, I'll arrange for you to see him."

The sergeant nodded yes and JB noticed the bright sparkle of tearing in the sergeant's eyes. "In all my life, I've never walked away from a fight. Our country is fighting for its life, and I want to be a part of the struggle! I will appreciate anything that you can do to prolong my usefulness."

They rode on in silence and soon arrived at the sergeant's house.

They sat on the patio, looking out over the Pacific. The house perched near the edge of a 100-foot cliff, above a long, narrow sandy beach. JB and the sergeant spent many hours running up and down the long beach and frequently swam far out into the ocean. JB's semi-annual visits with the sergeant had been alternated between the desert training base and the sergeant's home. JB and the sergeant competed physically during the past week, and both were grateful to relax in the warm afternoon sun. JB looked fit and healthy. The sergeant looked tired and drawn.

He thought about his meeting with the doctor. He had told Dr. Johnson about the assassination rumor, and the doctor answered, "Rumors have always been present, but this one scares me. I can't put my finger on it, but for some time now, I've felt uneasy about our vice president. I have no concrete evidence. It's just that something is not right. All I can say is, my gut feeling tells me something is rotten there."

JB replied, "I've told you about my investigation. I'm planning to start with our vice president and work my way down through the cabinet members and the high ranking congressional members."

The doctor answered, "I'll send you a copy of my file on the vice president to get you started and I'll send you information on how to contact a school chum of mine who is now a leading contemporary political historian. If I learn anything new, you will hear from me. You should know that I have the other four working on this same rumor. I'm concerned for the president, and I feel that something dreadful may happen soon. Do not waste time in your research, and I will contact you soon for another meeting."

Both slept in the warm afternoon sun.

Later in the afternoon, the sergeant awoke and shook JB awake. "Time to go, JB. I'll wait for you out front." The sergeant disappeared into the house.

JB got up and went inside to get his travel bag.

As they drove away from the sergeant's home, JB looked back, sensing that he would not return here again. He turned back to the front and caught the sergeant watching him. They exchanged knowing nods. Then, the sergeant looked straight ahead and drove quickly to the airport.

Once parked, the sergeant turned to JB and said, "The president needs you. Just relax, let it all hang out, and go after the bastards. So long as I'm alive, you can count me in, anytime, anywhere." The old sergeant's deep blue eyes were ablaze with anger.

He looked directly into the sergeant's eyes, nodded, and said, "Everything I do, I will do for us. I promise that I will not rest until I find out what is going on, who's responsible, and then bring them to justice. Justice being *our justice*." They shook hands and JB got out of the car. He leaned back inside and said, "Dr. David Protect will call you soon. I think he can help you. Good-bye, Sergeant Browning, and good luck." JB closed the car door, turned, and walked into the air terminal without looking back. He heard the car leave and his vision was blurred with held-back tears as he headed for the gate.

He was home by mid-evening and, after spending a few minutes with his family, went to his study to look over his mail from the past week.

Isabel followed him toward his study, glancing over her shoulder, making certain they were out of earshot from the girls. "JB, a large brown envelope was delivered by a uniformed military courier this afternoon. It looks important."

He stopped, turned, and enclosed her with his arms, speaking softly to her. "Isabel honey, I've been expecting the envelope. It's part of my investigation, so I shouldn't show you the contents. If you want to sit in the study with me, it's okay, but I probably should be alone for awhile."

She tiptoed, kissing him lightly. "I'll get the girls to bed, and I'll wait for you upstairs."

He went into his study and immediately noticed the large brown envelope. He scanned the outside and noted it had no return address or evidence of origin. He quickly opened it. Inside he found a thick packet of papers and records. The cover sheet was a personal resume of the vice president. Included with the resume were medical records; military records; and school records covering grade school, high school, college, and law school.

JB spent most of Sunday with his family but with a highly pensive feeling over what he might be about to discover.

Early Sunday evening, JB started reading the vice president's file. He spent the better part of the next twenty-four hours reading and rereading.

JB was interrupted by a telephone call about mid-morning Monday. He didn't recognize the voice but knew the purpose of the caller's message. It was a simple message: "Dr. Burr, Stanford, 415-365-8889." The caller hung up immediately.

JB made note of the name and telephone number, then placed a call to the number.

The friendly voice of a young lady answered, "Good morning, how can I help you?"

"This is Jim Barrlo, a friend referred me to Dr. Burr.

She replied, "Dr. Burr is expecting your call. When would you like to come in?"

"Tomorrow at two in the afternoon?" asked JB.

"Yes, that will be fine. Dr. Burr will meet you in Suite 202 at 9800 Welch Road at two o'clock. Do you need directions?"

"No," JB replied. "I'm familiar with the medical center. I'll be there at two o'clock tomorrow afternoon."

He hung up the telephone and resumed his assessment of the vice president's file.

He entered Dr. Burr's office five minutes before his appointment.

The lady smiled warmly and said, "You must be Mr. B."

JB swallowed hard and felt his desire stir. He met many beautiful women, but this lady stunned him—long, light blonde hair; blue eyes; high cheek bones; wide shoulders; large breasts; looking well-groomed with no visible makeup other than tinted lips.

She stood, then walked around the desk, extended her hand, and said, "Well, I'm Dr. Burr."

JB felt his face flushing, and his smile grew larger. He shook her hand, felt the firm grip, and replied, "I was expecting Dr. Burr to look like Aaron Burr! Somehow you just don't fit."

She laughed easily, saying, "Would you believe that Aaron Burr is one of my ancestors? Please, sit here on the sofa and tell me what I can do for you."

JB muttered, "Actually I got your name from a friend who told me you were a school chum of his, which explains why I was expecting someone a little older in years."

She laughed again, "Dr. Burr will see you in a few minutes. Dr. Burr is my father, but I also happen to be a Dr. Burr. You may call me Susan. I work with him. I've computerized the extensive files developed by my father. We've worked our way through several fellowships, adding that information to our data bank. I've also linked our computer into the National Historical Research Association Network, which includes unclassified federal and state information sources, and we're linked with all major universities around the world. We may not be able to tell you what someone is thinking, but we can tell you where they've been and what they've said during their lifetime. If you will tell me what you need, I'll have our computer bring up the information, while you become acquainted with my father."

"I need information about Vice President Houston. I have some information about him, but I need more."

"Consider it done. Now come with me and I'll introduce you to my father."

JB followed her into an adjacent office, admiring her stylish coiffure and chic business suit that stretched taut over the pronounced curves of her well-proportioned feminine figure.

She introduced him to Dr. Burr then left the office. She was back within ten minutes and handed him a thick file. Looking directly into JB's eyes, she spoke. "This file is as complete as you'll find anywhere so far as historical chronology is concerned. The file starts at birth and contains information as new as mid-morning today. Our new technology allows computer storage of photographs, so this file contains all photographs contained in public records. You should not have a problem deciphering this information, but if you do, please call me, anytime, day or night."

Her father was oblivious to the electricity being exchanged between his daughter and JB.

JB was smiling and thinking, *Oh, so vibrant and so much like Isabel!* He nodded slightly and said, "Thank you for the offer. No doubt I'll need some assistance so you can be sure that I'll be calling you soon."

Susan left the office, and he turned to Dr. Burr. "Doctor, you obviously know that Dr. Johnson asked me to call you. I have no idea what he told you, but I'll tell you that I'm involved in a serious investigation of Vice President Houston, and I won't pull any punches. You may be jeopardizing your safety by cooperating with me."

The doctor smiled. "Mr. Barrlo, I have known Tom Johnson for many years, and if he referred you to me for help, I have no compunction about helping you. You're welcome to every scrap of information that I have and if you think of anything more that I can help you with, you must let me know."

"I'll do what I can to minimize your involvement, and I appreciate your trust."

They shook hands, and JB left the doctor's office.

Outside he encountered Susan. "Thank you, Susan, you've been more than helpful." Her exciting and lingering handshake dwelled in his mind, as he excused himself and left the office, anxious to return home to begin his reading.

During his drive home, the image of Susan kept interfering with his thoughts. JB had not strayed during his marriage, but Susan's stunning beauty and female magnetism was a problem.

After arriving home, JB went immediately to his study. He accepted the Susan dilemma, put her out of his mind for the moment, and settled down to digest the Burr file on the vice president.

JB was impressed by Dr. Johnson's file until he began reading the Burr file. The doctor's file was a good chronological summary of the vice president's life, but the Burr file was huge by comparison. The vice president's family tree was carried back to the fourteenth century, and every branch was complete. The biographical section was almost a day-by-day accounting of the vice president's life from birth until the present. Minute details covered all major and minor events, and there were no unexplained voids or lapses anywhere in the biography. Photographs were inserted, so as JB read about the vice president's life, he saw the pictorial changes taking place. Dr. Burr's high speed computer had printed the report in five minutes. It took JB two days to read it.

JB sat back, rubbing his eyes and relaxing his aching body. He had read and absorbed a huge amount of information during the past forty-eight hours. He thought, *What I need is a good physical workout, a hot shower, and a good night's sleep.*

JB went to his bedroom, changed into his running clothes, went outside, and ran hard for five miles.

JB slowed to a walk and continued walking for fifteen minutes, allowing his body to cool down. He went inside, took a long hot and then cold shower, dressed casually, and went downstairs for a light dinner with his family. Throughout their marriage, he shared the chores of raising the girls. He took his turns with nighttime feedings and learned early how to keep them dry. He and Isabel shared the selection of the names, Lisa and Lori, and now that the girls were four and three years old, the evening dinner was his favorite time of the day. It was a joy to hear the girls excitedly tell about their daily activities.

He was asleep early that evening and slept soundly until six the next morning. He awoke feeling rested and lay in the warm bed with Isabel cuddled up against him. He thought about Susan and grew strongly erect. He felt embarrassed by his Susan thoughts, so he put her out of his mind and turned his attention to Isabel. He knew all of her body, and without conscious thought, he began his prelude to loving her.

JB cuddled her close, and as they lay together in the afterglow of their satisfaction, whispered, "Isabel, you're magic for me, I can never get enough of you."

She giggled and lovingly clutched his growing erection. "What do you feed this thing anyway?"

"I feed him Isabel," and she made love to his hardness.

They arose soon after. Isabel got their children ready for nursery school, and he packed a bag. He planned to spend a few days in Texas. The vice president was born in a small town northeast of San Angelo, and JB intended to visit the vice president's birthplace. He was uncertain what he expected to learn, but he wanted to see the town where Houston was born and hoped to find old time residents that could tell him early life facts about the vice president.

JB's plane landed at the Dallas-Ft. Worth Airport late in the afternoon. He rented a car and drove west on Interstate 80 to Abilene where he spent the night in a motel.

He was up early the next morning and on his way south to Ballinger, a small Texas town located on the Colorado River.

The main street was two blocks long. JB spotted the *Tribune* sign painted on the window of a small single storied brick building and pulled over to park in front of the newspaper office. The street was deserted, and JB was greeted by a rush of hot, humid air when he opened the car door. It was early, but the temperature climbed quickly after the sun came up.

JB went inside the newspaper office. He heard the clatter of a typewriter and a rail-thin gray-haired lady looked at him. She smiled pleasantly, stopped typing, and asked, "Good morning, young man, what can I do for you?"

JB smiled in return and walked over to her desk. "My name is Jim Barrlo. I'm a political historian, and I'm interested in your most famous citizen, our vice president. If possible, I would like to read through your old editions to see what I can learn about Vice President Houston and his birthplace."

She eyed him warily and said, "You look like one of them investigators that like to snoop around in other people's business."

JB laughed easily and replied, "No, Ma'am, not me. I'm a college professor from California. I've read all about our vice president, so I feel it's time for me to visit the place where it all started. I don't expect to learn anything that I don't already know but as a historian it's exciting for me to actually see the places that I read about. I must say, the information that I've been reading did not mention this sweltering heat."

She smiled again and seemed to warm up to him. "Well, I reckon it won't do no harm to let you read our old papers. Just be careful with them, they're old and fragile, and of course, don't tear anything out. You come with me now and I'll get you started."

JB followed her across the office and through the door into a room full of vertical cabinets. She explained that each cabinet contained copies of the weekly papers for the year listed on the cabinet, all in chronological order. The weeklies hung on wooden rods so that he could take out four weeks together.

JB went to the cabinet for 1900, and she showed him how to open the cabinet and remove the papers.

JB thanked her and she left, saying, "Come and get me if you need any help, and please be careful with my papers."

JB settled down to feast upon the information.

JB felt the trickles of sweat running down his body but was soon absorbed in reading the old papers and completely forgot the heat.

JB looked at each page carefully and spotted the birth announcement, baptismal notice, and various other items about the vice president. By midafternoon he was up to 1916. While leafing through a weekly edition, JB spotted the vice president's name in a headline on page two. The vice president was then thirteen years old and an avid Boy Scout. He had been severely injured while on a camping trip to Lake Brownwood. The news article explained that another of the Boy Scouts had been tossing his scout hatchet against a tree stump. The hatchet bounced off the stump and struck the vice president's right foot. Houston almost bled to death before they got him to a doctor in nearby Santa Anna. The doctor was able to stop the bleeding and mend the wound with twenty-five stitches. JB recalled the notation in the vice president's medical record about a scar on his right foot. JB reread the article, entered the data into his notes, and continued reading through the newspapers. Obviously the wound had little effect, as the paper was full of athletic exploits and accomplishments by the vice president during his high school days, most notably his talent as a boxer. During his junior and senior high school years, he was the Texas state light heavyweight champion. The many articles were interesting reading inasmuch as the vice president won his titles with enthusiasm and stamina rather that with inherent talent. He simply wore out his opponents and then put them away when they were helpless to his onslaughts. He continued his boxing exploits through his college years at TCU and developed definite cauliflower ears by the age of twenty-two. His nose was broken numerous times, and his left eye would always wander whenever he became overly tired. JB thought, *Actually the thickened eyebrows lend character to his facial features and give a menacing look.*

It took JB three days to read through all of the weeklies up to the present. He made notes about each reference to the vice president, but he discovered nothing that had not been contained in Dr. Johnson's file or in Dr. Burr's file. By the time he was finished, he appreciated the completeness of Dr. Burr's file and had the sinking feeling that had wasted the better part of a week's time.

He finished his reading, thanked Miss Simpson, and tipped her generously.

She accepted his stipend with relish. "Thank you, young man! Y'all come back now, hear?"

He reread all of the Dr. Burr files and his notes from the Texas trip. He felt stymied in his search for clues. He was tempted to ask Dr. Johnson for contacts within the FBI and CIA, but he knew from Dr. Johnson that those organizations could be and probably were infiltrated. He spent a restless day again rereading parts of his files. He sensed that an important direction or clue eluded him, but he couldn't put his finger on it.

That evening David popped over to let JB know that arrangements were in place for the sergeant's consultation.

They sat in JB's study.

David was explaining a new idea that he was working on. David stopped talking and sat quietly, watching JB.

JB was deep in thought and didn't realize that David had stopped talking. JB's attention snapped back to the present and he said, "I'm sorry, David, my mind is somewhere else tonight. Please, don't think I'm not interested in your work. I've got a big problem, and I can't figure out a solution."

David laughed and said, "Whatever your problem is, you were really zeroing in on it. I stopped talking two minutes ago and you didn't notice. Why don't you use me for a sounding board. Maybe I can help you."

He looked at David and thought, *Why not?*

"Well," JB started, "I've got this theory that something is amiss about our vice president. I've spent considerable time reviewing his files. Something in these files is not right, but I can't spot the problem."

David sat quietly and waited for him to continue.

"You're a medical doctor. Let me show you his medical records. Maybe you can spot an irregularity." He removed the medical file section from Dr. Burr's report and spread the pages out on the table.

David whistled, "Wow! You've really got a file here. I don't think I've ever seen anything so organized and complete." The written dialogue was supplemented by photographs, and the file told everything about the vice president.

JB left the room for about an hour and David proceeded to review the files.

David was pouring over the files and looked up as JB entered. "Whoever did these files sure knew what they were doing. It's all here. I don't see anything particularly unusual but this file certainly covers all the bases so far as the medical side is concerned."

While David talked, JB idly looked through the notes from Texas. When David stopped talking, JB said, "Take this foot wound, for example. I read about it in an old newspaper. It's in the medical file, and they've taken pictures of the scar during his recent physical examination."

Looking perplexed, David asked, "When did you read about it?"

"I was down in Texas a couple days ago, reading old newspapers. The accident happened in July 1916. The vice president was cut by a hatchet while on a Boy Scout camping trip. He almost bled to death before they got him to a doctor."

David went back to the medical files. He reread a few pages, then looked at JB. "The file refers to a laceration to his right foot when he was thirteen years old, closed with twenty-five stitches. The photo shows a scar on the right foot. Let's look at the photo under a lens." The computerized photo outlined the foot, and the scar was visible.

JB brought over a map reading lens, and together they looked at the photograph under the lens. JB noted the scar and counted the twenty-five stitch marks. He started to speak, then noticed the funny look on David's face.

David asked, "How old is the vice president?"

"Sixty-three." He frowned and David went back to the map reading glass for another look.

"JB," David whispered, "I doubt this scar was made by a hatchet blade. More importantly this scar is not fifty years old!"

JB waited for David to continue.

"The vice president is well over six feet tall. I would guess he wears about a size twelve shoe. When he was thirteen years old, he would've worn about a size eight. As the body matures and the foot grows larger and longer, certain parts of the foot change more than other parts. If you look at this scar, the stitch marks on each side of the scar are too symmetrical. As the foot grew, each stitch mark would have moved a little differently, and after fifty years, the spacing should be much different than what we're looking at. I would guess the scar we're looking at is not more than ten years old, at the most, fifteen years."

"David, it's important that you don't ask me any questions, and it's important that you don't discuss what you've seen and what we've talked about tonight." He continued, "Would you please look at the photos in the file and tell me if the ears, eyes, eyebrows, nose, and overall facial features show signs of damage from years of boxing."

David spread the photos out under the bright desk lamp and studied them carefully. Some minutes later he spoke. "I have a funny feeling about these photos. At first glance, the ears look like a fighter's ears, but if you look closer, the cartilage of the middle part of the lobes is firmly intact. The outer edges seem to hang over. Although the nose looks like it was broken, it's too perfect. If you look at the lips, you'll notice the symmetry is intact unlike what you would expect from lips battered many times."

JB held up his hand. "For the moment, please leave your thoughts and questions here and go on home. I promise I'll explain everything to you at a later time."

David nodded slightly and smiled. "JB, you have my word. No one will hear from me about this evening. Call me if you want to talk further, and be careful; take care of yourself. You know by now you can trust me, and if ever you need me, all you must do is ask."

David reached out, and JB took the handshake. "Thanks, David, I appreciate what you've said."

JB stepped back to let David pass, and David left the house.

JB sat for a few moments, gathering his thoughts, then picked up the telephone, and dialed the Bethesda number.

"Good evening, Bethesda Research Center," the operator said.

"This is Apercu calling. May I speak with the doctor?"

"Thank you, sir, good night."

The telephone line went dead. JB slowly hung up his telephone receiver, reached over, and turned out the desk lamp and sat in the darkness, waiting for the telephone call. All at once he went numb, and a chill ran up his back! The implications of what David pointed out were staggering! The vice president was not the same person who grew up in Texas and worked his way through the political offices. Somewhere along the way, an impostor was substituted. "How? When? Where? Why?" The why was the most self-evident.

The questions shot through his mind as the telephone rang. JB picked up the receiver and answered, "Hello."

"You called?"

"I need to see you, soon."

"Can it wait until tomorrow?"

"If need be, but it's urgent!"

"You should leave now. Go to Springline Aviation at the Concord Airport. A jet will bring you here." The telephone line went dead.

He went upstairs. "Isabel, I have an emergency that I must take care of. I must go to Washington. I'll call you if I get a number where you can reach me, and I'll probably be home late tomorrow."

JB kissed her deeply, and she sighed and smiled. "Oh honey, call me when you can. I love you very much," and he said, preoccupied, "I shouldn't be gone long. Stay close to home, and I'll be in touch."

JB was at the airport in twenty minutes and spotted the lighted sign for Springline Aviation. He parked his car next to the general aviation center and went into the lighted office.

"Good evening, sir, can I help you?" The young man behind the counter watched him carefully.

"My name is Biloxi. There should be a plane here for me."

"Yes sir. Go through the brown door over there, walk straight down the hallway, and out the door at the far end. You'll see the flight line. Wait there in the lounge, and you'll see your plane in a few minutes. They're fueling it now, and the pilot should be here anytime. Have a good flight, sir."

JB thanked him and went out to await the plane, wondering, *What made me use Biloxi?* As he watched, he saw a tall, athletic looking man walk across the concrete apron and go aboard the small jet.

The fuel truck finished, and the plane's engines came to life. The plane hurriedly taxied to the ramp, adjacent the Ready Room.

As JB entered the main cabin, he saw the pilot standing in the doorway to the pilot's compartment. The man smiled, put out his hand, saying, "Good evening, JB, my name's Roger. I'll be your pilot tonight. You can sit in the back or up front with me, take your pick."

"I'll ride up front with you."

Roger turned and dropped into the left seat, JB in the right.

"Start reading me this checklist." Roger handed a clipboard to JB.

They quickly ran through the checklist. Roger touched the throttles and asked the tower for clearance as they taxied to Runway twenty-nine.

The engines whined!

They were quickly airborne. JB was startled by the velocity and angle of their takeoff. The plane climbed to 25,000 feet; leveled off; and took a heading of ninety-six degrees, all preset into the computer.

By the time they crossed the Sierras, their altitude was 42,000 feet, and they were far above the cloud cover. The dark sky twinkled with the millions of stars; the engines whispered now, as the sleek plane raced along at almost 500 knots.

Roger looked over at him, smiled, and said, "You've probably flown in small jets before, so I would guess that you were surprised by the takeoff and climb out. Look at the instruments, you'll notice that we're cruising at 490 knots. Our speed may give you a clue that this aircraft is no ordinary small jet."

"I noticed our takeoff," JB replied, "and I see our cruising speed. Do you mind telling me what we're flying in?"

"Not at all," said Roger. "This is a souped-up version of a North American Sabreliner business jet. The airframe has been beefed up, and we're powered by a couple of 4,000 pound thrust turbofan engines. I use this plane and three more exactly like it in my business."

"Which is . . . ?" JB asked.

"Our country's military air force needs constant combat training. I contract with the government to provide combat speed aircraft for our air force jet jockeys to practice against. This plane will easily break the sound barrier in flat-out flight, is easy to fly, and is very maneuverable in flight at less than five hundred knots. We call it shadow boxing, and I drive the air force, navy, and marine corps fighter pilots crazy in our training sessions."

JB wondered about the connection between Roger and the doctor.

"We'll be arriving in Washington D.C. before sunrise. You look like you can use some rest. Why don't you go back and relax for awhile. I'll wake you before we arrive, but before you crash, you'll pardon the expression, fetch me a cup of black coffee from the galley."

JB found the galley and passed a cup to the pilot, then moved into the rear cabin, laid down on the lounge chair, and was soon fast asleep.

JB felt the hand on his shoulder and was instantly awake.

"Time to rise and shine, old buddy," Roger said. "There's plenty of coffee and a couple of snacks in the galley. Bring 'em up front and join me."

They sat together in the sun-brightened cockpit, sipping the hot coffee. The radio was alive with messages, and he saw the radar, tracking other planes in the vicinity. Roger was alertly watching for other aircraft and busy talking to Air Traffic Control, making his way through the heavy traffic.

They received priority landing clearance, and Roger flew a straight-in approach.

"We're fifty miles out, and we'll be on the ground in about eight minutes."

JB remained silent and watched Roger casually but skillfully bleed off their airspeed and jockey the plane into a perfect approach.

Roger reduced speed to 300 knots and settled the plane into a steep descent. He maintained their airspeed at 300 knots until they saw the runway lights, then flared the plane, and dropped their airspeed to 110 knots.

The touchdown was smooth, and Roger slowed the plane with a roar of the thrust reversers, and in a few moments they were taxiing off the main runway toward a group of small private hangars. As the plane came to a stop, Roger pointed ahead. . . ." There's a car waiting for you over by the hangar." Roger held out his hand. "Good luck!"

JB accepted the outstretched hand, shook it firmly, and replied, "Thanks for the fast and smooth trip. Good luck in your dogfights with the friendly military."

He jogged across the tarmac toward the waiting car. The driver opened the rear door and said, "Good morning, sir, the doctor is waiting for you."

He got into the car without a word and settled back. He noticed the car was heading away from Bethesda.

They drove for about ten minutes, then turned off the freeway onto a county highway, and headed north. JB pretended to doze and noted the driver carefully and continually watching him in the rear view mirror. They drove on for a few miles, then slowed and turned off the road onto an access road leading up to an old farmhouse. The car pulled around behind the farmhouse, drove into a large garage, and stopped.

The garage door closed behind them as the driver opened the rear car door.

JB got out and followed the driver through a door in the rear of the garage. He expected to be going outside. Instead the door led to a stairwell heading down. They followed the stairs into a well-lighted hallway, moving along the hallway to a closed door.

The door swung open as they arrived, and the driver stepped aside to allow JB to enter the large room.

He saw Dr. Johnson seated on the sofa in the rear of the room.

The doctor stood as JB walked over to the sofa and they shook hands. "Well, JB, what's on your mind?"

"Doctor, I've found evidence that our vice president is not who we think he is."

"Sit down," the doctor said, "and tell me about what you've found."

He explained what David had said the evening before, then JB sat back and waited for the doctor to speak.

The doctor watched JB carefully and when JB finished speaking, he asked, "What do you make of your information?"

JB shrugged and said, "I'm not sure but I believe that our vice president is an impostor. He doesn't live up to his medical records. It looks like his facial features have been altered, to make him look like the real Houston, and I think they made a critical error in trying to disguise an old foot injury. The injury is an obvious discrepancy. How and where they made the change I don't know, but I do know what I read in those old newspapers. The accident happened in 1916. The physical exchange of the vice president could've occurred anytime, but it was definitely planned at least ten years ago, inasmuch as the scar on the vice president's foot is about ten years old. I have a nagging feeling that we have a mole in the White House, and that mole is our vice president."

Dr. Johnson was quiet for a few moments, then let out a long sigh and said, "JB, one of the scenarios I've prepared is exactly what appears to have happened. I've discussed it with our president many times. Our president has always been alert to anything out of the ordinary that might occur but he has never spotted anything unusual regarding the vice president. It may be because the switch occurred before the president and vice president became closely acquainted, so the behavior pattern of the vice president would've remained constant throughout their relationship."

"What should we do?" JB asked.

"We certainly cannot ignore this development. The vice president is a mole and in place. There's no doubt, an assassination plot is going to be carried out, so the plant can assume the presidency. Come to think of it, the vice president has been persistently insisting our president should stop over in Dallas after visiting the Space Center in Houston next week. We're expecting a huge crowd in Dallas to greet the president. What better time and place to execute an assassination plot."

JB sat silently and waited for the doctor to continue.

"JB, you can freshen up and rest in the next room. I must have some time to talk with our president. There's a valet in there to take care of anything you want or need. Please excuse me for awhile. I'll let you know when we can talk again. It shouldn't be too long."

JB nodded, got up, and went into the suite next door.

The doctor went into the small office off the end of the conference room, picked up the red telephone, and waited for the president to answer. Within a few moments he heard, "Good morning, Tom, what do you have?"

"Mr. President, we have evidence that your vice president is an impostor, and I feel strongly that an assassination plot is at hand."

"I'll take your word on the evidence. I guess we'll just have to be on our toes and be ready for any attempts to kill me."

"Mr. President, will you consider canceling your trip to Texas?"

"No, Tom. I feel it's important to visit the Space Center and the Dallas stopover is too far along in planning to allow a cancellation without political embarrassment for our congressional friends from Texas as well as the governor."

"You could pretend an illness."

"No deal, Tom. I can't start hiding out and changing my lifestyle just because we've got a crackpot running loose or because we think there's a plot to kill me."

Dr. Johnson was saddened by the cold dread of fear for the president's life. The upcoming trip to Texas frightened and frustrated him. It was obvious he couldn't persuade the president to cancel the trip, and total protection was a myth. The crowd control would be difficult, and the time and route through Dallas would present numerous opportunities to kill the president. The FBI was already checking out several threats from Texas. "Mister President, you're well aware of the current rumors. We must take them seriously! The Cuban Secret Police dispatched Santana and the FBI tracked him from Tampa to New Orleans before losing him. The FBI feels Santana is headed toward Texas, but I'm wondering if Riccotto is hiring The Satan to get vengeance against you and your brother because of your harassment to his organization over the years. And we can't forget *Ueber-Mensch*! Anyone who taunts the World Police Organizations with assassination threats and calls himself Superman must be reckoned with. Why expose yourself unnecessarily?"

"Tom, I told you! I won't curtail my activities and work because of rumors, so make the arrangements. I'm going to Texas!"

"Yes, sir." The doctor hung up the telephone.

He knew the main deterrent would be to alert all governmental and civilian police groups. He thought about his last line of defense and now decided that he must bring his five special agents together and protect the president at any cost.

The doctor picked up the other telephone and spoke to his trusted assistant. "Two of my special agents are in Washington now. I want the other three here within the next six hours. We will assemble in my planning office at 1500 this afternoon." He hung up the telephone, sat back with a deep sigh, and let his chin fall down against his chest.

The doctor's body was drenched with a cold sweat, and he realized there would be no turning back. He did not trust the police agencies involved and felt a screaming frustration his five trusted agents would not be enough to offset the well-planned, coordinated attack surely to come in Texas.

JB slept soundly. The old sergeant had told him many times, "When you're between skirmishes or battle, rest as much as possible. Just close your eyes and forget about the outside world. The better rested you are, the better you can respond."

It was almost 1500. The doctor directed his aide to awaken JB, instruct him to freshen up, and to join the doctor in the adjacent conference room.

JB heard the doctor's aide enter the room, felt his gentle shake, and heard the instructions.

He headed for the shower. He turned the water on hot and stood soaking for almost five minutes. Then he turned it to cold and forced himself to endure the uncomfortable cold water for two minutes. He turned off the water and rubbed himself dry with the fluffy towel. His skin tingled, feeling warm after the cold water. He felt good. Wide awake, ready and anxious to get to the problem at hand. He dressed quickly and rushed to the conference room.

JB entered without knocking. He looked around the room and saw Dr. Johnson sitting at the head of the conference table. Two men were seated on one side of the table; a man and a woman were seated on the other side. He was surprised to see Roger seated at the table.

All eyes were upon him.

JB returned their inquisitive looks and then looked to the doctor for instruction.

Dr. Johnson nodded toward the end of the table, and JB took his place.

The eyes watching JB now turned toward the doctor.

The doctor waited for a few moments before he spoke. "JB, you've met Roger. I choose not to introduce you to any of the others. Each of you should look at the faces of the others in this room and henceforth know that you can depend upon the people you see here. Some of you know I call you the compendium. Each of you has been similarly trained so let's move ahead with the crisis at hand. There's a serious plot against the life of our president. The threats received so far are being checked out by the FBI and our other security people. These threats are probably smoke screens. We do not know what the real threat is or where it will come from. I will tell you this; JB has found solid evidence our vice president is an impostor. JB also saw some strange actions by our secret police during the assassination attempt in San Francisco. Until we find more solid clues, we can only guess what's planned, but my conjecture is we're facing a threat beyond our wildest imagination. The vice president must be a part of the plan. Our presidential Secret Service could be a part of the plan. This is definitely more than an individual with designs upon becoming our president.

"The vice presidential situation points to an international conspiracy, but we all know our president is targeted for death by several underworld leaders because of his anti-crime drive. This situation is well out of control so we must put our heads together and plan our defense. As a starter, I asked the president to cancel his Texas trip next week. He refused, which came as no surprise to me. I'm going to furnish each of you a detailed copy of the president's itinerary and then we'll disperse. I feel that we would waste our time if we tried to set up avenues of escape and protective measures. I think we'll be better off allowing each of you to review the president's itinerary, and then make your own plans to intervene in any attempt to kill our president. I may decide to merge your plans."

The doctor pointed to a stack of papers and said, "There are five copies of the president's itinerary for next week; each of you should take one. JB, Roger will fly you back to your home. The rest of you should return to your homes, study the itinerary, and make your plans. Time is of the essence. After I leave this room, I want you to stay for five minutes. Do not talk. The less you know about the others, the better. You've all been trained to withstand interrogation, but who knows what can happen, and if you're captured and questioned, the less opportunity for you to expose the others, the better. Burn the faces of others into your memory so that you'll recognize them without hesitation, even when in disguise." He paused, looking around the room, then continued, "Get on with your plans, and let's hope to God that we're able to intervene and protect our president." With that the doctor left the room.

The five sat quietly, each looking intently at the others. Roger was firmly fixed in JB's mind. Now he sat and intently studied each of the others in turn. He was surprised to see the woman. While not beautiful, she was comely, and she exuded a mien of confidence. He studied the other two carefully, and all eyes were drawn back to the lady as she suddenly arose. She slipped her sweater partly off her right shoulder and turned her body. All could see the small tattoo, and JB smiled and thought, *A ladybug! Beetle is not a proper name for her, so I'll think of her as Papillon; that's close enough!"* She tugged the sweater back onto her shoulder and returned to her chair. He visualized each of them: *Roger, tall, stately, athletic and well conditioned, confident, his nose aquiline; the all American boy.*

Papillon, tall for a woman, about Susan's height, slim and fit, dark hair, well-tanned, her left ear lobe pierced slightly low as compared to her right. He thought, *If Sergeant Browning trained her, she's the prettiest killing machine around!*

Sandy, boyish looking, sanguine hair, many freckles, his rotund appearance deceiving; not many people wear a watch inverted to the inside of their wrist!

Woody, JB mentally smiled. *Mahogany skin, could be ebony and ebony could mean hardwood so, I'll call him Woody!* He mused further. *Skin, hair, eye colors are easily changed. I must fix in my mind their inner reality.*

And he continued absorbing an essence from each of them. The way they sat, breathed, moved, looked at the others, and on and on. He would eventually learn their real names as Roger, Kathleen, Kelly, and Stephen, but Stephen would always be Woody, Kelly would always be Sandy, and Kathleen would always be Papillon.

He sat watching the others arise, take a copy of the itinerary, and leave. As the last one left, JB arose, walked over, and picked up the last copy of the president's itinerary. He found Roger waiting outside. "Let's go, JB, we've got some traveling to do."

He grimaced at the pilot and said, "Show me the way to go home."

They left the building and found a limousine waiting for them. Without their asking, the driver headed for the airport. They were soon airborne, headed west. JB and Roger had not spoken since leaving the doctor's building. He looked at Roger several times and found Roger staring at him. Neither spoke, and each smiled knowingly, hoping to tempt the other to speak from nervousness. Obviously each felt sure of himself because no words were exchanged.

They reached cruising altitude, and Roger trimmed the aircraft out at 600 knots. They flew along in silence. Roger busied himself. JB chose to break the silence. "I'm going to read the president's itinerary out loud. You listen, and if you hear anything unusual or have a particular concern about any part, please tell me."

It took him thirty minutes to read through the detailed travel plans. When he was finished, he looked over at Roger and asked, "Any particular part bother you?"

"Well, it sounds like there will be many opportunities for an assassination attempt, but if I were asked to pick the most likely spot, I would choose Dallas."

"What part of Dallas?" JB asked.

"Some place outside, probably while driving in the open-top car," Roger replied.

JB smiled and said, "You and I have obviously received similar training. If I had to pick a spot, it would be in Dallas, in an open-top car and among the many buildings. I feel they will try to shoot the president, probably from several directions at the same time. They will likely use a diversion and then attack from an opposite direction."

JB was startled by a flashback to the many hours he and the sergeant sat in front of the computer screens, watching, analyzing, and trying to puzzle out the many different plots presented by the computer on how to assassinate someone in a public place. He could recall a scenario where the target's car passed a group of midrise buildings, and the initial attack came from behind. JB had flunked that test because he had selected auto acceleration and weaving of the car to prevent further attack. The initial attack was a diversion, and his choice took the victim directly into the real attack, and all was destroyed. He realized death could come to the president immediately if heavy weapons were used. However, it could be expected that the attackers would plan to be able to escape so the heaviest weapon to be expected would be an automatic rifle or a satchel charge type of explosive. Stationary explosions would probably not be used, because the presidential motorcade route was invariably changed at the last moment, and weapons heavier than a rifle were difficult to conceal or move around. JB and the sergeant had studied thousands of different variations of attack, and the most successful attack was a three-stage one. The first stage was the diversion, the second stage the finishing attack, and the third stage was the back-up in case the second stage was unsuccessful. JB was thinking, *The potential assassins would have gone through similar training and will come up with the same answer, a three-pronged attack.*

JB and Roger flew on in silence for awhile. Roger spoke first this time. "I'll be leaving you at Concord. We'll surely meet again, and I'm looking forward to working with you. We've got a tough problem to handle, but I feel confident that we can come through."

JB replied, "I feel the same. I think Dr. Johnson is wise in having each plan our own defense, so we don't have all of our eggs in one basket. We've received similar training, so we think somewhat alike, but I'm sure each of our defenses will be different. Let's hope so."

Unbeknown to JB, Dr. Johnson later contacted the other four and brought them together to review their plans to protect the president. He had explained, "Each of you is unusual, talented, and well trained, but JB is on a plateau above all of us. His skills, dexterity, and competence are immense, almost immeasurable. To make best use of his talents, we will leave him alone, and he will ferret out the assassins. The four of you should work together, coordinate your ideas, and design flexible escape plans. You should assume that JB will take on the assassins, and you must respond to whatever happens–be ready as his support team. There's always the likelihood that I will be eliminated. If that happens, you should look to JB for guidance; he will be in charge. I have not told him your names, and he feels that you're remaining nameless will protect all of you. That isn't completely wise. The four of you should become acquainted, using discretion of course. I've withheld his name from you as added protection for him in the event one or more of you is taken and interrogated. Now, JB knows your faces, so if I disappear, you should attend Christmas Eve midnight mass at St. Mary's Cathedral in San Francisco. I will make certain that JB knows you'll be there."

They soon landed at Concord. JB left the jet, walking away toward the parking lot without looking back. He knew he would meet Roger and the others again soon, and he dreaded the thought of failing.

Early next morning, JB telephoned Dr. Burr, as he needed to discuss the information contained in the vice presidential file. Dr. Burr agreed to meet with JB at two o'clock that afternoon.

At precisely two o'clock JB entered Dr. Burr's office. JB looked around expectantly, hoping to see Susan, but the front office was empty. JB walked across the room and knocked lightly upon the door.

He heard Dr. Burr. "Come in please."

JB entered.

"Hello, JB, it's nice to see you again."

"Good afternoon, Dr. Burr. Thank you for letting me come to see you today. I know you're a busy man, but I need to confirm some information you furnished me about our vice president."

"That shouldn't be a problem. What can I help you with?"

"Your file made reference to an old injury to the vice president's right foot, and there was a photo of the right foot, showing the scar. Can you tell me the source of your information?"

Dr. Burr responded, "Every bit of information in our files is referenced as to its source. Let's call up the vice president's file and take a look."

Dr. Burr turned in his chair to face the computer terminal sitting alongside his desk and entered a command. Dr. Burr swiveled the computer screen around to enable JB to see the information displayed. Dr. Burr paged through the file until the photo of the vice president's foot was displayed on the screen. He keyed in another command and the informational source was displayed across the bottom half of the screen: "Physical examination, June 14, 1948, Bethesda Naval Medical Center, Bethesda, Md. Examining physician, Dr. Wells."

Dr. Burr looked inquiringly toward JB.

JB asked, "Can you print that picture?"

"Yes, of course."

JB heard the quiet clatter of the printer located alongside the computer.

"Can we look at the medical records and find reference to the vice president's foot injury?"

Dr. Burr keyed in another command, and the vice president's medical record appeared on the screen. Dr. Burr scrolled slowly through the medical record, looking for information regarding the foot injury. The file was lengthy. It was a chronological report, including photographs, of all known medical records on the vice president from birth up to the present date. They scrolled through the chronological records, and as the years passed, the vice president had red measles at age six, chicken pox at age eight, and occasionally was seen by a doctor for the usual childhood maladies. He routinely received smallpox vaccination and other vaccines.

JB watched and waited for 1916. "Stop," cried JB, "there it is."

Sure enough, a detailed report of the ax incident verified the accident. They read slowly through the doctor's report. Twenty-five stitches were used to repair and close the wound, and the seriousness of the injury was apparent. Houston lost a considerable quantity of blood and was kept alive by the quick and accurate treatment furnished by the young medical doctor on duty in the emergency room that day. They read on though the subsequent medical records and noted recovery was rapid. The wound was mentioned in the medical examinations for the next three years. Then no further mention was found. They read on through the years–high school, college, and then the military. He halted the search and asked Dr. Burr, "Can you go back to the foot injury in 1916 and give me your reference?"

Without answering, Dr. Burr quickly scrolled back the record and keyed in his request. The reference was pulled up onto the screen: "Stillwater Texas County Hospital, October 21, 1955, personal review and photographs by August Burr."

JB looked at Dr. Burr and asked, "You did this research personally?"

"Yes. The vice president was a phenomenal young Texas politician, running for the governor's office. The National Democratic Party hired me to look into his background. They were planning to have Houston give the keynote speech at the next year's Democratic National Convention as a stepping stone on the ladder to national politics. They wanted to be certain no skeletons lurked in the closet as to his background. I took my job seriously and spent a month in Texas gathering information. I was able to give them a clean report, and obviously the young man from Texas has done well."

"Did you have any problems gaining access to the medical records?"

"None whatsoever. There was only one hospital in the area, so I went to the administrative office, explained what I needed, furnished my references, and the files were made available to me."

"Could I do the same today?" asked JB.

"I'm afraid not. The hospital was totally destroyed about two months after I gathered my notes."

"What happened?"

"Texas is famous for its tornadoes. One of the biggest on record swept through that part of Texas, destroying everything in its path. It passed through Stillwater and destroyed over half the town and killed over a hundred people.

The hospital was leveled, and the records probably ended up somewhere in New Mexico."

"Let's go to 1938. As I recall, Houston was first elected to congress that year. I'd like to see his medical record for 1938."

Dr. Burr scrolled forward to 1938. Having been elected to congress that year, the vice president became a federal employee and was required to take an annual physical examination. They scrolled slowly through 1938 and found the physical examination report. The Identifying Marks Section listed a birthmark and several scars, among them a scar an the top of the right foot. No other comments related to the scar.

JB suggested, "Let's go on through the file."

Dr. Burr scrolled forward and JB watched as the years went by. They stopped the screen to review each physical examination report and all of the examination reports listed a scar on the top of the right foot. When they were finished, JB asked, "Dr. Burr, how do you get the annual medical reports for our vice president?"

"I send my requests to the Governmental Records Section. The files are public domain, and I can obtain any file on any public figure for a small fee."

"What if you needed background information pertaining to part of a file that you had purchased?"

"What do you mean?"

"Well, for example, your file on Houston shows he was injured when he was thirteen years old and furnished a detailed medical report to explain the injury. Can you ask the Government Records Office to furnish a similar report to support the scar-on-right-foot notations?"

"I could ask for it but as I explained to you, the early medical records covering the vice president were destroyed in the tornado."

"But why wouldn't the vice president tell the examining doctors what had happened? Most doctors are inquisitive and will ask their patient about a scar that large and make notations in the medical report."

"The Government Records Office has a section to handle special requests, and I deal with them regularly. I'll call my acquaintance early tomorrow morning and ask for detail to support the medical examination. If I ask for expedited service, I'll have a response the same day. Ring me tomorrow afternoon."

"I'll call right after lunch. If you need to be away, please leave the information with Susan."

"Susan's gone for the week, skiing in Utah. I'll be here!"

CHAPTER ELEVEN

JB decided to go to Dallas. He didn't have a particular plan worked out; but he felt certain an attempt would be made to kill the president. He booked a seat on a late afternoon flight from San Francisco then packed a suitcase for the trip. The explosives he selected to take along would be easy to conceal in his checked baggage. The handgun, silencer, and ammunition were of more concern. He broke the pistol down into its many parts and placed each part into its designed storage place within the suitcase. The suitcase was designed for transporting handguns and ammunition, so the contents avoided the obvious airport security x-ray scanning of checked baggage. He packed his most powerful handgun, a .518 magnum. The gun would bring down a 1200-pound bear at 300 feet. Used in close combat, it simply blew the target apart. He recalled the first time Sergeant Browning demonstrated the pistol. "Keep your eye on the dummy," and the stuffed target exploded into fragments. At that time, JB thought, *Whew, fire this thing in a closed room and you don't need to hit your target, the noise will scare it to death.*

JB sat in his study, waiting for the afternoon to arrive so he could call Dr. Burr. In the meantime, he mentally reviewed everything he learned about the vice president. The evidence continued to point to an impostor acting as the vice president with an opportunity to become the next president of the United States if something happened to President O'Sullivan. He kept thinking over and over, *It must be one helluva plot to have been moving forward for the past twenty to thirty years. Whoever is behind it is patient and covered the bases thoroughly. Well, almost thoroughly.* He would know more after talking to Dr. Burr this afternoon.

JB ate a light lunch, and deciding he couldn't wait any longer, picked up the telephone and dialed Dr. Burr's office.

"Good afternoon, Dr. Burr's office," a young male voice answered.

An alarm went off in JB's mind. "May I speak with Susan Burr please."

"I'm sorry, Miss Burr is not here at the moment. Please give me your name and telephone number, and I'll have her call you when she returns."

"Oh, I dated Susan when we were in college, and I've stayed in touch with her and her father. Perhaps I could say hello to Dr. Burr." The electronic panel alongside his telephone indicated that a trace had been initiated. The timing indicator told JB he had another twenty seconds to break the connection to avoid a trace.

"Dr. Burr is in a meeting at the moment. Give me your name and telephone number, and I'll inform Dr. Burr that you called."

The timer was down to ten seconds as JB spoke. "I have another call coming in; I'll call you back in a few minutes." He hung up the receiver. Something was wrong at Dr. Burr's office! Could it be that Dr. Burr's inquiry to Washington about the vice president's medical records has triggered action by someone to silence him? JB was worried, feeling saddened by the thought that Dr. Burr and possibly Susan would be harmed.

Without hesitations JB dialed the emergency room at Stanford Medical Center. The emergency room receptionist answered promptly. JB identified himself as Dr. Burr's attorney. "I've been informed that Dr. Burr was taken to your emergency; what is his condition?"

She responded, "Dr. Burr is no longer here. If you want further information, you should call Dr. Burr's personal physician."

JB thanked the receptionist, hung up the telephone, and sat back with his eyes closed.

JB remained quiet, allowing his mind to assimilate what was happening and fitting it into the overall scheme of information. He felt a momentary fright about Susan's safety before he recalled that she was in Utah, skiing. He was now certain that Dr. Burr had been eliminated, so he might as well get on with the Dallas trip.

He telephoned David. "David, JB. I'll be away for a couple of days. I'll appreciate your looking in on Isabel and the girls."

"Of course, JB, I'll handle it. I have a meeting at Stanford, if you need a lift to the airport, be glad to drop you there."

"Thanks, David, good idea. I'll be ready in a few minutes. Just honk."

He found Isabel in the kitchen, preparing supper. "Honey, I need to leave. I'll call you from Dallas to let you know where I'll be staying and when I'll be home."

Earlier they discussed her taking the girls to visit her parents, but she was adamant. "I want to stay home! We'll be okay. Don't worry, I can always call David or Cosmo if something comes up."

An auto horn tooted.

He enfolded her into his arms and held her tightly for a moment before deeply kissing her. With a feeling of foreboding, he reluctantly left.

Before his flight was called, JB telephoned Cosmo. "Cosmo, JB here. I'm leaving town for a few days. I'm working on the case that your grandfather told you about. I don't know what I'm getting into, but I may need help. I want you to know any call you get from me will be ultra-urgent."

"JB, no questions asked. You call, I'll handle it. If I'm not here, they will find me. Tell whoever answers that your name is Palermo. They will know I must be reached immediately."

"Thanks, Cosmo, and one of these days, I'll be able to tell you what's going on. There's one more thing, I'll feel much better if you'll have someone watch my home, keep an eye on Isabel and the girls."

"No sweat, JB, I'll use my best men. Take care of yourself and call me if I can help."

They exchanged good-byes, and he found the loading gate.

JB arrived at the Dallas-Ft. Worth Airport at midnight Tuesday. The president would arrive on Friday, so JB had two full days to prepare.

He slept fitfully, his mind searching for clues among the information he gathered about the vice president. Still without answers when he awoke, he accepted he would have to move blindly until the action started.

JB knew the city would be virtually shut down on Friday with many streets closed to traffic until after the president left the city.

Before retiring, JB ordered a breakfast and morning papers to be delivered to his room at 0700 the next morning.

The room service waiter knocked and delivered the breakfast tray and papers. JB immediately opened the newspaper, scanning the articles. He found what he was looking for, and his shoulders sagged as he read, "Noted historian collapses and dies." He read on, "Dr. August Burr collapsed early yesterday and died of an apparent heart attack. Dr. Burr was stricken while eating lunch at a local restaurant. He was rushed to nearby Stanford Medical Center where he was pronounced dead upon arrival. Dr. Burr was a noted political historian born in . . . ."

JB dropped the newspaper and sat looking out of the window, across the city.

JB used several hours on Wednesday locating and buying a used motorcycle. He searched the morning newspaper, found a motorcycle he liked, and then negotiated with the seller. He paid cash and delivered it to a motorcycle repair shop for servicing to be completed by Thursday afternoon. It would be ready early Friday morning. He consumed the rest of Wednesday and all of Thursday driving around the downtown area in his rented car. By late Thursday, all possible routes were thoroughly visualized and stamped in his mind. He also looked at every building along the various routes and selected the most dangerous spots that could conceal an assassin with a weapon. He looked over the parks, grassy areas, overpasses, tall trees–any place that might be used to launch an attack. As he checked the various alternative routes, he eliminated the more dangerous routes, and concentrated on the innocent looking ones. He knew the route selected would not have dead ends. The tall buildings would be unobstructed, so they could be watched. Parks with many trees would be avoided, and an escape route would always be available in the event of a blocked street. JB visualized the most logical routes and finally settled upon Delaney Boulevard as the safest and easiest to control. All of the possible routes had bad spots, and Delaney was no exception. There would be a two-minute interval where the motorcade would have to nearly come to a stop, make a sharp left turn, and be dangerously exposed until the president's car could accelerate away from the building. This particular route left the president vulnerable from three different angles. The bright side was that the president's car would be quickly in and out of the danger area.

Thursday night JB ate an early dinner and placed his daily call home to his family. Afterwards he fashioned a dozen bombs, the size of golf balls. The bombs were stable, detonating upon a measurable impact, and designed for noise and concussion. Used in close quarters, they would disable the unsuspecting.

He checked out of the hotel at 0700, took a taxi to the motorcycle repair shop, picked up his motorcycle, and was at the Dallas-Ft. Worth Airport by 0900. He disposed of his suitcase and extra clothing. He carried a small soft leather bag containing the small bombs and his pistol. He did not intend to be present when the president's plane landed. He wanted to be in the vicinity and then tail the motorcade.

Air Force One arrived on schedule and JB picked up the motorcade shortly after the plane landed. The first stop for the president was a breakfast meeting at the Veterans of Foreign Wars Memorial Hall in downtown Dallas. The president was scheduled to arrive at 0945.

JB hung back about half a mile to avoid observance by the tailing police escort and arrived in the area about five minutes after the presidential party. The first stop was to last for an hour and fifteen minutes. Precisely at 1100 hours, President O'Sullivan would leave the Memorial Hall and head downtown for a political luncheon at the Dallas Convention Center. Hundreds of politicians would be present along with all local, county, and state dignitaries. The only question yet to be resolved in JB's mind was what route to reach downtown?

His vantage point was two blocks from the Memorial Hall and allowed him to see which way the motorcade turned as it left the Memorial Hall. Either direction, JB would know the ultimate route and would reach the most dangerous spot long before the motorcade arrived.

The motorcade pulled away promptly at eleven o'clock, traveled one block, then turned right.

Bingo! thought JB.

JB reached the Delaney Boulevard section of the motorcade route several minutes ahead of the presidential motorcade. Streets throughout Dallas were jammed with people. The crowds didn't know the motorcade route but all hoped the presidential limousine would pass their way, so they could glimpse the president and his wife.

JB parked his motorcycle and started looking around the area. He saw secret servicemen on top of every building and standing in many windows of the buildings. The overpass was closed and several policemen patrolled back and forth across the overpass. JB stood near a grassy knoll and would see the motorcade turn the tight corner down among the buildings. The motorcade would then accelerate toward his vantage point and pass quickly underneath the overpass, moving down the wide boulevard to the Convention Center.

He thought that if anything was going to happen, this had to be the spot!

JB moved back and behind the slatted fence at the rear of the grassy knoll and ran to his motorcycle parked beneath the trees. He was about to open the small bag on the rear of the motorcycle to retrieve his pistol when he noticed three men standing behind the slotted fence. One man was a uniformed policeman, and the other two appeared to be Secret Servicemen, dressed in dark suits. one man was talking on a hand held radio and JB froze! They had not seen him but he was near enough to get a good look at the man talking on the radio.

He knew the face! Where? How? And then it hit him full force. *It's too good to be true!* It was the same face he had seen outside the Palace Hotel in San Francisco, and the same man who shot the innocent bystander JB pushed in front of the gunman. The scene flashed in front of his eyes, and he was immediately sure this same man was again involved in trying to assassinate the president.

JB ducked down, checked for passing pedestrians, then crab-walked around his motorcycle and down the street, past the cars until he was behind the three men. The one on the radio stopped talking, and, from the roar of the crowd, JB knew the presidential motorcade was approaching.

The uniformed policeman left the other men and went around the fence to stand on the grassy knoll. The two men pulled large pistols from beneath their coats. The pistols looked like high powered magnums and both were equipped with silencers.

Without hesitation, JB ran toward the gunmen.

One of the men spotted JB, much too late.

As the gunman swung around, trying to bring his gun toward JB, JB lashed out a vicious kick that crushed the man's kneecap and tore away tendons and cartilage. The man gasped in pain. JB continued toward the gunman, buried his stiffened right hand deep into the man's throat, crushing his larynx and destroying his breathing passage. In one continuous, fluid motion, JB continued into the second gunman with a spinning kick to the face, then broke the man's arms with quick, strong hand chops. As he went over backwards, JB was immediately upon him, crushing his chest with a strong kick.

JB crouched, picking up one of the silenced pistols.

The uniformed policeman heard the commotion and looked searchingly toward the fence.

The motorcade turned the corner and came toward the grassy knoll.

The policeman took a step toward the fence.

JB raised the pistol and shot. "Bullseye!"

He heard the crowd roaring its greeting to the approaching motorcade. He glanced quickly toward the approaching presidential limousine then turned his attention to the buildings beside and behind the president's car.

He saw the puff of smoke before he heard the firing noise as someone fired at the president. He swung his pistol up and squeezed off three rapid shots toward the puff of smoke. He didn't see the shooter and couldn't tell if he hit his target. One thing for certain, his three shots would've disrupted any subsequent shots from that window.

JB heard the screams and saw the crowd moving in panic. Some people were running away; others were cowering on the ground.

He did not waste time observing the panicked crowd. He calmly swept his gaze cross the other buildings and continued on around to the overpass. He spotted three men standing on the south end of the overpass with weapons raised and pointed toward the approaching motorcade.

JB turned his gun toward the overpass. He heard several quick gunshots and saw the three diving for cover. He smiled and thought, *I've got some pals working the crowd.*

He glimpsed the motorcade as it passed and saw the president's wife cradling the slumped president. A Secret Serviceman jumped into the back seat with the president and shielded the president.

The motorcade accelerated rapidly, and JB knew it would head directly to Parkland Hospital.

JB ran to his motorcycle, stabbed viciously at the starting crank, and heard the engine catch. He jammed down the gear shift, goosed the throttle, and released the clutch. The motorcycle leapt forward, and he smoothly accelerated the screaming bike. He had memorized the route to the hospital, so he concentrated on driving the motorcycle through the winding streets.

JB arrived at the rear of the hospital in just under three minutes.

JB parked the motorcycle against the building and took his pistol and several of the bombs from the leather bag. He pushed the pistol down into his waistband and donned the white medical doctor's smock. He designed the white doctor coat with inside pockets. He put the small bombs into the coat pockets, pulled the coat down over the pistol, and ran into the service entrance. He knew the emergency rooms were down the hallway and to the right of the linen department.

JB reached the linen service entrance and heard tires screeching. He swung around and saw two delivery vans arriving. The doors flew open, and the drivers leaped out with their pistols aimed and ready. He recognized both drivers—Sandy and Woody!

JB stepped out into the open and they acknowledged his presence with a wave of their pistols, then fanned out on each side of the loading dock to protect and secure the rear of the hospital.

The scene was near chaos. Secret Servicemen grabbed the gurney from the emergency room attendants and tried to push everyone out of the area.

A young doctor ran along the passageway, yelling at the Secret Servicemen to leave the gurney alone and to clear a pathway for the patient.

A burly agent took charge, settled down the staff, and cleared the way.

The attendants quickly pushed the gurney to the ambulance unloading area, ran to the president's car, and prepared to unload the victim. The young doctor was right on their shoulders and directed the unloading of the victim from the car. They placed the president on the gurney and ran, pushing it before them into the emergency operating room.

JB anticipated the move and was there ahead of them, holding open the emergency operating room door.

As the gurney was pushed into the emergency room, JB saw the gaping wound on the right side of President O'Sullivan's head. The president was drenched with blood, and the attendants handling the president were splattered as well.

JB was appalled. Aside from the horrendous head wound, the loss of blood would surely be fatal.

They quickly moved him from the gurney to the operating table.

Several other doctors and nurses pushed their way into the room and moved around the operating table to assist the young doctor.

JB heard the young doctor shouting orders. "Start packed red cells into his right arm, match his blood, and start whole blood into his left arm. Give me a scalpel; I'm opening his throat!"

The young doctor cleared the president's air passage and then called for epinephrine to stimulate the heart. The other doctors and nurses connected the president to a heart monitor and an automatic respirator.

JB heard someone excitedly announce, "No heartbeat, no pulse!"

The young doctor took the epinephrine-filled syringe with a six-inch needle, plunging it directly into the president's heart.

Moments passed, silence lingered.

"We've got a heartbeat, we've got a pulse, we've got blood pressure, 80 over 40, coming up, slowly."

The president was fighting off death.

Secret service agents continued pushing into the room. JB saw the vice president and the president's wife standing just outside the operating room door.

He looked back at the scene around the president and saw two new doctors pushing the young doctor away from the operating room table. Several agents encircled the operating room table and stood facing away from the table. The young doctor was pushed up against JB by an agent trying to manhandle the young doctor out of the room.

JB stepped between them, moved against the agent, and jammed his stiffened fingers up under the agent's rib cage. The pain immobilized the agent long enough for JB to apply pressure to his neck, causing him to black out.

The young doctor looked at JB and asked, "What in the hell is going on?"

"I don't have time to explain. They're going to let the president die. We must get him away from those doctors!"

Just then the operating room door opened and the vice president stepped into the room.

JB watched him intently.

The vice president looked over the heads of the onlookers, directly at the Secret Serviceman in charge, and nodded his head. The Secret Serviceman loudly announced, "Everyone out of the room, clear this room, now!"

The agents began herding the nurses and attendants out of the room.

JB spotted Woody and Sandy across the room watching him for a signal or instructions. JB knew they must act immediately. He whispered to the young doctor, "We need you, stay with me!" JB reached inside his jacket, took out two bombs, and flung them against the operating room wall.

The noise was deafening.

Many of the agents pulled out their pistols, looking for attackers.

JB drew the pistol from his waistband and fired into the crowd of agents. Woody and Sandy started karate chopping down others. JB calmly continued shooting agents, while Sandy and Woody sealed off the operating room.

The room was a blood bath.

The doctors around the president stood, wide-eyed, looking at him. The vice president cowered against the wall.

JB shot the doctors.

He heard explosions outside in the hallway and turned to the young doctor. "We must get the president out of here!"

The young doctor yelled, "Get him on the gurney. I'll grab whatever supplies I can find, and we'll go out that back door. It leads to the linen supply department; we can find a way out."

JB leaped over the bodies laying on the floor. Woody and Sandy heard the doctor and joined JB at the operating room table. Together they gently moved the president to the gurney. They laid the bottles of blood atop the president and started wheeling the gurney toward the back door.

The young doctor threw medical supplies into a draping sheet, bundled it up, and ran for the same door.

JB heard more explosions outside and ran, shakily, toward the door. They wheeled the president down the short hallway and found themselves in the linen room.

JB ran to the outside exit door and saw the vans backed against the loading dock. He checked to see if it was clear to go outside, then gestured for the attendants to wheel the gurney outside.

The young doctor ran ahead and opened the rear door of the nearest van. Quickly, they wheeled the gurney into the van. The young doctor and Sandy went in with the president. Woody closed the rear doors of the van, scrambled into the driver's seat, and cranked over the engine.

JB leaped into the other front seat. "Get going fast!" JB yelled. The van lurched away from the dock. JB looked back toward the hospital and saw the door on the dock burst open. Roger and Papillon ran for the other van. JB's van went around a corner of the building, and he lost sight of the other.

He had no plan for their ultimate escape.

They reached the local boulevard, turned right, accelerated, and moved into traffic. JB looked back and spotted the other van moving up behind them.

The radio came to life. "Butterfly to Leader, Butterfly to Leader, answer please."

He picked up the microphone and replied, "Leader, go ahead please." It was Roger!

"Do you have a plan? Over."

"No."

"Turn right on Highway 41, about a mile ahead. Drive north for twelve miles and look for Eden Field exit. Take that exit, go right for about two blocks, and you'll see the hangars. Look for my plane, you'll recognize it. You rode to D.C. in it last week."

"Roger, Roger." JB smiled nervously and felt relieved to have friends in the other van.

"Leader, we're dropping back a couple hundred yards. Keep your eyes open."

JB watched the other van slow and drop back into traffic. They reached the Highway 41 exit, turned right and headed north on Highway 41. JB calculated they would reach Eden Field in about ten minutes.

JB saw the black limousine speeding up the freeway toward their van. JB rolled down the passenger door window, took out several of the small explosives, and watched the mirror to time his toss. He reached out of the window and tossed a bomb into the air. It hit the ground in front of the speeding limousine. The concussion from the bomb explosion caused the black car to swerve but the car continued accelerating.

A bullet came through the rear window of the van, shattered the glass, and whizzed past JB, hitting and smashing the windshield on the right side.

The black car was catching up quickly. JB saw the other van tailing the black car.

He called to Woody, "Slow down and pull over to the side of the road!"

Woody braked the van and pulled off onto the shoulder of the highway.

The black car roared around them and cut in sharply to stop in front of the van.

The blue van now moved in behind the black car, smashed into the rear, pushing the car off the roadside and into the deep ditch. Papillon jumped out of the van and lobbed an object under the black car. There was a thunderous explosion, and the black car was engulfed in flames.

He saw the steam coming from the engine of the blue van. The collision with the limousine had obviously damaged the radiator. He reached over and honked the horn. The doors of the blue van burst open, and Roger and Papillon ran toward them. Papillon and Roger piled into the rear of JB's van, and they pulled away from the roadside.

They accelerated up to seventy.

They reached the Eden Field sign then turned off, spotted the hangars, and turned into the side road, continuing around to the backside of the hangars where they screeched to a halt beside the jet.

The rear doors opened. All hands sprung out. Roger ran to the plane, opening the side door, while the others fanned out, forming a defensive guard.

JB climbed between the seats into the back of the van and helped the young doctor prepare the president for transfer to the plane.

JB heard the jet's engines begin to whine and looked at the young doctor.

The doctor nodded yes.

JB went to the rear and called the other men over to help transfer the president into the plane.

They rushed the president aboard the plane. JB looked at the others. "Does anyone know who's coming?"

All three shook their heads no.

Sandy spoke, "We need to dispose of the van. You've got a plane. Get going and find a place to care for the president. Keep in touch through the doctor. You should get out of here now. We'll watch the road for you until you get airborne but please hurry."

Sandy, Woody, and Papillon jumped into the van and drove toward the highway.

JB spotted the telephone booth against the hangar wall. He ran over to the telephone and dialed Cosmo's telephone number. The call was promptly answered by a deep, gruff voice. "Hello."

"May I speak to Cosmo?"

"Cosmo's not here."

"Palermo."

The voice on the other end of the telephone line replied, "Stay on the line; it will take a few moments to reach him." JB heard the man calling Cosmo to the phone and then, "JB, this is Cosmo."

"Cosmo, I need help, fast. I need a fully secured hospital with a full scale operating room. The place must be totally private, no one else around. I have a plane that can reach any location in the continental United States within three hours. Time is important!"

"JB, do you know Palm Springs?"

"Yes," replied JB.

"Specifically, the airport at Bermuda Dunes. The runway is 3,200 feet long. Is that long enough for you?"

"Yes, somehow we'll get in and out."

"It is an uncontrolled field, but use the flight service frequency just before you arrive. You will not get a response. There will be no other aircraft going in or out until your plane is in and out. Get into the airport fast and taxi to the apron of runway twenty-one. An unmarked van will be waiting."

"Roger, Cosmo. Now, call David Protect. I've told him that I might need his help. Have him at the airport to meet us and tell him to be prepared to handle a serious and possibly fatal head wound. I have another doctor with me. We'll be there soon as possible; our ETA is about two and a half hours from now."

JB hung up the telephone, sprinted to the waiting plane, dove up the steps, and pulled the door closed behind him.

Roger was at the controls and looked back over his right shoulder toward JB, waiting for instructions.

JB nodded go and the plane moved down the ramp as Roger quickly ran through the check list. They reached the runway, made a left turn, and accelerated.

The plane left the ground smoothly and departed the pattern toward the north. JB leaned over Roger's shoulder and spoke quietly, "Go west. We have help waiting for us at Bermuda Dunes, near Palm Springs. Do you know that area?"

Roger smiled and replied, "I know the Southwest. Most of our business is handled over the unpopulated parts of Arizona and Southern California."

"The airport will be ours. No other traffic in or out. We are to advise Flight Service just before we land, using the normal frequency. Land runway twenty-one and disguise your message any way you want to avoid leaving a trail; then, taxi to the end of the runway 21."

Roger answered, "JB, go back and help the young doctor. Let's hope we can pull this thing off. As you can imagine, it will be interesting hearing what comes out of Dallas. If the doctor doesn't need you, come back here and I'll fill you in."

JB went to the rear cabin, saw the young doctor tending to the president. JB offered his hand. "Thanks for coming along, doctor. By the way, I'm JB."

The young doctor smiled ruefully, "I'm John Andrews, and I wish to hell we could've met otherwise."

JB asked, "Anything I can do to help you?"

"Get me a hospital operating room and a neurosurgeon, fast."

"We should have you in an operating room in less than three hours. Will the president make it that far?"

"There's no way to tell. It looks like the bullet was coming from an oblique angle and just clipped the upper right side of the president's head. The impact tore away a large piece of his skull and exposed his brain. The brain appears to be intact, but I'm sure he has considerable intracranial bleeding. His involuntary muscle control is functioning, so I think his heart will keep working, and he's continuing to breathe on his own. There's no way for me to determine if his conscious mind will work again. You can see that his eyes are totally dilated and he's catatonic. I'm keeping his exposed brain covered with bandages soaked with saline and I've given him a large dose of antibiotics. The bleeding has mostly stopped, but we must tend to the damaged blood vessels inside his brain, or the continued seepage of blood will destroy it."

"We'll be met by a talented, imaginative surgeon, and the two of you will have to handle the president from here on in." JB looked at his watch, then said, "It's twelve o'clock. We should be on the ground in two and a half hours. Keep the president alive until we get on the ground, and then you'll have all of the tools you need. And, doctor, you've done a great job. Let's pray that you're able to keep him alive."

"Thanks JB, and please call me John."

JB turned and walked forward to the cockpit.

"How's the president doing?" asked Roger.

"He's alive; all we can do is hope for the best." JB sat down into the co-pilot's seat, "Now, what did you want to tell me?"

"Well," Roger said, "it'll be interesting what comes about in Dallas. The question is, how will they explain the disappearance of the president? I've been monitoring the news programs and they're all reporting the president as dead from a gunshot."

Roger dropped the plane down to about 100 feet above the desert and headed west, traveling at 575 knots.

JB looked at the charts hanging on the instrument panel. Roger reached over and placed the plotter over their route to Palm Springs. They would fly north of Abilene, turn to the southwest across a huge area of relatively uninhabited territory, then south of Odessa and Pecos before sweeping northwest between Las Cruces and Almogordo. The route then paralleled Interstate 10 into Arizona. They would wind their way northward through the Mazatzal Mountains, turn west about thirty miles north of Phoenix and parallel Interstate 10 to Bermuda Dunes.

Roger saw JB looking at the avionics. "These warning devices will keep us clear of cities. You'll notice that we're on auto pilot. Our Terrain Clearance System enables us to fly underneath radar sweeps, so we shouldn't be detected. The guidance control system also allows us to fly low at high speed. I'll climb a bit when we travel through the mountains. Otherwise, the G forces could harm the president. I've set our course to keep us away from controlled air spaces. I hope we'll make it across without being detected. I've got two planes working against the air force at Luke Air Force Base. I know the areas they're working, so we should be okay. I'm monitoring the military frequency. If we're noticed, I'll hear the alert and we can adjust our route."

Roger slowly added power and dropped the plane lower.

JB noted the airspeed and altitude, thinking, *Six hundred-fifty knots at 100 feet feels like we're traveling a couple thousand miles an hour!*

To prevent the desert landscape from blurring, JB had to look far ahead of the plane. He watched Roger adjust the various instruments. Roger pointed to a spot on the chart, and JB was amazed at the distance traveled. They tuned in a civilian news broadcast. It was now being reported the president was dead, and the vice president was sworn in to replace him. The president's plane would soon leave Love Field, taking the dead president and the new president back to Washington. The radio news reported the president died from a head wound. A suspect was arrested and the murder weapon had been recovered. There was no mention of the dead agents in the grassy knoll area; no mention of the dead agents in the hospital; no mention of the freeway incident.

JB felt uneasy as he thought, *No doubt, a huge cover-up is in progress, and the framers of the plot now have their man in place as the new president.*

The plane veered sharply to the right in a course correction. JB looked at the compass heading, and they were traveling due west. As he watched, the compass swung to northwest, and he felt the plane making the adjustment. "Course adjustments aren't too bad. We'll have to slow down when we get into the mountains because we'll be tracking on the terrain. I'll take us up a little higher in the unpopulated areas to keep our ride from feeling like a roller coaster. We've just passed into New Mexico, and we'll be in Arizona in twenty minutes. Why don't you see how our passenger's doing?"

JB nodded, got up, and walked back to the rear cabin. The young doctor hovered alongside the president.

"How is he doing, John?"

"No big changes. Blood pressure is dropping, but it's okay, and his eyes are still dilated. His catatonic state has not altered; doesn't look good for recovery. How much longer?"

"We should be there in about an hour and a half. The pilot's doing his best to give us a smooth, level ride."

"What's the word out of Dallas?" the doctor asked.

"It looks like a big cover-up. After we get down and you're able to take care of the president, we can talk about today. Why don't you go up front with the pilot for a few minutes. I'll keep an eye on the president."

"No thanks. I'm okay and I don't want to leave the president, even for a moment. I would appreciate a soft drink."

JB brought John a cold orange soda from the galley, then went back to the cockpit.

CHAPTER TWELVE

JB sat in the second seat for the next hour. He marveled at the maneuverability of their small plane as they worked their way through the rugged mountains.

They flew up the canyons, over the mesas, around the buttes, always within several hundred feet of the ground.

Roger constantly made computer and instrument adjustments.

The pilot pointed toward the map and placed his finger at the California border, just above Blythe. JB saw they had crossed over into California.

"How much longer?" He asked.

"We should be on the ground in less than twenty minutes."

The pilot was busy, so JB looked back toward the young doctor and said, "Twenty minutes."

John nodded okay and JB turned forward and resumed looking for other aircraft. He noted their airspeed, 620 knots, and their altitude, just over 160 feet. A glitch in the computer control or an erroneous instruction from the pilot would send them into the ground at almost the speed of sound.

As they passed north of the Chocolate Mountain Gunnery Range, the radar screen picked up several blips.

The pilot spoke, "Probably some navy pilots taking gunnery practice. I don't think we have to worry."

They flew on, winding in and out of the mountain passes, up and down over the terrain.

When they passed north of Indio, Roger clicked on the radio to a pres-elected frequency and quietly said, "We're here to visit the Date Gardens, one minute away," swung the plane southwest, and crossed over the Interstate Freeway. He reduced the throttle setting, and the plane flew along in an eerie silence.

JB saw a string of runway lights in the distance.

Their airspeed was down to 200 knots and slowing rapidly for final approach. Flaps and gear down. Now a flare . . . and they hit the runway hot at 150 knots. The touchdown was perfect, and he felt Roger gently slowing the plane as they rolled along the landing strip toward the end of runway 21.

The pilot saw the van, swung the plane around, and braked to a stop about thirty feet away.

JB went to the door, released the locking lever, and pushed the door open. The ladder was down.

JB saw Cosmo and David racing toward the plane.

John untied the straps securing the gurney and pushed the gurney toward the door, saying, "We're ready, let's go."

JB leapt to the ground, Roger jumped from the cockpit to help the doctor, and they began removing the president from the plane. Cosmo and David helped JB handle the gurney down to the asphalt runway and to the van parked near the plane. Cosmo opened the rear doors of the van, while David and John were bent over the president, talking in low voices. Roger stepped down from the plane, looked at JB and put out his hand. "Good luck, JB. Tell Dr. Johnson when you need me, and I'll be wherever you want." They shook hands, and Roger jumped back into the plane.

The door closed, and the plane sat idling, waiting for the van to pull away.

Cosmo and JB helped the two doctors load the gurney into the van. David and John went into the van with the president and it quickly pulled away. Cosmo signaled JB to follow him to the nearby car.

The jet's engines roared loudly, and JB looked back. The plane started rolling. Roger gave him a salute and the plane quickly accelerated down the ramp toward the downwind end of twenty-one.

JB turned and ran to the car. The rear door was open, and Cosmo was waiting in the rear seat. He got in, slammed the door, and the car sped away.

"We'll be at the hospital within fifteen minutes. JB, why don't you sit back and tell me what's going on."

"Cosmo, I don't know where to start so I'll just tell you to be patient and trust me. That man in the van is President O'Sullivan. The president was shot in the head, and there's a big cover-up going on. They intended to allow President O'Sullivan to die from the gunshot wound, or if needed, they were going to finish the job on the operating table. For the moment, we need to do all possible to save President O'Sullivan's life."

Cosmo looked sadly at JB. "Jesus, what a situation."

JB saw the tears glistening in Cosmo's eyes before Cosmo averted his face.

"What's going on Cosmo?"

Cosmo looked back at JB, reached over and grasped JB's arm and said, "JB, there was an explosion in your house this morning."

JB sat, frozen, wide-eyed, speechless. He felt cold, and he gritted his teeth to keep from crying out.

Cosmo continued, "When Isabel started her car this morning, probably to take the kids to school, a fire bomb exploded. It destroyed the car, your house, and everyone in the car and house. When you called me, I couldn't tell you." Tears were streaming down Cosmo's cheeks and he continued, "I swear on my family's honor, I'll find who's responsible for what happened, and I will kill them in the lowest manner possible."

JB inhaled deeply, turned, and looked out of the car window. He couldn't talk or get his mind to accept what Cosmo had told him. He sat, frozen.

They rode in silence.

JB felt the car slow and halt briefly at the guard station. They entered what looked like a country club and drove down a long two-lane boulevard, lined with royal palms, flowers everywhere. The road wound to the foothills, up and over the low mountain range. They went up a second mountainside and turned into a large asphalt parking lot, behind a low, ranch-style adobe house.

The driver got out and walked around the car and into the house.

Cosmo and JB sat in the back seat of the car. Finally Cosmo got out, went around to open JB's door and said, gently, "Come on, JB, let's go in."

He looked up at Cosmo, and Cosmo saw the cold, controlled fury in JB's eyes and thought to himself, *Heaven help whoever did the job.*

The two doctors worked well together. David looked at the president's wound and thought, *It's a miracle he's alive.* Putting that thought out of his mind, he asked the young doctor, "Tell me everything you remember, from the first moment you saw him."

The short ride from the airport was over before the young doctor finished telling his story.

The van screeched to a halt. Two orderlies stood waiting with a gurney. David vaulted from the van and yelled, "Gently but quickly, let's get him to the operating room."

Once on the sidewalk, they quickly wheeled the gurney through the open doorway adjacent the garage. The doctors watched their patient as the orderlies moved the gurney down the brightly lighted, white hallway.

They entered a small room. An orderly turned to David and said, "Your dressing room is on the left. When you're ready, we'll put your patient on the O.R. table."

David looked through the windows into the operating room. It was obviously well-equipped, and two nurses were waiting next to the operating table. He turned to the young doctor. "Let's get him on the table now, then we'll scrub. By the way, I'm David Protect."

"I'm John Andrews. I've heard of you. I hope you're as good as I've heard; our patient needs the best and a ton of luck."

David nodded, and the orderlies opened the door and helped them move the gurney to the operating table. They connected the automatic respirator, the heart monitoring machine, the electroencephalograph, and replaced the intravenous bag with a new supply of packed red cells.

David checked the president's pulse and found it rapid and weak. The heart-lung and brain monitoring machines were functioning properly.

John spoke to the nurses, "Drape the patient and stabilize his head, looking left. Then scrub and be ready to go in five minutes."

David and John went immediately to the dressing room. They stripped off their clothing and stepped into the shower. David stood under the shower, the hot water cascading down over his head and body. The warm water helped him to relax as he thought about the grueling hours ahead. John had miraculously kept the patient alive. David had been shocked when he saw the wound but even more shocked when he saw the patient's face. *The president! My god, what's going on?* He thought to himself, *Forget about the president. Concentrate on what must be done.* He thought back to his recent surgery experiences, trying to relate ideas to the problem at hand. He thought, *The internal bleeding must be stopped. The only hope for recovery is if the damaged blood supply system continues to furnish enough blood to the president's brain.* He turned off the shower and toweled himself dry. He walked over to the stainless steel sinks and scrubbed. Standing next to John, David explained his plan. Using the encephalograph, they would trace the flow of blood. As the damaged areas were located, he would try closing the arterial or venous wounds with internal cauterization. If that failed, they would have to play it by ear. They would also need to close the open wound on the right side of the president's head.

John had protected the wounded area. The local bleeding was controlled by small clamps, and it appeared they would be able to close the wound, using a minimal amount of plastics for reconstruction. They planned to tackle the internal bleeding problem immediately. They donned sterile surgical gowns and finally their surgical gloves.

They returned to the operating room and went immediately to the operating table. David positioned the electroencephalograph against the president's head, turned on the machine, and they read the printout. John shook his head in resignation as they noted the damaged blood channels. David switched on the nuclear imaging apparatus then injected the radioactive contrast solution into the president's carotid artery. They saw a jumble of veins and arteries and several blotches on the screen, indicating damaged veins. As the solution coursed through the president's cranial vascular network, bleeding spots were marked on the imaging plate. The examination took about fifteen minutes and noted six blood seepages. Four of the spots appeared to be inactive, probably stopped due to clotting. Two spots were seeping blood and both doctors knew the seepage must be stopped to prevent further damage, and it might well be their attempts would be too late.

He commanded the nurse, "Pass me the cauter-injector," and the ordeal began. The delicacy of the procedure increased mental tension, and he felt a deep concern about attempting the operation with an unfamiliar operating team.

With painstaking care, David guided the thin flexible tube into the carotid artery, up through the maze of the cranial vascular network, positioning the tip of the flexible tube precisely against the damaged section of the artery. Then he slowly pushed the resistance wire through the tube until the tip of the wire rested against the damaged spot. He reviewed the marking spot, satisfied himself the wire was correctly positioned, and then increased the low voltage. He watched the damaged spot darken before he reduced the power. Too much burning would damage the artery beyond repair. Too little burning would not stop the bleeding. David felt the frustration of uncertainty in the procedure but knew he must rely on his judgment and instinct.

Without hesitation, David began retracting the wire. The flexible tube could not be moved with the wire inside. The wire must be removed and the flexible tube withdrawn to a vascular junction and then rerouted to the other bleeding spot.

The first repair had taken an hour and a half, and at one point, twenty minutes passed without a word being spoken.

The young doctor and the nurses were spellbound at the sureness and painstakingly gentle movements of David. With a slight twist, he started the tube toward its second target. As the tube moved, millimeter by millimeter, he recalled his mentor's message during training in neurosurgery: "Do it right the first time. You will not get a second chance. The cranial vascular system is sensitive to intrusion, and the arterial walls will collapse if you try to use the artery wall to guide your tube. You must allow the blood flow to center the tube in the artery. Then allow the blood flow to pull it along to your destination. It may take an hour or it may take six hours. You must be patient and allow whatever time is needed. If you fail the first time, there will be no second time." David was concerned partial retraction of the tube would trigger a vascular collapse. The vascular network was complicated and twice he took a wrong turn. Consequently it took over two hours to reach the second leaking area. He positioned the tube adjacent the damaged area and started the arduous task of inserting the wire.

Finally the wire was in place. As a nurse mopped his brow for the eleventh time, David rechecked the marking spot, found it to his liking, and increased the power.

They watched the damaged area change to a darker color.

David cut the power and muttered, "Nothing more we can do with this. If they're sealed, he's healed, and let's hope the other bleeders have cured themselves. We've pushed our luck doing the second repair. There's no way to do another at this time."

The retraction procedure took another hour, and when David finally removed the flexible tube from the president's artery, they all let out a sigh of relief.

The young doctor continually monitored the president's vital signs and now reported adequate blood pressure, almost normal pulse, and unobstructed breathing. They checked the president's eyes. Both eyes were fully dilated.

David was worried. "There's nothing more we can do inside his brain. Let's take care of the local damage and close up the head wound."

The young doctor hesitated, looking at David.

David smiled, "John, you did a great job getting him here. Go ahead and finish the job."

The young doctor nodded and asked the nurse for a bone tweezer.

For the next two hours, David watched John carefully check the entire wound area, removing torn tissue and crushed bone fragments. When the wound area was cleansed, he inserted several soft plastic supports and pulled the torn skin back to the president's scalp. The torn skin was sutured into place and the wound bandaged.

The young doctor looked up, and David could read the fatigue.

David looked at the wall clock and was surprised at the time. It was almost midnight.

The doctors and the nurses moved the president onto the gurney, and the interns pushed the gurney into an adjacent private ICU. The monitoring equipment was connected, readings checked, and a dextrose drip started.

"Doctor," one of the nurses said, "we will watch the patient at all times. Both of you can use the suite next door. If you feel like eating or need anything, pick up the telephone and tell the operator. Please, don't worry about your patient. If any problems come up we'll awaken you immediately. And by the way, I've scrubbed with many excellent surgeons, but I've never seen anyone pull off what you did earlier. There's no doubt, the patient owes you his life."

David smiled and responded, "I should warn you he's far from out of the woods, but I could not have tried that crazy stunt if Doctor Andrews hadn't done the impossible in keeping the patient alive. Thank you for helping us. We'll be sleeping next door. Let's hope what we've done is enough to bring our patient back."

The doctors left the ICU, and the nurses turned their full attention to the comatose president.

JB and Cosmo observed the doctors at work in the operating room and listened to the muted conversations between the doctors and nurses. They sat at their observation post, watching the activity below and talking quietly about the events of the past few days. JB asked, "Tell me what you know about the bombing."

"There's not much to tell. It happened around eight o'clock this morning. It was one helluva explosion. I was having breakfast with Ilona, and our house shook from the blast. Seeing the smoke, I ran the two blocks to the corner of Woodhill Drive and saw what remained of your house engulfed in flames. The heat from the fire was intense, and the house was totally shattered. The ones on each side were badly damaged and also on fire. The fire and rescue trucks arrived and quickly controlled the blaze. They searched the ruins, hoping to find survivors, but there were none. Your station wagon was shattered and burned. It appears that Isabel and the girls were inside the car when she turned on the ignition and set off the bomb. It was a powerful bomb, and I'm sure highly flammable material had been placed around to ignite when the bomb exploded. It looked like a small atomic explosion had hit. When I saw the utter devastation, I knew a bomb had been planted, so rather than help search the wreckage, I watched the streets, looking for any suspicious looking people. The sidewalks were crowded with onlookers so I watched the rear of the crowds. I saw a tall, thin white man walk away from the crowd, down the street, and around the corner. I tailed him and saw him get into a dark colored sedan and drive away. It looked like a Chevrolet, but I'm not sure. I was able to get most of the license number, and I've got my people checking for the car's ownership. I should have an answer by tomorrow morning. I overheard people in the crowd talking to investigators and they were telling the authorities that you were home with your family. They probably think you were killed in the blast along with them."

"What about your men who had been watching my family?"

"I found their van around the corner. It was empty. We haven't heard from either of them, so it's my guess they're dead and disposed of."

JB sat silently, trying to piece together what had taken place. He had a gut feeling he had been pinpointed from his inquiry to Dr. Burr about the vice president. *Perhaps they recognized my voice, and although unable to trace the call, maybe thought I was at home?"* Dr. Burr had been eliminated and they probably felt that JB had now been eliminated as well.

JB thought of Susan. She had not been present during his last visit with Dr. Burr. JB turned to Cosmo, "Would you have someone find Susan Burr and bring her here. Her father was murdered, and the same people likely murdered my family, thinking they would get me. She's innocent but will probably also be targeted if they find her. Her father mentioned to me she was on a ski trip in Utah. She's probably back in Palo Alto attending to the funeral arrangements for her father. Have someone look after her, and bring her here after the funeral."

"JB, when are you going to tell me what's going on? Someone murdered a man you visited, murdered your family thinking they would get you, and we've got the president down there in the operating room, fighting for his life. You've got to admit this whole thing is bizarre!"

"Cosmo, I'm not able to tell you all of the details. All I can tell you is I'm working for the president and for our country. The new president is an impostor and controlled by unidentified person or persons. If I can discover who controls the new president, perhaps I can unravel the total picture. I hope contacts with the new president will lead us to the culprits and the people responsible for murdering Dr. Burr, my family, and only God knows how many more."

Cosmo spoke, "JB, it does no good to watch the operation going on down below. Let's get some rest and then see what tomorrow brings."

JB was mentally and physically exhausted. He nodded despairingly, yes. They arose, left the room, and went downstairs to their sleeping quarters. When JB was alone, the mental image of his dead family haunted him and the chilling reality hit him full force! "I made a fatal error, and my innocent wife and children were murdered by someone expecting me to be their victim." Vomit gushed forth through his mouth and he gagged. The constriction around his chest made him gasp!

In the adjacent room, Cosmo heard pounding on the wall and wailing as JB grieved.

JB swallowed several Seconals, and before they took hold, he thought, *Being alive is a hell on earth and I'll bear their cross forever! Please, please let me find them, let me get my hands on the one responsible for the killings!*

Finally he slept.

JB awoke with a start, looked at the bedside clock, and was amazed it was 0900.

He felt refreshed after shaving and showering but was sick at heart with the loss of his family. He was anxious to find out the president's condition, so he dressed hurriedly and left his bedroom. To extinguish his sorrow, he focused on the condition of the president.

Cosmo sat on the floor in the hallway, outside the bedroom door. He stood, looked JB directly in the eyes, and asked, "Are you okay today?"

"I'm fine, and Cosmo, thanks for putting yourself on the line for me."

"Forget it, JB. I can never fully repay you for your kindness to my grandfather and for saving my father's life. Now let's see how the president's doing."

JB followed Cosmo through the maze of hallways until they reached the I.C.U.

The doctors had just finished checking the bandages on the president's head and were checking the steady flow of information from the electroencephalograph. David grabbed the president's charts and beckoned for JB to follow him into the adjacent room. JB followed, and after entering the room next door, closed the door.

"JB, his heart is strong, regular, and his breathing is good. We're getting no output from his conscious mind. It may be that parts of his brain were destroyed, or it may be temporary swelling. I think we repaired the damaged arteries, but we may have been too late. On the other hand, he could be affected by temporary blockages caused by the blood let loose around his brain. His body could absorb the excess blood and allow those parts of his brain to resume functioning. All we can do is wait, and it may take days, weeks, months, or even years. There's no way to tell."

"When can we move him?"

"In a few days. He must remain quiet for the next seventy-two hours. Then we'll see. What do you have in mind?"

"We must get him out of the country, to a place for his recuperation. I have a plan, but it involves much traveling. We'll need you to come along. Can you get away for a couple of weeks?"

"I need to get back to my office and clear up a few matters. Then I can go with you. Any traveling the president does must be done with him connected to all of these machines. One slip and we lose him."

JB nodded. "Cosmo will get you home and arrange for your return."

David spoke, "JB, Cosmo told me about Isabel and the girls. It was a brutal thing to happen, and I wish there were something that I could do for you or to the ones responsible."

A somber JB replied, "Thank you, David. I feel nauseated, and I hurt physically because of what happened, but the past is out of my control. I've dedicated myself to keeping the president alive and to finding the ones responsible for what happened to my family. I will avenge their needless and heartless deaths and I'll give my life to keep the president alive."

David left for home soon after.

The young doctor seldom left the president's bedside, and JB sat alone in the den, overlooking the golf course, planning their escape from the United States but also feeling his karma transmigrating him into another existence. He silently agonized over his compassion for the families of those he had slain, visualizing their broken hearts and shattered dreams.

CHAPTER THIRTEEN

JB called Dr. Johnson's number and left a number. Within a few minutes, the telephone next to JB rang.

JB answered, "Yes?"

"Hello, JB. It looks like we've pulled it off. What can I do for you?"

"I need Sergeant Browning. In fact I'll probably need him for the rest of his life."

"You know the score, JB. He won't last more than a few months, and he'll need medical attention."

"I'll take care of the sergeant. I need someone we can trust, and I feel he will appreciate serving his country during his final days."

"Done, JB. I'll notify the sergeant. Now, what's the prognosis?"

"Too early to tell. We'll relocate during the next few days. I'll be in contact." JB hung up the telephone receivers. There was a light knock on the door and Cosmo entered. "I've got four good men watching Susan. The funeral is this morning. After the funeral they'll bring her here. Just so you'll know, your father-in-law has made funeral service arrangements for your family. The service and burial will be Monday in Monterey. You're included."

JB sat watching Cosmo, then replied, "Thanks, Cosmo. Any problem with Susan?"

"We spotted a man tailing her, and we're watching him every minute. If and when he makes his move, we'll take him out."

JB nodded and leaned back in his chair, closing his eyes. His chest felt as if it would burst from holding in his agony. Cosmo sat down across from JB. Neither spoke, JB unable and Cosmo knowing that JB needed time to regain his composure. They sat for over an hour without talking.

Finally JB cleared his throat and spoke, "I've decided where we should take the president. We'll need your help."

Cosmo nodded yes and said, "Tell me."

"I want to take the president out of the country. You remember the two houses you helped me buy in Positano? He'll be safe there, and we can have Signora Boronio care for him. The houses are private and have enough room for our group. We should move him soon. David says that we must keep the president connected to the monitoring machines. I know that you can arrange a chartered plane to fly him out, but it would have to be a large plane and would require us to go to a large airport. I'm concerned that all airports are being watched. We cannot take a chance on being found out. Can you arrange a ship to pick us up in Mexico? I can have Roger fly us to the ship."

Cosmo thought for a moment, then answered, "We have a ship in Houston picking up oil drilling equipment. It is due to sail tomorrow for the Middle East. Perhaps we can arrange a rendezvous off Mexico. We have a private airstrip near Cancun. Roger could fly you there, and we'll transfer you to the ship on one of our fishing boats. Then we'll meet the ship off the coast from Positano with another of our fishing boats and take you there."

"Let's do it; no reason why it shouldn't work. Everyone should be here by Sunday, and we should be able to leave then, provided the president is stable."

Cosmo excused himself to make the arrangements.

JB wondered, *How can we invade Positano with all these people and not attract attention?*

JB telephoned Dr. Johnson and then sat back, waiting for the return call. It came quickly. "Hello," JB answered.

"What can I do for you?" the doctor asked.

"I need Roger here at 1600 Sunday afternoon. Have him pick up Sergeant Browning and land, same as before. He knows where. We'll be waiting for him and be out of the airport soon as he's refueled."

"Anything else?"

"No," replied JB. "Wait, there's one thing . . . I'm going to tell Roger about my plans. I want you to have the other three contact Roger. I want them to know, just in case something happens to me, you, or Roger."

"Anything else?"

"No, not for me. For your information, he's okay for now. We don't know if he'll recover but, thanks to you, he's alive." JB hung up the telephone.

JB spent the afternoon watching television, listening to radio news, and reading the papers brought him by Cosmo. The nation mourned its dead president. The funeral was scheduled for Monday. Political dignitaries from around the world were flying to Washington to attend the funeral, and the dead president lay in state at the rotunda in the Capitol. People stood in a block-long line to view the casket.

JB found no mention of the dead agents in Dallas and was puzzled as to who was in the president's casket. As he read on, he thought, *The cover-up continues, but the perpetrators must be alarmed at the disappearance of the president. Unless they really didn't know! Could it be possible?*

JB thought back to the hospital emergency room in Dallas and replayed the chaotic scene over and over in his mind. The blasts of the small bombs; shooting down the agents; his mind focused on the agent standing next to the doctors working on the president and he could vividly recall seeing the agent take several gunshots into his face and head, blasting away his features before he fell to the floor next to the operating table. Could it be possible they were using that dead agent's body as the president? Or could it be possible they actually thought his body was that of the president? If the cover-up extended to the Special Board already named to investigate the assassination, they would not pay attention to autopsy details.

JB intently watched the afternoon and evening news broadcasts; the more he watched, the more convinced he became that it was possible they were unaware the president had been removed from the scene.

It was early evening when Cosmo and the young doctor came to JB's room.

Cosmo had their evening meal served.

JB was unable to eat.

During and following the meal, John explained the president's condition: "He's stable; blood pressure is 120 over 80; breathing is okay; head wound is healing normally; the head wound will require some re-constructive surgery; we're continuing to feed him intravenously; he does not respond to stimulus, and his eyes remain fully dilated. It's looking more and more like his brain was seriously damaged, although we have brain action shown on the EEG."

JB told them, "You know the plan, Cosmo. I want to leave here Sunday afternoon. Roger will be at the airport at 1400, and David will be back but he'll need help caring for the president, so John, we need you to come with us."

Cosmo answered. "That'll work. I'll make certain they're ready to receive you."

John spoke, "They must be investigating my disappearance so I can't go back to Parkland. I've come this far. I wouldn't give up the opportunity to see this through to the end. I just wish I knew what was going on."

JB smiled at the young doctor. "I'll admit, this whole thing is incredible, but you've got to have faith in us. We're doing the right thing."

"I've never met you before, but I believe you. I hate to think what would've happened to me and the president if you hadn't been there in Dallas. You lead the way, I'll follow."

118

Cosmo and John arose to leave.

The doctor reached into his coat pocket, took out a vial, and handed it to JB. "One of these will do you good. When you're ready to sleep, take one. I promise that you'll sleep soundly. It won't make you groggy tomorrow, but you won't be worth much tonight. You need the rest, take it."

JB took the vial of pills from the doctor, opened it, and swallowed one pill.

Cosmo and the doctor left the room, and JB sat down, looking out the large window and up toward the star-filled evening sky. He sat and quietly cried for his lost family, hating himself for what had happened to them.

Susan sat on his bed, watching him come awake.

JB's eyes opened, looked at her, then closed again.

She lay down beside him, letting her head fall into the crook of his arm.

JB felt her warmth. He enclosed her in his arms, pulling her close and hard against him.

She was sobbing quietly.

He stroked her hair with his free hand and felt tears gathering in his eyes. He forced himself to hold back his sobs. The back of his throat ached, his ears and eyes hurt, but he remained quiet, gently stroking her, trying to ease her grief.

Susan stopped sobbing, shuddered, and relaxed against him. After awhile she pulled her head back and looked into his face. His eyes were brimming with tears. She reached up and touched his lower eyelid with her finger and several tears spilled from his eye, running down his cheek to their pillow. She wiped away the tears with her finger, reached up, and kissed his cheek. She put her head upon his shoulder and closed her eyes.

They lay together for over an hour, each clutching the other, tightly.

JB relaxed his arm and whispered into her ear, "Thank God you're safe."

They lay together for awhile longer before she pulled away from him and sat up on the bed. "I'm so confused and frightened. I was heartbroken because I was away when father had his heart attack and needed me. Then yesterday, when those awful men tried to pull me into their car. I wouldn't have had a chance. Some other men came from nowhere and saved me."

JB looked at her. "Please, tell me everything that happened."

Susan continued. "They shot the driver and the man who was grabbing me. Then they took me around the corner to their car. I was frightened, so I started kicking and screaming. I didn't want to get in. One of the men grabbed me in a bear hug and I thought I was a goner. Then he whispered to me, 'We have been ordered to bring you to JB. We aren't going to hurt you, so please come quietly.' I acquiesced and here I am. Would you please tell me what is going on?"

JB sat up beside her. "Look, I need a shower. Let me get dressed, then we'll have some breakfast and I'll tell you what is happening."

"Okay, JB, but I'm not letting you out of my sight. I'm still so frightened!"

JB smiled at her. "That's fine with me, but the steam from the shower might take the curl out of your hair."

"Okay, I'll wait, but please hurry!"

He was back in a few minutes, and together they went in search of the dining room.

David returned in the late afternoon and Cosmo arranged for all of them to dine together early in the evening. Their traveling group would be the president, the two doctors, Susan, JB, and the sergeant. Roger would fly them to the ship and Cosmo would return home. Following dinner they met in Cosmo's study to review their plans and preparation for departure. Cosmo had cautioned JB not to tell anyone their ultimate destination, so the group knew only that departure would be early the next afternoon.

The meeting broke up early, and JB remained to talk privately with Cosmo. All arrangements were made. The ship would move slowly past the Cancun area, about twenty miles from shore. The plane would land at the private airstrip near Cancun, and they would be met by a van. The van would take them to a fishing boat at a private estate, a few miles north of Cancun. The boat would find the ship and come alongside on the seaward side for the transfer, and the ship would stop dead in the water for the few minutes needed for the transfer of passengers. Roger would refuel at the private airport and return immediately to Arizona. Private quarters were arranged aboard the ship and no crew members would see the passengers. The Atlantic crossing would take five to six days, then another day in the Mediterranean would bring them to their destination where another fishing boat would be waiting to take them ashore. The transfers would be made under darkness.

JB slept soundly until 0700 Sunday, arose, and took a long hot and then cold shower. Cosmo was waiting when JB came out of the shower. JB looked questioningly at Cosmo and Cosmo nodded yes.

JB turned to Cosmo. "Tell me what you've learned."

"We located the car. It's a government car from the pool at San Bruno. The car checked out last Wednesday morning and was turned in Friday afternoon by a George Jackson. Jackson is an FBI agent assigned to Special Investigations in San Francisco. We know where he lives, and we now have him under surveillance."

"Cosmo, I cannot allow him to live. I will go with our group today and make certain the president gets aboard the ship, then I'll come back ashore and have Roger fly me back to the Bay Area. I must say good-bye to my family and I'll need transportation to Rome on Wednesday."

"When you get to San Francisco, call me. I'll take you to him. As for Rome, I'll arrange for you to board the plane as a crew member. With a disguise, you should not be spotted, and I'll let the signora know you're coming."

The doctors were busy preparing the president for the trip, and they selected the equipment, materials, and supplies needed for the trip and afterwards.

JB sat with Susan in the dining room. He was unable to eat but managed several cups of coffee while calming her anxiety about the coming trip.

The morning passed slowly for JB.

The equipment, materials, and supplies were loaded into a van and another van was readied for the president.

The doctors rode with the president, JB and Susan with Cosmo in a car.

The three vehicles arrived at the airport ten minutes before Roger was scheduled to land. They drove to the west end of the runway, parked, and waited for the plane.

Precisely at 1400, the jet touched down. The plane's door was already opening when it came to rest, and the vans backed to within ten feet of the plane's open door.

The first van quickly unloaded, and the supplies were stowed aboard. The president was taken from the second van and gently loaded aboard the plane. The entire process took about ten minutes, and during this time, the plane was refueled.

JB turned to Cosmo. "Thank you, my friend. I'll see you soon."

They embraced and JB ran to the plane, following Susan up the ladder. The jet taxied to takeoff position, did a quick clearing turn, then accelerated down the runway and into the air.

JB turned and the sergeant was looking toward him from the cockpit. The sergeant appeared gaunt but JB could see the excitement and pleasure in his eyes. They shook hands firmly, and the sergeant said, "You cannot imagine how welcome was your call!"

"We need the best, so I called for you. In case you didn't notice, that's our president in the back. He's seriously wounded and it's our job to protect him and give the doctors a chance to bring him back to health."

The sergeant nodded and smiled, one of his few smiles. "I've prayed for a chance to go out in style!"

The plane finished its climb-out and immediately dropped down to 160 feet altitude, heading east.

They flew low and fast, avoiding the populated areas and traveled the 3,300 air miles in a little over six hours.

They touched down about one and a half hours before midnight. It was after midnight when the fishing boat pulled away from the dock and headed out into the gulf to rendezvous with the ship.

The fishing boat plowed through the water at fifteen knots. The ocean was calm, but it was a moonless night, very dark, and the fishing boat was traveling without lights.

JB went to the small bridge and watched the ship's captain searching for the large ship. A transponder was beeping, and the sweep on the radar screen picked up their target.

The captain glanced at JB and spoke, "We'll rendezvous the ship in about an hour. It's traveling slowly, about twenty miles at sea. The area is clear, so we shouldn't have a problem."

JB went down to the passenger compartment and relayed the captain's message to the group. He sat beside Susan and put his arm around her shoulder. She had somewhat recovered from the shock of learning that her father had been murdered and she nestled her head against him, smiled tentatively, and whispered, "Do you think we'll make it?"

JB squeezed her shoulder. "We'll make it. There's no reason why everything shouldn't work out for us. Our present goal is to protect the president and help him with his recovery. David and John will need all the help they can get, so pitch in and help them as often as you can."

They sat in silence, listening to the heavy throbbing of the diesel engines pushing them toward the ship.

The engines slowed and their boat rolled slowly on the smooth ocean.

JB and the sergeant went out onto the deck and saw the large ship looming over their fishing boat.

Their captain expertly brought the small boat against the port side of the large ship and stopped their boat adjacent the open hatch. The crewmen on the fishing boat placed fenders between the fishing boat and the large ship to protect the small boat, then went fore and aft with landing gaffs to hold the small boat steady against the larger ship.

Crewmen from the large ship passed two lines to the smaller boat. The lines were secured and kept the small boat steady. The captain ordered JB to commence the transfer.

JB nodded to the sergeant, "Go aboard the ship."

The sergeant carried an automatic pistol as he leapt aboard. He checked the adjacent passageways and signaled to JB, "All clear."

The doctors readied the president for the transfer, placing him in a concave metal stretcher. JB helped the doctors move the stretcher adjacent the hatch and then used the ship's derrick to guide the stretcher onto the deck of the large ship. The doctors followed the stretcher across.

Susan looked at JB, looked at the ship, then looked back at JB. He smiled, kissed her gently, and held her arm to help her step across to the large ship.

The crewmen quickly passed the equipment and supplies across to the other ship and then cast off the lines.

The captain of the fishing boat turned up his boat's engines, and the small boat turned away and circled around, astern the large ship, heading back to shore. JB could see the wake forming behind the large ship as it commenced its journey off into the darkness.

JB stood on the fantail of the fishing boat, saw the name *Festina Maru* through the mist as he crossed her stern, and watched the large ship until it disappeared into the darkness. He had not told the group that he was going back with Roger.

After boarding the *Festina Maru*, all were busy attending the president and making sure the equipment and supplies were stowed for the coming trip.

An officer received them aboard and directed them to their quarters, two suites totaling eight rooms, aft of the hatchway where they came aboard. The quarters were amidships to minimize the pitching at sea.

David and John immediately took the president to the aft compartment of the suites, moved him onto the hospital bed furnished by the ship, hooked him to the monitoring machine, and restarted the ever-present drips to keep him alive.

Susan accompanied the doctors. The sergeant alertly watched the ship's seamen move the equipment and supplies into the suites.

The suites consisted of a large room for the patient, an adjacent room setup as a laboratory-office-treatment center, a large dining room-lounge, a storage room, and four bedrooms.

After the president was taken care of, they assembled in the dining room.

They stood silently, each looking at the others and looking for JB. The sergeant spoke up. "JB went ashore." He surveyed the group, then continued. "Doctor Protect, you will be in charge. The president's condition and survival is our number one concern; nothing else matters. I'm along to provide security, so I will inspect our quarters and the surrounding area to gauge our safety. I suggest that we use a single door for our quarters, and all of the other doors should remain locked at all times. We will establish a watch to ensure the president is never alone."

David looked at the group. "Thank you, Sergeant. I feel it's important for us to work together. The sergeant is the expert on security. Therefore we will follow his advice on security measures. John and I will spend our time caring for the president's medical problems. Susan, you'll be in charge of logistics, coordinating the delivery of our meals from the ship's kitchen and handling our communications with the ship's captain and crew. We must all take part in the constant watch over the president. I suggest that John, Susan, and I rotate the watch, four hours on, eight hours off and the sergeant should spend all of his time at security. Susan, you prepare the watch list, starting with my taking first watch. The dining room is the farthest room from the president. Let's make the dining room our entrance and exit door. Sergeant, you take the sleeping quarters nearest to the dining room. Susan, you take the next bedroom. John and I will take the back bedrooms, nearest to the president. Make your search, Sergeant. Susan and John, get some rest."

David went to the president, checked the president's condition, then settled down at the nearby desk to plan the next few days.

David and John spent every waking moment either with the president or sitting together in the dining room, lounge, or office, discussing the president's condition.

The president's vital signs remained within acceptable limits but he remained comatose.

Susan arranged their meals, took her turns in watching the president, and if not sleeping sat with the doctors during their discussions. She understood most of what they discussed, often surprising the doctors with her probing questions about the president's condition, leading them toward treatment alternatives not previously considered.

The daily watch routine and their secondary chores kept them busy every waking moment, and none were able to sleep enough to become fully rested and restored. The sergeant was ever present, and the other three wondered if he slept at all. David and the sergeant ate a few meals together and alone. On those occasions, David learned what he could about the sergeant's condition.

The sergeant never complained, but David could see the jaundice in the eyes, lack of appetite, and the tiredness on the sergeant's face. From these outward appearances, David realized the sergeant was seriously ill.

They sat, sipping their coffee, and David listened. "I get the feeling they were stumped. They told me if it was congenital, it would've shown up when I was a baby. The doctors told me that I'm still getting some liver function, but the damage done by my drinking could not be reversed." The sergeant continued. "That's when I decided that you're my only hope. My doctors assumed that I'm a drinker since men in the military have that reputation, but Doc, I don't drink, never have, never will."

David sat quietly for a few moments, then asked, "Sergeant, tell me about your life."

"I grew up on a corn farm in eastern Nebraska. My mom and dad worked hard, and I worked hard for as long as I can remember. We raised corn for eating and corn for animal feed, and I used to think there's enough corn on our farm to feed the world, but, of course, I had never been outside the county, so I had no idea how big our world is. I went to school, studied hard, and played ball. If the war hadn't come along, I would've gone to the university on a football scholarship. The hard work on the farm and my mom's good cooking turned me into a strong, well-built young man. But when war was declared, I did what most young Americans did–I volunteered for the service, and that's how I got into the marines. I served in the South Pacific during World War Two. When people say South Pacific, they think of Hawaii or Tahiti. It was nothing like those places. It was a living hell and I saw many of my friends blown away by Japanese or wasted away by jungle crud. I think that's where I became a man. The hardest part was moving the body bags back to the beaches, knowing that my friends were inside those shiny, black bags. One day I sat on a beach looking at a row of those bags, and I cried like a baby. I vowed to do all that I possibly could to keep my shipmates alive. I stayed in the marines, and I served in Korea, and I was at Chosen. I kicked plenty of asses, keeping my men moving, and we walked and fought our way out of the Chosen Reservoir but I knew that every ass I kicked gave that young marine a chance to live. I first served in 'Nam before it was Vietnam. I was a Special Military Advisor to the French Army, and I was there when the Vietcong kicked Frenchie's ass. The French Army was mostly foreign legion types, and they thought they were tough until the Vietcong got hold of them. We were lucky to get out alive." He paused and then continued, "I served a total of three tours with the corps in Vietnam. It got worse each time, but I couldn't leave the young, inexperienced marines. Our boys needed all of the help they could get, so I stayed on and saved as many lives as possible. It seems that all I've been doing since the Pacific Campaign is trying to keep someone alive, and now, here I am, trying to help keep the president alive. I can promise you that whoever might come after the president couldn't possibly be as bad as what I've seen and experienced in the South Pacific, Korea, and Vietnam. So you take care of the president, give me as much time as possible, and I'll keep the bad guys off your back."

"Sergeant, I've learned not to accept anything as a final answer. The human mind is unbelievable, and I've found many solutions to what appeared to be dead end situations. I forget about finality and spend my time searching for an answer or a way to change a particular situation or condition. JB told me that you've been diagnosed as terminal. That diagnosis may well turn out to be correct, but I choose to approach your problem in my own way. If you'll give me your medical file, I'll read it over, and then we can start looking for a way to beat your problem. By the way, one question, "Did you catch malaria when you were in the South Pacific?"

"I never went into the hospital with malaria but I remember how we all turned yellow from the quinine pills we were told to take. Those pills were bitter, but I always took them so I never got sick."

The sergeant continued. "JB told me that you're an unusual doctor. I like your style, and like I said, everyone goes sooner or later. I just want to be around to protect the president."

"Thanks sergeant, I'll read your file tonight and we'll talk again tomorrow."

Later that evening, David walked into the office and the sergeant's thick medical file was on the desk.

David awoke early and went immediately to the dining room, hoping to find John. John was sitting with the sergeant, drinking coffee when David entered. "John, I need your help! Last night I read the sergeant's medical file and I've got a big question in my mind about their diagnosis!"

John replied, "Get yourself a cup and let's talk!"

The sergeant stood and excused himself. "If you don't mind, I'll leave you gentlemen alone. I need to check our security."

David hesitated a moment, then spoke. "John, just listen to me, don't ask questions, just hear me out and try to find holes in my logic." He continued. "They diagnosed the sergeant with cirrhosis of the liver. They've done all the usual tests but found no sign of lymphomas, you know, Hodgkins; they found no sign of leukemia, nor did they find any sign of myelofibrosis. They did find him with amyloidoisis. To refresh your memory, amyloidoisis is the accumulation of various insoluble fibrillar proteins in amounts sufficient to impair normal functions. We call it a sago spleen. They haven't diagnosed the cause of his problem. They've diagnosed a present condition that is being caused by some unknown. I think the sergeant has congestive splenomegaly, which is what's causing the thrombosis of veins and external compression in his liver. And I think it may be caused by an infectious and inflammatory disease—malaria! And if so, we need to test ourselves immediately. If the sergeant's spleen is the culprit, we can either fix it or take it out and I hope his liver will regenerate and keep him alive. I also suspect a large part of his discomfort is caused by tissue hardening in his pancreas."

"David, your logic is sensible and I think right on! If you're right, the parasites must have lain dormant all these years and just recently started releasing into his bloodstream. That would explain his irregular low grade fever and his headaches. It almost sounds like he caught it when he was in the South Pacific, but the quinine he was taking suppressed it, and the parasites laid dormant for all those years. I would also guess that he's basically immune to malaria, but the parasites caused the spleen irregularity and subsequently, his cirrhosis. We'll need to also test ourselves to be sure we haven't picked up the bug."

By the time the ship approached Positano, the sergeant's condition was confirmed and also that no others had been infected, and plans were being formulated to handle the sergeant's spleen problem.

Roger waited at the airport. The plane was refueled and they were airborne.

"I'm taking a more direct route back to Phoenix. We'll be traveling low over some rugged mountains. Get some sleep if you can."

JB knew that rest was important, so he strapped himself into a passenger seat and closed his eyes.

JB was awakened several times during the flight when the plane either dropped down over a mountain or rose quickly to avoid flying into a mountain.

The cabin light came on and JB heard Roger. "JB, we're in Phoenix, time to rise and shine."

The plane landed at Lively Field adjacent the commercial airport and taxied to Roger's hangar. Crewmen were awaiting to attend to the plane.

Roger and JB left the plane, and JB followed Roger into a private office inside the hangar.

"It will take about half an hour to service the plane. Let's relax, have a cup of coffee, and you can tell me where you want to go."

"Half Moon Bay. Cosmo has a car there, waiting for me. I'm going to drive down to Monterey, say my last good-byes to my family. Afterwards I'll find the man who murdered them and make him tell me who's responsible for the plot, then to Italy to meet the ship to get the group safely ashore and settled down."

CHAPTER FOURTEEN

The trip to Half Moon Bay took a little over an hour. JB said good-bye to Roger.

Roger replied, "Call Dr. Johnson if you need me or contact me in Phoenix if you can't reach him. Good luck with the president."

"Thanks, Roger. I've got a feeling that I'll need you soon."

JB left the plane and walked to the small terminal building. A man sitting in the waiting room looked up as JB walked in. The man put down his paper, stood up, and walked out the side door.

JB followed and found the man waiting outside.

The man handed JB a set of car keys and pointed to a light-colored sedan parked nearby.

JB drove down Highway 1, through Santa Cruz, and on around the bay to Monterey. His family's funeral was at ten o'clock at All Souls Church on Alvarado Street.

JB parked on the street, a block from the church and sat, watching the people arrive. He saw a few familiar faces—Isabel's relatives, some school friends, and his heart skipped a beat when he saw Dr. Johnson, dressed in black, enter the church. He paid particular attention to the two men in the car parked across the street from the church. The two men carefully scrutinized each person who walked into the church.

The services lasted about an hour. Then four caskets were carried from the church, placed into black hearses, and the funeral procession drove to the Cypress Point Cemetery. The two men watched the caskets being loaded into the hearses and then followed the cortege.

JB tailed along behind the procession and parked his car outside the cemetery. He walked around behind the area where the internment was being made and stood watching as the caskets were placed at the grave sites.

The final prayers were said, and JB watched as the crowd dispersed.

The two men watched all of the people come and go.

Isabel's parents remained at the grave sites and watched as the caskets were lowered into the ground.

JB stood in his hiding place, silently repeating his prayers for Isabel and their children.

Isabel's parents left the cemetery, and the two men got into their car and drove away.

JB watched as the graves were filled. Still in his hiding place, he knelt down and said his final good-byes.

JB noted the license number of the car driven by the two men. Cosmo would identify the owner of the car, but JB felt certain the car was driven by the government agent he was planning to kill.

JB retraced his route back to Santa Cruz, then changed directions and traveled over the hill to San Jose and north to San Francisco.

JB stopped at the outskirts of San Francisco and called Cosmo, "I'm ready, Cosmo. I want to move on him now!"

"Do you have a plan?"

"Yes. Where is he and is he driving a car?"

"He's back in his office and yes."

"Meet me at Mickey's in twenty minutes."

"I'll be there."

JB drove into San Francisco on the Bayshore Freeway, took the Ninth Street turnoff, and found his way to the warehouse building at Tenth and Howard. The sign on the building read, "Mickey's Towing Service."

Cosmo waited outside. They shook hands, and Cosmo asked, "What do you need?"

"I need someone to finger him, identify his car, and I need to know what time he leaves his office."

"He usually leaves soon after five o'clock. Here's a picture of the man and his car." Cosmo handed JB two black and white photographs, one of the man and one of an automobile.

The photo of the man was head-on, and JB immediately memorized the face and body characteristics. The car was a gray Chevrolet. He handed the photographs back to Cosmo. "Thanks, Cosmo. Now where is his office and where is his car parked?"

Cosmo reached into his car, picked up his carphone, and dialed a number. He listened for a moment, then put the receiver down. "The car is parked in the reserved section in front of the Federal Building. There are four angle-in parking slots used by the FBI. His car is in the second slot from the right."

"I'm going to take a tow truck and snag his car as he leaves his office. Have a taxi cruise along behind me and have someone on the sidewalk to identify the tow truck and tell him Tenth and Folsom. I'm hoping he'll have another agent with him who has a car and will follow me. Otherwise, let's have the taxi available for him. Can you have this warehouse cleared of people?"

Cosmo nodded. "Yes, no problem. How much time do you need?"

"I should be finished by six-thirty."

"Okay, let's go!"

JB picked out a tow truck, started the engine, and drove out of the warehouse. He looked at his wristwatch–ten minutes to five–and drove across Market Street toward the Federal Building. He cruised by the Federal Building and spotted the Chevrolet. He drove around the city block and double parked alongside the Federal Building.

JB waited until a minute before five, then pulled slowly around the corner, toward the parked car. He looked in the rearview mirror and saw a taxicab pull around the corner and stop, with it's "occupied" light on.

JB drove slowly up the street and stopped next to the parked cars and waited.

The two men left the Federal Building, walking toward the parked cars. The tall man was his target. JB swung the tow truck around and backed up to the gray Chevrolet, jumped out, and placed the grapple hook under the rear bumper. He ran back to the cab, revved the engine to lift the rear of the car off the ground, shifted gears, and pulled away. He heard the men shouting at him. He watched his rearview mirror. The men ran to another car, jumped in, and backed out into the street. JB turned left onto Polk Street and headed toward Market. He saw the other car run the red light and come after him. The taxicab was following behind the other car.

JB drove through the yellow light at Market Street and was across before the other car caught the red light and was unable to cross because of the heavy traffic. He slowed going down Tenth Street past Mission Street and saw the car coming after him. JB passed Howard Street, signaled for a left turn, and pulled the tow truck and the Chevrolet into the warehouse building.

JB pulled the switch to drop the car, leaving enough room for another car to pull inside the building. He leaped from the tow truck and ran to the wall and stood beside the overhead door next to the entrance.

The other car came through the door and screeched to a halt. JB pushed the switch to close the overhead door and quickly walked up to the driver's side of the car.

The tall man opened the front door on the passenger side and jumped out.

The driver started to open his door, turned his head, and looked into the barrel of JB's silenced pistol.

JB shot him between the eyes, turned, and leveled his gun at the other man.

The tall man heard the door closing and the muffled gunshot. He turned, reaching for the handgun under his coat. The man froze when he saw JB and JB calmly instructed him, "Move your hand another inch and you're dead."

The man stood, sizing up JB. The man's eyes adjusted to the shadows inside of the building, and they grew large when he recognized JB.

"Raise your hands and turn around."

The man appeared to calculate his chances, then slowly raised his arms and turned around.

JB walked carefully around the car and over to the tall man. "Put your left arm behind you, slowly. Now, put your right arm behind you, slowly."

The tall man stood with his arms behind his back.

JB walked up behind the man and snapped shackles onto the man's wrists. JB ran his free hand up the man's body, searching for his pistol. JB was ready for the backward kick, aimed at his kneecap. He eluded the kick easily, grabbed the man's arm, swung him around and, and, standing face to face, fired a bullet into the man's left foot.

He screamed and fell to the floor.

JB grabbed the collar of his victim's coat and dragged him over to the rear of the tow truck. JB hooked the towing device under the wrist shackles, then reached over and pulled the lever to raise the tow bar. The man was lifted off the floor, and JB heard the tendons breaking in the man's shoulders as the tow bar lifted him off the floor.

The man screamed in pain. He swung from the tow bar and groaned loudly.

JB stood, waiting for the man's eyes to focus, then asked, "Do you know who I am?"

JB had seen the recognition in the man's eyes earlier. The man hesitated, then said, "We thought you were dead."

"I'm very much alive. You're the one who's dead, almost. You will be dead soon if you don't answer my questions."

"I've got nothing to say to you."

"We'll see." JB reached under his coat and pulled out a knife. He flipped it open and placed the tip inside the man's right nostril. "This knife can easily slip up through your nose into your brain."

The man's eyes were filled with fear.

JB lifted the man's necktie and sliced through the tie with the knife. The man's eyes widened with fear as he saw the sharpness of the knife blade. The man stammered, "I can't tell you anything. I just follow orders. I don't know anything!"

JB sliced away the front of the man's shirt then put the knife blade against his victim's pectoral muscle.

The man's eyes followed the knife, and he moaned loudly when blood appeared from the incision.

"I want you to know the sharpness of the blade before I begin asking you questions."

"You may as well kill me and get it over with! I can't help you!"

"I don't plan to kill you quickly. You committed a heinous crime when you murdered my wife and children. My goal is to find the person who gave you the order to fire bomb my home. If you don't tell me, I'm going to slice open your belly and let you hang here and die in agony. I'll let you hang for a week if you can live that long. Now you have a shred of a chance to live if you give me answers. Who ordered you to kill my family?"

The agent's eyes were filled with tears from the pain and fright. "If you let me live, I'll tell you!"

JB remained silent, waiting for the man to continue.

"I'm a special agent and I report directly to the director. He called me last Tuesday and ordered me to eliminate you."

JB stood looking at his victim, "Did you kill Dr. Burr last Tuesday?"

"No. That was handled by my partner. He's the one you shot a few minutes ago."

"How about Dr. Burr's daughter?"

"That was assigned to two other men in our office. We haven't heard from them since last Friday."

"Did you have anything to do with the attempt to assassinate our president at the Palace Hotel?"

The agent's eyes widened and he gasped, "How do you know about that?"

JB did not answer and after a few moments, the man continued. "You've got to understand, I'm just a small cog in the organization. I'm only one out of two dozen terminal operatives and I'm trained and paid to follow orders."

"Who does your director report to?"

Sweat trickled down the man's torso as he replied, "You've got to understand, I don't know anything more."

"You're wrong, I do not have to believe you and I don't. I will not ask you again—who does your director report to?"

The man looked at JB and shuddered from the cold, icy look in JB's eyes. "They'll kill me for sure if I talk and no one has told me the details; I've only heard rumors." The agent was talking fast, negotiating for his life. "They couldn't control the president. His political party heads felt they had been double-crossed. The president's wife was fed up with the president's philandering so she made her own fortune selling inside information to the director. We cracked the president's Secret Branch once but lost our man when he killed himself." The man paused, and JB could see the realization appear in the man's eyes, "You're part of the Special Branch aren't you?"

JB took out his pistol and aimed the end of the barrel against the man's forehead, above his eyes. "So long as you keep talking, you have a chance to live."

The agent shook his head, resignation in his eyes. "You have no intention of letting me live. I'm through talking."

JB shot him. Revenge was bittersweet, but he learned more about the plot against the president. Sweet because he had avenged the wrong to his family, but bitter because it was an evil for an evil. The remorse he had felt eased his compunction.

JB went to the pool car and opened the trunk. He removed the dead agent from the driver's seat; placed the body into the trunk; and then went to the tow truck, lowered the tow bar, removed the hanging victim, and placed the body into the trunk as well. He opened the overhead door and looked outside. Cosmo was sitting in the rear seat of the limousine parked outside the warehouse.

Cosmo beckoned JB over. "Get in, JB. We'll clean up the mess. The car and the bodies will disappear forever."

JB got into the back seat next to Cosmo.

Cosmo gave a signal to the driver, and the limousine pulled away from the curb, made a U-turn, and entered the traffic flow down Tenth Street toward the freeway.

They rode in silence.

JB's eyes were closed, and he rested his head against the back seat headrest. He felt empty, drained. The killing didn't ease the pain or the aching for his lost family. There was no measure of satisfaction from the killing, and he wondered if he would be able to go on with his work.

They drove down the freeway in darkness, and Cosmo could see the wetness on JB's cheeks.

Neither spoke until the car stopped at the cargo station at the International Airport. Then Cosmo spoke. "JB, nothing in this world is worth more than family and friends. I've been your friend. Now I want to be your family. I wish that I could share your grief for your lost family. All I can do is reaffirm our honest friendship and invite you into my family. A cargo plane is cleared and ready to leave for Rome. Your friends in Positano will be expecting you. I wish you Godspeed and tell you to let me know if you need anything."

JB opened his eyes, nodded his head slightly, and got out of the car and walked around to the other side.

Cosmo got out and stood facing JB.

JB opened his arms and stepped up to Cosmo, hugged him tightly, and muttered a choking, "Thank you, Cosmo, I wouldn't have made it without your help."

Cosmo returned the embrace and replied, "Go, JB, they're waiting for you, and you've got much to do. Keep me informed."

JB stepped back, shook hands with Cosmo, and followed the waiting crewman through the gate to the flight line.

JB slept during most of the fifteen hour flight to Rome and was rested when they finally arrived. He changed into a crew uniform before landing.

The crew members left the plane together and were cleared through customs with a cursory examination of their passports.

JB left the group outside the airport, hailed a taxi, and headed for the bus station. He was soon aboard the bus for Naples where he changed to the bus that traveled down the Amalfi coast.

JB sat looking out the bus window at the blue sea far below and remembered his first drive down the Amalfi coast in the Alfa. He dozed awhile, and when he awakened was surprised to find the bus entering Positano.

He walked away from the bus stop, turned left on Giovanni Street and, felt his calf muscles resist the steepness of the street. He saw the church and remembered, *Please come to Signor Boronio's funeral mass.* He turned his eyes ahead, looking for the Boronio house. A familiar voice hailed him, "JB, please wait!" Guido strode toward him.

JB smiled and shook his head, "Guido, Guido, Guido," and they exchanged a strong embrace.

"Your house is ready and waiting. I've even got an extra dory if you think you can still catch fish!" Guido laughed and clapped him on the back.

"I want to stop by and say hello to Signora Boronio."

"She's expecting you. You couldn't have gotten past her house without a fight. She's excited to see you."

"How's your family, Guido?"

"We have a new daughter to go along with our son. She's beautiful, just like her mother."

"And Carmine?"

"He's ahead of me. They're expecting their third son any day now. They're very happy!"

"And the signora?"

"She has aged, but she's a magnificent woman. Of course, I don't have to tell you. She lives to help others. So, what brings you to Positano in late November?"

"I've got five people coming in, and Guido, trust me, we need your help. But it's too early for me to tell you all that's happening. It could turn into a rough situation before it's over, and I don't want you or anyone else unnecessarily harmed."

"JB, you stood up in my behalf when I hardly knew you. You helped me meet my wife, handled Salvatore, and unselfishly stepped in to help the Boronio family. If you need help, I want to help you!"

"Thanks, Guido. Let's see what happens."

Signora Boronio sat on the porch, watching them walk toward her home. As they came closer, they could see her smile, and JB waved to her.

She stood as JB walked up the steps and opened her arms for him.

They hugged and reluctantly he released her and stepped back. "Signora, what a lovely sight."

She smiled at him. "My tears are from the joy of seeing you. I've missed you so much!" Her eyes told of her longing for him, and he returned her love without speaking.

"Come in, tell me how you've been and how long you will stay."

They went into her house. She brought hot coffee. They sat, sipping the coffee.

"Signora, I'm bringing people here. One is an important person who has been badly injured. Two of them are doctors, to care for the injured one. Another is a young woman marked for death, with no place to hide, and the last is a dear, dear friend of mine who is probably near death. He has chosen to spend his last days protecting the others I'm bringing here. The doctors are skillful, but I need your help in nursing and caring for our patient. You will be paid very well. The young woman can help, but we need your expertise in patience and caring to bring our patient back to good health. I will meet their ship late Saturday night and bring them here on a fishing boat. We cannot allow anyone in the village to know what we're doing, and it's important for us to know if any strangers come into town, asking questions and looking for me or anyone in our group."

Without hesitation the signora responded. "My friends are spread throughout this coastal area. If anyone asks questions about you, we'll hear it and let you know immediately. As for the rest I look forward to helping you and your patient. My son is now married, so I live here alone with my two youngest daughters. I have plenty of time to help."

She turned to Guido. "Guido, please go now and tell Carmine and Salvatore that we'll have a welcome home dinner for JB at my home tonight. All of you should bring your families and come at five o'clock. Go now, I need to talk with JB for a few minutes." Guido kissed her cheek and left the house.

After the door closed she turned to look at JB. "Your eyes look dead. Something terrible has happened. Please, tell me."

JB told her about the last few days and when he told her about the death of his family, she gasped and crossed herself.

They sat without speaking for a moment. The signora placed her hand on JB's and broke the silence. "JB, terrible things happen to each of us at some time or another. We cannot change what has already happened. All we can do is to pick up the pieces and go on with our life. The ones of us fortunate enough to have families and loved ones must look forward to the future and let our loved ones show their caring for us. Memories are of things that have passed, dreams are for what is yet to be. You lost an important part of your life. They are now a memory for you. You still have a family who loves you, so please, let us share your grief, let us show you our love, and let us help you to dream about what is yet to come!"

JB pushed his chair back, stood up, and stumbled toward her. She stood, and they embraced. She felt his strength as he held her tightly, and she heard his quiet sobbing as he cried, his face pressed into her hair. She stroked his head and softly crooned her love. When he was quiet, she pushed away from him. "Now, JB, we must talk."

JB looked at her, released his tight embrace, and walked over to the window.

She followed behind and bowed her head against the back of his shoulders. "JB, we should not discuss your group, the important person you mentioned, or the reason you're here whenever my son is present. He has treated me and his family with love, but I fear that he is still involved with his old group."

JB nodded his understanding and turned to face her. He took her face between his hands and looked into her face before he gently kissed her mouth. "I must be the luckiest man on this earth to have met you and been loved by you. You restore my faith in humanity. Now I'd better get out of here before I take the combs out of your hair."

She smiled and stood on tiptoe so she could kiss him in return. "These combs have been in my hair for too long. If you don't take them out, I'll take them out and come searching for you!" She stepped back. "You make me crazy. Get out of here before I make a fool of myself."

JB laughed, kissed her lightly, and headed for the door.

She watched him leave and followed him to the front porch, calling to him, "Five o'clock and don't be late."

JB turned and waved as he walked down the hill, calling, "Five o'clock."

JB walked to the bottom of the hill and turned up the street toward the bistro. The bar and cafe were full of fishermen. He knew many of them, and they greeted him profusely. Papa John poured drinks for the house, and JB felt he was among close friends. He stayed for awhile, saying his hellos to his friends.

JB left the cafe at four o'clock and walked up the street, past the fish stalls and fishing beach area. Nothing had changed. He walked inside his house and found it neat and clean, with food and wine in the kitchen. He went into the bedroom. His clothing was hung in the closet, fresh and neatly ironed. He smiled and said to himself, *Signora, you're something else.* He shaved, showered, and dressed in fresh clothing, then went out to his front porch to sit and wait for his friends.

JB watched the families walking toward his house. Guido and Carmine each carried a small child, and the mothers walked hand in hand with the other children. Lucia and Ruby were alive and beautiful. All showed their happiness, and each hugged him tightly and kissed him energetically. He couldn't help but notice the momentary lingering when Ruby kissed him. He squeezed her hand and spoke. "You look lovely, Ruby, show me your little ones." The children were shy at first but soon were holding tightly to his hands as they walked up the hill to the signora's house.

Salvatore arrived ahead of them and JB met Salvatore's new wife for the first time. She was frail but exquisite with a bewitching twinkle in her eyes.

Salvatore's wife helped the signora prepare the evening meal, and the signora was obviously pleased with her new daughter-in-law. The two youngest daughters took the children into another room, the twins went into the kitchen to help prepare the meal, and the men sat in the living room, talking and drinking wine.

JB arose and went into the kitchen for another glass of wine. Ruby saw him, took his glass, and refilled it with wine. She handed JB the full glass. "Thank you, Ruby, it's good to see that you still have a twinkle in your eyes."

She spoke. "You started the fire in my heart, and it will always burn brightly for you. I am happy with my life, but I'll always long to be with you!"

He felt pangs and sat quietly until supper.

Following the sumptuous meal, the men sat on the front porch, and the women cleaned the dishes. The women soon joined them, and together they watched the last of the evening's sunset. Afterward they walked down the steep street to their homes. JB carried one of the small children asleep on his shoulders as far as his house, then handed him to Guido.

JB sat on his front porch. It was a cold evening, and he sat in the darkness for over an hour before he heard the noise inside his house.

JB went inside, and the moment he entered the dark bedroom, he could sense her presence. He undressed in the darkness, then went to the bed and lay down beside her.

Her body was warm and welcoming, and when he started to speak, she kissed him fiercely and said, "No promises, no commitments, just love me tonight!" Her soft body received him with an urgency that soon turned into a prolonged passion. Their hearts, souls, and bodies blended into a breathless and satisfying love.

The signora left him at midnight. Without her knowing, JB followed after her to ensure her safety, then returned to his house and slept soundly until the following morning.

JB arose mid-morning. As he walked to the bistro, he stopped at the fish stalls, and found the signora and her daughters busy cleaning the fish from the morning's catch, preparing them for sale. The daughters greeted him excitedly. "*Buon giorno!*" The signora said her good morning with her eyes, and, as usual, he marveled at her total beauty. The signora called to him, "Supper is at five o'clock. Come early if you wish."

"I'll be there, good luck with your fish today." JB walked on to the bistro.

He dined with Signora Boronio and her youngest daughters. After supper the daughters cleaned the kitchen, dishes, and cooking pots. JB and the signora sat on the front porch and watched the daylight fade away. He described the group that would arrive late Saturday night and explained the security problems. After awhile he realized he was babbling on and on, while she sat, relaxed and with her eyes closed.

"Have you heard anything that I've said?"

"Not really. I was remembering last night and planning how I can be alone with you again before your friends arrive. I will be at your house later tonight for awhile. Tomorrow night, my two youngest will stay with Ruby. It will be more comfortable for me if you would come to my house. In fact if your houses are too small, I would be pleased if you would stay at my home. We would have so much time alone to make love that your knees would be too weak to allow you to walk down the hill!"

JB laughed. "Signora, you're too much woman for me. I couldn't possibly make love with you more than two or three times a night. You need a real man!"

"I'm glad we can joke about ourselves. You know that I would give anything to spend the rest of my life with you. I also know it will not happen, so I'll just be happy with whatever time we can be together."

He arose to leave, called "good night" to the girls in the kitchen, kissed the signora lightly, and inhaled deeply. "Oh, what a lovely fragrance. You're intoxicating. I'll be waiting for you."

The signora watched him walk away, up the hill toward the hotel. Her eyes glistened with moisture, and she felt as if her heart would burst with love.

JB located a public call box in the hotel lobby and placed his call to Cosmo.

Cosmo informed him the fishing boat would arrive at the quay at 2000 hours Saturday. The *Festina Maru* would be off the coast from Positano at half past eight. They should be safely ashore before the Saturday night dance ended.

JB asked, "Is everything quiet?"

Cosmo responded, "Nothing is changed, everything looks okay."

As JB listened to Cosmo, he saw Salvatore walk toward the hotel, stop next to a black sedan parked on the street, open the rear door, and get into the car. The car drove away, and he was unable to see who was driving. He noted the license number and gave the number to Cosmo.

Cosmo replied, "Call me at eight o'clock on Friday. I'll tell you who owns the car."

JB hung up the telephone. "*Ciao*, Cosmo," then left the hotel and walked back down the hill to his house.

They lay together in the dark quietness of his bedroom.

"Is she special for you?"

He noticed the jealous undertone in her voice. "Who?"

"The lady coming with your group." She sounded piqued.

"Yes, she's special. Not like you, but yes, she's special."

Now inquisitively. "How is she so special for you?"

"She was there when I needed someone so much that I was almost dead. She helped me understand I still have feelings and my life did not end when my family died."

Expectantly, the signora asked, "Do you love her?"

"I care for her, but no, I am not in love with her. She's in mortal danger now and perhaps for the rest of her life because of me. I intend to do all that I can to protect her."

She hugged him tightly. "Thank you for telling me. You made love with me so fiercely tonight, I felt you were saying good-bye."

JB leaned over and kissed around her face and finally on her lips, letting the kiss linger. "Signora, when I say good-bye to you, it will be from my grave. As long as I live and breathe, I will never forget you or pass up a chance to be with you."

They kissed deeply, pushing their bodies together, each exploring the other and made love again.

JB returned to his house, assured the signora was safely at her home, and fell into a deep sleep that lasted until well into the morning.

JB closed the front door and walked up the street, in the opposite direction, away from the beach and fish stalls. The old concrete quay was at the south end of the small harbor, seldom used except by the motorized boats that occasionally stopped by. The quay was perpendicular to the street, about a hundred yards from his house.

He walked out onto the quay, discreetly investigating the entire stretch of concrete. He spent the rest of the day gathering items needed to handle the equipment and supplies arriving Saturday night.

JB ate supper with the signora and her two daughters. Following the meal, the two young girls gathered their night clothes and left for their older sister Rosa's house.

He walked up the hill to the hotel and placed his call to Cosmo.

"The car belongs to Lou Corcura. Corcura is presently a freelancer in the drug business. Salvatore and Corcura were cell mates at the Naples Prison, and it looks bad if Salvatore is mixed up with Corcura. Corcura would sell his mother for a quarter. You can imagine what Corcura would do if he learns about you. Be careful! Your group is still doing okay?"

"I'll handle the situation. Thanks, Cosmo, see you soon."

JB took a round-about route back to the signora's house, making certain he wasn't followed, and entered her house through the rear door.

JB left the signora's warm bed an hour before the village began to stir, walked home, and waited inside his house until he saw Guido and Carmine walking toward the fishing beach, then went outside and joined his friends.

"Well, good morning, JB, you're up early today."

"Good morning, Guido, good morning, Carmine."

They walked along in silence toward the beach. Guido glanced at JB. "Weather looks okay. We should do okay if the wind doesn't blow."

They continued on in silence. When the trio reached the beach, JB halted. The other two also stopped, and Guido asked, "JB, what's bothering you today?"

"I'm worried about Salvatore. Do either of you know anything about his after work activities?"

Guido replied, "We see him every day, here at the fishing beach, and we see him a couple of times a week at the signora's house. He comes to the bistro but not every day. As far as I know, he is respectful of his mother and sisters. Once or twice I suspected he might be treating his wife badly. Lucia and Ruby talked with his wife, but she denies any problems. Why do you ask?"

"I was at the hotel a few nights ago, and I saw Salvatore get into a car with a man named Corcura. It didn't look right, and I'm worried he's involved with his old pals."

"Corcura! That guy is bad," Carmine whispered.

"He's right, JB, Corcura is no good. He's been around the tourist area for years except when in jail. Anytime a tourist disappears, Corcura is suspected. He'll do anything for money, including murder. It is rumored he is pushing bad drugs among the tourists."

JB told them, "Keep an eye on Salvatore, he's up to something."

They nodded yes to him and then went to their boats.

He stood in the shadows and watched the launching of the boats. Salvatore was among the fishermen. It would be hours before the boats returned.

He walked back to his house, closed the shades, and slept until the afternoon. He ate a light lunch and sat on his front porch, relaxing, trying to control the excitement building in anticipation of the coming night.

CHAPTER FIFTEEN

JB sat through the sunset, knowing that his friends on the *Festina Maru* had the same sunset only a few miles away. At half past seven he got up; changed his clothes; went to the shed behind his house; pulled out the two-wheeled cart borrowed from Papa John, ostensibly to move a piece of heavy furniture; and started toward the quay. He was there in a few minutes. The day before, he spotted a good hiding place for the cart and he rolled the cart into the midst of two large cypress bushes. He made certain it was concealed, then turned and waited for the fishing boat.

JB heard the boat before he saw it, its diesel engines turning over slowly. The boat bumped gently against the quay, and JB stepped aboard. He heard a slight roar as the pilot revved the starboard engine, and the rear of the boat swung away from the quay. When the bow pointed back toward the open sea, the pilot engaged both engines in forward and increased the engine speed slightly.

They ran along quietly for several hundred yards, then the pilot steadily increased speed until they moved swiftly out to sea. The boat was totally dark, and JB did not see anyone. The sunset was gone, and the night was inky black. The boat changed course to the southwest and slipped by the small islands offshore. Whoever was piloting the boat knew the waters. The boat ran southwest for half an hour before coming to a dead stop. They drifted for a few moments, then the pilot slowly increased their speed and circled around the large shadow sitting in the water ahead.

They were on the starboard side of the *Festina Maru*, facing out toward the open ocean, and JB saw the dim, muted light coming from the open hatchway. JB stood back and watched the seamen materialize out of the darkness to handle the bumpers and lines from the ship. They secured the boat adjacent the open hatch, and he saw his friends waiting.

They came aboard quickly, and the stretcher was passed across. Without a word, the two doctors took the stretcher into the boat cabin. The boxes of equipment and supplies were transferred to the fishing boat, placed on the open aft deck, and the boat pulled away from the ship.

The pilot circled back astern the *Festina Maru* and set his course toward Positano.

JB checked the crates, found them secured, then went into the cabin. A large man blocked the door. "Good evening, Sergeant. I trust your trip went well."

"Everything is okay. Be careful where you step. The stretcher is on the floor to the right. The doctors are sitting next to the stretcher. Ms. Burr is standing on your left." JB turned to his left, took a step, and found Susan. She moved against him, laid her forehead on his shoulder, and whispered, "Thank God you're here! I still can't believe what's going on!"

He squeezed her gently. "Please relax and stand back against the wall. I need to talk to David and John." He let her go, turned, and squatted down on the floor next to David.

The boat rounded the peninsula, and JB saw the hillside lights of Positano. The cloud cover blacked out the moonlight and the boat slipped toward shore in total darkness. After turning the boat toward the lights of Positano, the captain reduced power and the boat slowed. JB distinguished the lights along the waterfront and saw the lights from Papa John's bistro. He saw the lights rotating to his left and realized the boat was turning. He heard a slight roar as the captain reversed the engines, and the boat gently bumped against the concrete. The seamen leaped onto the quay and secured the boat. JB heard the quiet activity, but all he could see were muted shadows moving on the dock. He stepped across to the dock, retrieved the cart from the nearby bushes, and returned to the boat. The supplies and equipment sat on the dock.

The sergeant stood away from the unloading activity, poised alertly with his automatic pistol at the ready.

The doctors carried the stretcher from the boat, Susan alongside of the stretcher, tending the IVs.

JB directed the seamen to load the supplies and equipment onto the cart and instructed the sergeant to protect their rear. JB went first, followed by the seamen pulling and pushing the heavily loaded cart. David, John, and Susan took care of the president, and the sergeant followed.

They moved along quickly, reaching the house in a few minutes. The larger house was set up to receive the president.

The sergeant melted into the darkness and scouted the area around the houses, looking for intruders.

The seamen quickly unloaded the cart, placed the boxes and crates inside the house, and JB led them back to the boat. The lines were cast off, and the boat quietly disappeared into the darkness, heading back out to sea.

JB returned to the house. David and John were examining the president, and Susan was taking notes and helping with the monitoring devices. The sergeant was nowhere to be seen but JB felt his presence.

The house had three bedrooms: kitchen, dining room, and living room. JB had set up the back bedroom as the president's ICU, the adjacent bedroom as a laboratory-treatment room, and had converted the living room into sleeping quarters to accommodate the men. Susan would use the other bedroom. The dining room was set up as a lounge-meeting room with a large table. Blackout draperies covered all of the windows which were to remain shuttered, and a rear pathway connected the house with JB's.

The others were busy so JB started opening the crates and boxes. The others joined him, and soon the equipment and supplies were unpacked and stowed.

They gathered around the large table in the dining room. JB described the area surrounding the houses and the Positano area in general. He explained. "It is important to maintain a low profile. Except for Sergeant Browning, you must remain inside at all times. Keep the window shades drawn, and don't answer if someone knocks on the door. Signora Boronio will be here daily to prepare our meals, clean the house, and do our laundry, and you should teach her to handle the president's basic needs. David and John, you will supervise the disposal of all used medical supplies, and Susan, establish a patient watch schedule and assist the doctors. Sergeant Browning is in charge of security. I'll be here to help with any problems that arise."

JB slipped out of the house and went up the hill toward the hotel. He found a call box and placed a call to Cosmo. As he left the hotel, he saw Corcura's car stop across the street, about a hundred feet away. He stepped into a dark doorway, took the small electronic listening device from his coat pocket, and aimed the device toward Corcura's car. Salvatore got out of the car and stood alongside the rear window.

JB listened to the conversation and was chagrined to hear Corcura telling Salvatore to find out who is visiting Positano and staying at JB's house. JB heard Corcura tell Salvatore to have the information by Sunday night.

Salvatore stepped back, and the car sped away. Salvatore turned and walked down the hill, not toward his own house, but toward JB's.

JB followed. Salvatore cautiously approached JB's house and crept up to the rear window. The house was totally dark, no noises or light coming from inside. Salvatore crept from window to window but was unable to see inside.

JB spotted the sergeant stalking Salvatore.

The sergeant smiled and whispered, "I watched you tailing him. Otherwise, I would've taken him out immediately. What's going on?"

"It's the signora's son, the one I told you about. He's mixed up with a bad group. I'm afraid we must take action to protect the president. I expect

143

the signora's son to nose around here tomorrow, trying to find out what's going on. Tomorrow night I'll take care of the other threat, and I'll arrange to resolve the problem with the signora's son."

As they watched, Salvatore gave up trying to look into the house and slunk away.

JB followed and watched Salvatore enter his own house. Satisfied the present threat from Salvatore was over for the evening, he returned home.

JB was awakened by the kitchen noise. He arose, went to the door, opened it slightly, and peeked into the kitchen. The signora was preparing breakfast for the group.

She saw the door open and saw him looking at her. She pouted her lower lip, then smiled at him and threw a kiss.

JB quickly showered, dressed, and went into the kitchen. The room was empty, so he went out the back door and walked to the other house. He entered and found the group in the dining room enjoying the breakfast prepared by Signora Boronio. He started to introduce the signora, but they laughed and waved him away. "We've met the signora, and we've tasted her cooking. Fantastic," said Susan.

The signora nodded her head toward JB.

JB smiled, sat down at the table, and she brought his breakfast.

Following breakfast they sat around the dining room table, discussing their situation. David explained, "We're getting signs of mental activity, but the president remains comatose, and both eyes are still dilated. His physical condition is good, considering what he's gone through. You should understand his present condition points to permanent, irreversible damage. The prognosis for his recovery is not good."

They looked at the other doctor. John said, "I wish it were otherwise, but I must agree with David. We can keep him alive physically, but with each passing day, hope for his mental recovery grows dimmer."

They sat silently for a few moments. Then JB spoke. "Of course, all we can do is hope for the best and go about out planning as if the president will fully recover. Now I'm moving Susan to another location for her protection."

Susan interrupted him, "No! I don't want to go!"

JB hesitated, placed his hand over hers, and continued. "Susan, please, allow me to continue. Now I feel it's important to keep you away from any further attempts on your life, at least for awhile. I've arranged to move you to a secluded farm in northern Italy. You'll be safe there. David, I feel you should do what you can for the sergeant and then return to San Francisco. We can arrange for you to receive a daily briefing from John. The signora will take care of the daily cooking and cleaning. She and her daughters will sit with the president as needed. I plan to return to the United States. The sergeant will remain here, devoting his time to protecting these houses from intruders. I'll make certain all of you are kept well informed about the president's condition."

Susan was obviously displeased but remained silent.

The doctors nodded their acceptance.

JB told David, "Susan is leaving at eight o'clock tonight. If you can resolve the sergeant's problem today, I'll arrange your passage, and you can leave with Susan. They'll drop you at the Rome Airport on their way north."

"I'll do the sergeant now. If all goes well, he'll be up and about within a few hours."

David got up from the table and beckoned for the sergeant and John to follow.

JB and Susan sat alone. He squeezed her hand, "Please, Susan, don't be frightened. The farm is safe. I will contact you often, and I'll be back soon."

She sat silently, looking at him. Finally she spoke, "I'll do as you say, but I want to help."

"There's nothing you can do for the president now. If and when the president awakens, we'll reevaluate our plans. I promise to include you at that time. Until then, I want you in a safe place. Please, trust me."

She nodded okay, stood up, and went to her bedroom to pack.

JB left the house and looked for Guido and Carmine.

David briefed John on the procedure and then commenced working on the sergeant. John watched with amazement as David skillfully inserted the thin flexible tube down the sergeant's throat and into his stomach, then beyond into the duodenum and up into the pancreas duct. At that point, he observed a calcification in the duct. He then passed a surgical wire through the tube. Attached to the end of the surgical wire was a device to grasp and remove the stone. He retracted the wire with the stone and then reinserted the wire, this time with the shunt at the end of the wire. He inserted the shunt into the pancreas duct, then retracted the wire, then the flexible tube. The entire process took twenty minutes. They revived the sergeant and watched him carefully for the next two hours.

By noon the sergeant felt much better and sat up on the operating table. David told the sergeant to rest for another two hours, then dress and go about his duties.

JB arranged to meet Guido and Carmine at the bistro to explain his plan. While the doctors worked on the sergeant, he returned to the call box and talked to Cosmo. "The signora's son is mixed up with Corcura, and he's snooping around, trying to learn what is taking place. I need you to arrange his parole revocation and get him back into prison."

"I'll take care of it today. The *policia* from Naples will pick him up within twenty-four hours. What about Corcura?"

"I'll handle him. Get rid of Salvatore soon, and we'll be okay." He broke the connection and walked to Papa John's. Following Sunday morning mass, Guido and Carmine walked down the hill to the bistro. They entered and walked back to JB's table, sat, ordered wine, and drank while JB explained. The three of them left the cafe together and walked to JB's house. He brought them into the house and introduced them to the doctors and the sergeant.

He spent the afternoon returning the cart to Papa John and preparing for the evening.

Darkness came shortly after five in the afternoon. David and Susan were ready to leave when JB came for them at half past seven. They followed him out of the house, and together they walked up the hill toward the hotel.

A block before reaching the hotel, he turned up a side street. The black limousine was waiting.

Josef got out of the car and greeted him with a strong embrace.

JB looked at David. "I'll be in touch within a few days. You've done a great job. Please, be careful."

They shook hands and David spoke. "JB, this whole thing is like a dream. I still can't believe what we've been through, but I'm ready to come back, anytime. As for the sergeant, his case may not be hopeless. I'm going to consult some associates about his condition. There may be a way out for him." David turned and got into the back seat of the car.

Susan gnawed her lower lip, tears ready to spill from her eyes. JB held her tightly for a moment and kissed her gently. "You'll be safe. I'll talk to you soon. Try to relax."

She looked questioningly and longingly into his eyes, seeing an honest caring but not seeing the love she looked for. She kissed him quickly and pulled away to get into the car. He closed the door behind her, signaled to Josef, and the car pulled away.

JB watched the taillights disappear around the corner. Then he went on up the hill toward the hotel.

JB positioned himself inside a dark alleyway, across from the hotel, and waited. He stood easily, knowing how to relax to avoid tiring his muscles.

An hour passed before he saw Corcura's car slide up across the street from the hotel. Corcura got out of the car and joined Salvatore at a table in an outdoor cafe, not far from the car. JB slipped on his old fishing hat, turned up his jacket collar, and walked toward the car.

JB walked unsteadily. The driver of Corcura's car saw him bump up against the car and lean against the front fender. He got out of the car, but JB recovered and walked up the street, away from the car. The driver yelled an obscenity toward JB. "Asshole!" He laughed and got back into the car.

JB walked around the corner and back through the hotel. He regained his original hiding place, took out his electronic listening device, and aimed it toward the two men sitting in the outdoor cafe.

Corcura raged at Salvatore, insisting that Salvatore learn what was going on at JB's house. "What do you mean, 'you don't know?' You took my money and I want answers, now! You better get off you lazy ass and find out what's going on! I WANT TO KNOW!"

Fearfully Salvatore nodded his head yes and spoke. "I'll find out soon! Just give me a little time!"

They pushed back their chairs and left the cafe. Salvatore walked away from the car. Corcura got into the car. It pulled around the corner, onto the main highway, and headed toward Naples.

JB walked to the corner and stood, looking toward the mountain north of town. The highway wound up and around the ocean-side of the mountain.

JB waited one more minute before pressing the detonator button . . . then, walked down the hill.

Late that evening, he placed the package underneath the bow deck of Salvatore's boat.

JB awakened early, looked in on John and the sergeant, then walked down to the bistro for his breakfast.

JB heard the commotion and joined the others outside. He followed the crowd to the beach, saw and heard the ruckus near the Boronio fish stall where two policemen struggled with Salvatore. He heard the signora screaming, "Oh my god, they're taking my son!"

Guido and Carmine consoled the signora as the officers handcuffed Salvatore and took him away in the paddy wagon. Guido turned to JB. "*Simplice y simplice*. Plain and simple, they found cocaine in his boat when he returned from fishing. What will happen to him?"

"If he violated his parole, he'll be sent back to prison."

Ruby and Lucia walked away with the sobbing signora.

JB entered without knocking. The living room was crowded with the Boronio family and friends. JB went over to the signora. She looked quizzically at him, searching his eyes with hers, seeking an answer.

JB returned her look, softened his eyes with compassion, and held out his open arms.

The signora bowed her head and stepped close against him, hugging him strongly.

JB held her tightly.

The signora cried against his shoulder for a short while, then released her hold and stepped back away from him.

147

JB reached up and wiped away a tear coursing down her cheek. "I'm so sorry, signora. I wish there was something I could do for you and Salvatore's family."

The signora continued searching his eyes, sighed deeply, then spoke. "It was in his destiny. He would be better off with God." She turned away from JB and went over to Salvatore's wife and child. The heartbreak she felt was more for her son's wife and child than for her son.

When JB awoke, he heard the signora in the kitchen preparing breakfast.

JB looked over when he heard the bedroom door open. The signora came into his room carrying a tray with coffee in a small pot, biscuits, warm milk, and serviettes. She set the tray on the table beside the bed and poured the steaming black coffee and warm milk together.

The signora watched JB sip the hot coffee, then spoke. "My son is gone. I choose to think of his goodness, and I will forget his wrongs."

JB continued sipping the hot coffee, not speaking.

The signora continued. "My son's incident yesterday prevented the town from talking about what happened Sunday night, just north of town."

JB sat, silent, not sipping the coffee, looking into the signora's eyes.

"They say a car exploded, killing two men. One of them was Corcura. He's the one my son was dealing with. They were in prison together. Did you know the man?"

"No. I never met him. I've heard of him, but that's all."

"Oh, I do not mourn him, he was trash. Some of my friends said they saw my son with the man at Café Georgia not long before the explosion. I pray my son did not kill those two men."

"Signora, for your peace of mind, I can assure you, Salvatore did not kill those men."

The signora looked directly into JB's eyes, smiled slightly, dropped her eyes and nodded. "I know, JB. We all do what we have to do and each answer to our own conscience and to our own God." She went back into the kitchen and continued her chores.

The next few days passed quickly and uneventfully. The signora became more adept in helping John care for the president and the sergeant recovered quickly.

JB was at the hotel Friday evening and precisely at nine o'clock placed a telephone call to Cosmo. "It's time for me to visit Washington. I need to leave tomorrow morning."

Cosmo spoke. "Same as outbound, except in reverse. Instructions will be waiting for you. It has been warm here during the past week. How about there?"

"Sunday was warm, but things cooled down quickly and should remain cool for awhile. See you soon."

They both hung up their telephones and JB went back down the hill. He kept to the dark side of the street and was adjacent to the signora's house when he heard her softly call his name. He halted, turned, and walked up to her front porch.

The signora was sitting in the shadows, almost invisible.

JB walked up onto the porch, over to her.

The signora stood, they embraced, he pulled her head back and kissed her. Her lips were warm and moist and she responded by hugging him tightly, pulling their bodies together. Their breathing became harsh and irregular. She released him and pulled her lips away from him. "Oh, JB, the magic is still there. I've missed you so much these past few days, knowing you were nearby and still not being able to be alone with you."

"I'm here now, but I will leave tomorrow for awhile. I want us to make love now so that you'll be fresh in my mind when I'm away."

Silently she turned, and holding his hand, led him into her house. "I expected this to happen. My young ones are with Ruby tonight."

They entered her bedroom, and without turning on the light, removed their clothes and lay down on the bed together. Their passion exploded, and they made love as if to consume one another. Time and again she reached a high plateau of passion, each time crashing down in a frenzy of physical love, only to begin a new climb to a higher level. "*Con amore, con amore. . . .*"

They made love throughout the night, and when JB finally slipped away, just before dawn, she followed him to the door and watched him disappear down the hill, into the darkness. She wanted to tell him she was sitting on her porch Sunday night and saw him go up the hill to the hotel. She saw Salvatore come down the hill, heard the bomb explosion, and then saw JB come silently down the hill. She knew of Salvatore's connection with Corcura. She had hoped against hope that Salvatore would break away from Corcura and wondered if JB was responsible for the drugs, and ultimately, for Salvatore's arrest. She was saddened by her thoughts but felt at peace, knowing that Salvatore's family was better off and safer with him gone.

CHAPTER SIXTEEN

JB spoke with the sergeant and John then went up the hill to town.

He caught the early morning bus to Rome, via Naples, arriving in Rome at mid-morning. He made his way to the airport and went to the air cargo terminal. The crew waited for him. He changed and went aboard the plane dressed as third officer. The plane took off, and JB went to the small lounge aft of the flight deck. He slept soundly during most of the fourteen hour flight.

The plane touched down at San Francisco in mid-afternoon. A customs officer boarded the plane and cleared the crew.

JB disembarked with the crew members and he met Cosmo in the adjacent office. "I need to go to Washington. If you can't take me, I'll need transportation out of here."

Cosmo replied, "I've got a plane waiting. You can do it with a single fuel stop. When do you want to go?"

"Now."

The plane landed at a corporate airstrip, a few miles from Dulles Airport. The pilot called a taxi through Navcom.

JB rode into downtown Washington and rented a room at the Americana Hotel. The hotel was located on Indiana Street and inhabited by drug pushers, drug users, whores, pimps, and derelicts. Indiana Street was also near the FBI headquarters, so for the next three days, JB became just another of the many homeless derelicts who hung out in the neighborhood.

JB spent long hours watching and recording the men and women entering and leaving the FBI building. Early each morning he saw the heavily-armored black limousine arrive. The same limousine seldom left the building until late at night.

By the end of the third day, JB selected his target.

She left the FBI building, walked to the corner bus stop, and boarded the K bus. JB boarded the same bus, went to the rear, and sat, watching his target.

The bus ran along its route for twenty minutes before she stirred, then stood up to leave. JB waited, then left the bus just before the doors closed.

JB stepped down to the street and caught a glimpse of her going around the corner. He walked to the corner and watched her walk half a block down the street.

She turned and entered an apartment house.

JB made note of the location, crossed the street, and caught a bus back to his hotel.

He was up early the next morning and waiting at the bus stop when she arrived to catch a bus to her work. He was cleanly shaven and neatly dressed. He stepped aside to allow her to board the arriving bus. She looked at him, and he smiled shyly and mumbled, "Good morning." She smiled back. The seats were filled, so they walked toward the rear of the bus and stood, holding the straps.

She was plain looking; well-dressed; and, JB guessed, in her late forties. As they walked to the rear of the bus and turned, catching the straps, JB noticed her quickly looking him over before she turned her eyes away.

They stood for a few minutes before JB started a casual conversation.

"Nice day."

She smiled.

"Work downtown?"

She nodded yes.

"I'm an electrician. We're remodeling a building near the FBI building." He saw her interest.

They rode in silence for a minute, then she spoke. "I work for the government. Actually, I work at the FBI."

"Golly! Sounds exciting!"

She smiled again. "Not really; it's kinda boring!"

As the bus approached the FBI building, JB told her, "Look, my name is Jim. It's been pleasant talking to you."

She replied, "It has been pleasant. My name is Mary. I hope you have a nice day."

They got off the bus, and JB smiled and waved to her as he walked up the street toward his hotel.

She waved back and walked across the street to the FBI building.

That evening he waited at the bus stop when she arrived.

"Hi, Mary, how was your day?"

She smiled and replied, "Awful. The director was in a terrible mood today. How was your day, Jim?"

The bus arrived and they boarded together. They sat together during the twenty minute ride. They talked easily, and he prodded their conversation with innocuous questions.

When their bus stop arrived, she said, "Oh, what a fast trip! Seems like we just got on the bus."

They stepped down and stood in the street. She seemed reluctant to leave, so he suggested, "Look, it's early. Would you join me for a drink? After all, it's happy hour all over Washington."

She smiled, relieved. "I'd love to, but there's no place nearby, except for that awful bar across the street."

JB turned to leave. "Oh well, maybe we can make it another time."

She hurriedly spoke, "I live just down the street. Why don't you come by, and I'll see what I have."

"That would be nice. Why not?"

They walked together to her apartment.

JB heard the nervousness and excitement in her voice and noted the trembling of her hands as she fixed the drinks. He walked over to her, put his hand over hers, and said, "Let me fix the drinks; you're going to break the glasses."

She laughed nervously, and when JB didn't remove his hand, she turned to face him.

He looked into her face, leaned closer, and kissed her gently upon her lips. He pulled his face away, and she continued standing there with her mouth half open, her eyes half closed. He heard her breathing accelerate, so he kissed her again, harder.

JB took command at just the right moment. He placed his hand on the back of her neck, tenderly massaging as he sympathetically observed how tense she was. "Mary, you have a whole month's worth of tension there."

"Yes, I suppose I do."

"It just happens I'm a real expert in giving back rubs."

The room seemed to heat up ten degrees before they reached the couch.

After they each took a few sips of scotch, JB placed the glasses on the coffee table and motioned for her to turn and lie down, first removing her shoes. He began lightly pressing the heels of his hands on each side of her neck and rubbing in symmetric oval strokes. As the muscles relaxed, he lifted his palms and moved lower on each side of her spine, just a few inches.

She whispered, "Oh, that feels exquisite."

Lower then lower. . . .

"Where have you been all my life?" she sighed.

She turned from under him and enclosed him with her arms.

JB moved his arms around her and they embraced tightly, prolonging their kiss. The kiss turned passionate, and she began stroking his body with her hands.

JB was rock hard, and she felt him through their clothes. She pushed hard against him.

JB stroked her buttocks and pulled her against him, moving her from side to side. He relaxed his grasp, and she continued moving against him. He continued kissing her and began to remove her clothes.

She unbuttoned his shirt and was trying to unbutton his trousers. When she was naked, he stood and removed his trousers. She groaned when she saw his hugeness and reached for him. JB pressed her down onto the couch and lay down beside her. She measured him with her hands, moving from the base to the tip of his rigidity. Her feathery touch increased his craving, and he saw longing in her eyes. She whispered huskily, "I don't even know you! What am I doing?"

He gazed into her eyes and, by degrees, he persistently whetted her ecstasy until he saw consent, then acceptance. Finally she yielded to his prolonged stimulation.

Their bodies were as one. They lay, locked together, gasping for air, sweaty from their exertions, and the night went on and on.

JB lay on his back, wide awake, thinking.

She awoke, cuddled closely against his warm, naked body. She kissed his body, just above his left breast, tasting the salt of the dried perspiration from their sweaty night of lovemaking. She reached down to fondle him and whispered, "How about one to start the day?" and they made love again in the early morning darkness.

They arose together, showered, shared a cup of coffee, then hurried to the bus stop.

They left the bus together, and JB told her, "I'm finished at noon today. Why don't we meet for lunch?"

She replied, "It's such a bad neighborhood. I never go outside our building for lunch. Why don't you come to my office at noon, and I will have lunch sent in from our kitchen?"

"Fine with me," JB responded.

"I'll leave a pass for you at Security. They'll bring you to my office."

JB kissed her then walked quickly away.

He arrived at the FBI building at noon, wearing wire-rimmed glasses which distorted his features, making his face look wide and flat. The security officer at the front entrance gave him a pass and escorted him to her office.

He made mental note of the floor plan of the building and noted the director's corner office at the end of the hallway on her floor.

She greeted him warmly and led him into a small lounge adjacent her office.

During lunch JB prodded her with innocent questions about the daily routine inside the FBI building. He learned the director normally left the building late at night, always accompanied by three bodyguards.

JB probed further. "Doesn't all this make you nervous? All these guards and secrecy?"

"Oh, one is always inside the director's office. The other two stay in the two offices on either side of the hallway. I see one of the guards occasionally. His office is between mine and the director's, and he comes through my office to the lounge for his short breaks."

They continued talking, and JB changed his questions, asking her more personal questions about herself and questions about her office routine.

"Director Simpson is away today. He'll be back tomorrow but then he's gone again next week, conducting a seminar in Quantico. I must be here every day to handle his correspondence, but there's not much for me to do."

"Great," JB replied. "Why don't we have lunch again tomorrow; enjoy the early afternoon together."

"That would certainly shorten the workday," she laughingly replied.

JB saw her eyes glazing over with desire.

She moved closer and spoke. "How about another back rub session tonight? I'm feeling a bit tense again. . . . "

"It's possible."

She continued. "I want you there when I get home. Just thinking of you will make this a long afternoon."

JB's visitor pass expired at 1400, so he quickly kissed her when the security guard knocked on her office door. He accompanied the guard to the security station, turned in his pass, and left the building.

JB spent the remainder of the afternoon planning and preparing for the following day. He waited at the corner bus stop and they walked quickly to her apartment.

They spent the night exploring and loving.

The next morning, JB rode downtown with her, kissed her good-bye, and told her, "I'll be there at noon. Make it a light lunch so we can have more time together."

She squeezed his hand. "I'll be waiting for you; don't be late."

JB arrived precisely at noon, took his security pass, and followed the guide to her office.

She greeted him warmly and led him into the large, plush inner office. They embraced and she breathlessly pushed him away. "Let's eat quickly, I've been thinking of you all morning, and I'm aching for you."

She dialed the telephone switchboard. "I'll be away until two; please hold my calls." Her back was turned toward JB, and she failed to notice his hand drop the small capsule into her glass of iced tea.

Moments later, while sipping the iced tea, she complained, "I'm feeling strange and dizzy; it must be love."

JB reached over to pat her hand and caught her head falling forward, preventing injury to her face. She collapsed, out cold. He carried her across the office and laid her on the leather couch. She would be unconscious for at least three hours, more than enough time for him to execute his plan.

JB inched open the inner-office door which led to the adjacent office and peeked through the narrow opening. The director's bodyguard sat facing the hallway, watching through the one-way mirrored wall. JB removed the ballpoint pen from his shirt pocket, carefully aimed the point toward the bodyguard, pressed the firing button, and hit the agent in the back of his neck.

The bodyguard slumped back in his chair, paralyzed, then dead from the poisonous dart fired from the innocent-looking writing instrument. JB slipped into the room, crawled across the floor to the dead guard, checked for a pulse, making certain he was dead. JB then crawled to the door leading to the director's office, stood up, and slightly opened the door.

The director sat in his office chair, his back toward JB, looking out his office window toward the Capitol.

Another bodyguard was standing alongside the director, also looking out of the office window.

JB reloaded the pen and shot the guard in the side of his neck. He slumped to the floor.

The director looked alarmingly at the dead guard.

JB edged into the room, tiptoed over to the director, leaned down, and whispered into the director's ear, "Make one movement, make any noise, and you're dead."

The director stiffened but remained quiet, not moving.

JB pushed the chair from behind the director's desk and guided the director, still in his rolling chair, out of his office into the adjacent one.

The director's eyes widened when he saw the bodyguard slumped in the chair.

JB wore what looked like a western style belt. In reality, the belt unfolded into a long leather strap with which he tied up the director. Then, covering the director's mouth with a piece of wide tape, he held an inhaler under his nose.

The director held his breath. JB punched him in the kidney, forcing him to gasp for air.

He inhaled just enough and lost consciousness almost immediately.

He went back into the director's office; crossed to the opposite door leading to the third guard's office; cracked the door; quickly used his pen, and returned to the director.

Using another inhaler, JB revived the director.

The director's eyes fluttered open, blinked a few times, then focused on JB.

He watched the director's look of uncertain questioning change to recognition, then hardness. JB smiled; took his hand from his coat pocket; and unfolded his fingers to show two vials, each with a needle attached. He selected one of the vials, pulled up the director's shirt sleeve, jabbed the needle into the director's arm, and emptied the vial. The vial contained a low dosage of LSD in saline solution.

The director's torso lurched against the leather straps, his head shot backwards, and his eyes rolled upward. His scream came out as a grunt through the adhesive tape over his mouth. The spasm lasted fifteen seconds, then the director slumped forward, his face sweaty and pale.

The director looked up as JB pulled the tape from his mouth. Some of the director's mustache came away with the tape and caused him to grunt again from the pain.

"The first jolt was to get your attention. This other vial contains a modified version of thiopental sodium and will help you tell me what I want to know. In the event it doesn't work, I have several more vials containing other variations of sodium pentothal and more of that delightful LSD you just finished enjoying."

The director strained against the leather strap and said, "I have a gut-feeling that you were responsible for the disappearance of my two agents in San Francisco."

"You're correct, Mr. Director, and one of your agents told me all about you and your plan."

The director scornfully replied, "I don't believe you. All of us are trained to resist interrogation and die before breaking."

"You cynical son of a bitch! You're making a serious miscalculation. The will to survive is stronger and more logical than any computer or training program. The mind can be trained and programmed to do many things but cannot be forced to kill itself. You will answer my questions!"

The director did not respond.

JB continued, "I want the names of everyone involved in your plan to control the United States government."

The director sat, without speaking, looking at JB.

JB removed the cover from the needle, then injected the solution into the director's arm. JB pulled up a chair and sat down, facing him.

The director's facial features relaxed, and his head leaned over toward his shoulder.

JB asked again, "Tell me the names of everyone involved in your plan to control the United States."

The director remained silent.

JB understood what was happening. The director had systematically practiced being interrogated while under the influence of sodium pentothal and was trained to block out all speech while under the influence. JB removed the vials from his other coat pocket, selected the vial with a black cover over the needle, and held it up for the director to look at. Then he removed the cover, pushed the needle into the director's arm, and injected the liquid.

The sloe-eyed, relaxed expression on the director's face turned to a tense, wide-eyed, frightened stare. JB injected a placebo of a deadly poison commonly used by agents to commit suicide. The director's mind and body was fooled into thinking it was fast approaching death. The spasmodic jerking of the involuntary muscles confirmed the deadly symptoms, and his heart stopped beating. The director gasped for air, his face turning blue from lack of blood circulation and oxygen. JB calmly selected another vial, this one with a white cap over the needle. He removed the cap and injected the contents into the director's arm.

The spasmodic jerking stopped; the director's heart resumed beating normally, and, after a few moments of violently gasping for air, he resumed breathing normally as well.

JB sat quietly, watching the director try to regain his composure. Then came the telling signs of panic and fear. JB thought to himself, *I've penetrated his subconscious.* He reached into his coat pocket for another vial, took it out, and held it up in front of the director's eyes.

The director lurched backward when he saw the black cover over the vial's needle. Sweat beaded on the director's brow, his right eyelid ticked nervously, uncontrollably; tears starting to gather in his eyes.

JB pulled the black cover from the needle and sat, looking at the director.

The director's subconscious mind took control, telling him the contents of the vial would kill him this time.

He was startled and lurched backward again when JB spoke. "Do you remember my question?"

The director's eyes never left the needle, and he slowly nodded yes.

"Well then, is it necessary for me to repeat my question? Should I put down this needle and pick up a writing pen?"

The director continued nodding his head slowly up and down, yes.

JB replaced the black cap.

The director's eyes followed JB's hand, and relief flooded across his face when the needle was placed on the table, still in full view.

JB took a pen and a small writing pad from his inside coat pocket and sat, waiting for the director to speak.

The director spoke, lifelessly. "The vice president or, I mean, the new president."

"Senator Anros.

"Senator Bimert.

"Senator Berlow.

"Senator Vikering.

"Senator Sterland.

"Senator Peters.

"Senator Roadley.

"Senator Yelloway.

"Senator Johnbury.

"Senator Transcott.

"Senator Yowdall.

"Senator Conway.

"Representative . . . . "

On and on, the list grew. The director recited the names; twelve senators, four representatives, an admiral of the Navy and a general of the Army, both members of the joint chiefs, the director's two top assistants, the director of the Federal Reserve Bank and his assistant, five CEOs of large vital corporations and investment banking houses, two university presidents, and several names from wealthy old-line American families.

The director droned on and on.

JB listed name after name, and as the list grew, he felt bile rising from his stomach, making him feel like throwing up.

The names came slower. Obviously the director was thinking hard to recall all.

Fifteen minutes passed before the director stopped talking.

JB stared incredulously at his notebook. It was full of names, page after page of popular public figures and American heroes. He looked at the director and asked, "Yourself?"

The director nodded yes.

JB almost whispered, "What's your plan after taking over the U.S. government?"

"We've commenced infiltrating other countries. We have agents in high places in France, West Germany, Japan, and the United Kingdom. I do not know names of any agents involved in those infiltrations."

"I want the name of your control in Moscow."

"There is no control in Moscow."

"Who do you work for?"

"The Cartel."

"What cartel?"

"The Cartel of Moneta."

"What is The Cartel of Moneta?"

"It is a group of men who control the world, politically and economically. The group perpetuates itself, and when I gain control here, I will be nominated for the next vacancy."

"Tell me more about them."

"The group was responsible for World War One and World War Two. They set up the confrontation between the United States and Japan, to bring the United States into the war, and they eliminated President Roosevelt because he would not use the atomic bomb on Japan. Stalin decided that he would rule the Soviet union under his own plan, so they eliminated him. A top civil rights leader failed to follow orders so he was eliminated. The president's brother will go. A middle eastern leader will go. The Shah will go. The list goes on and on. The group was formed in 1914 in Zurich and used

158

World War One to gain international economic control. They meet once each year, always in Zurich."

"Who are they?"

"I don't know."

"Where are they located?"

"I'm not sure. I'm called to Zurich once each year for a briefing. All I can tell you is they're becoming impatient."

"Impatient over what?"

"Impatient with our progress. Your president was a big stumbling block, and his close advisors, especially his doctor friend, have been uncontrollable. We'll move ahead now that we've replaced the president, and his doctor friend has been taken care of."

"What do you mean, 'taken care of'?"

"We finally found him. He's no longer a problem."

"What happened to the doctor?"

"Read the newspapers tomorrow. You'll find his funeral date."

Doctor Johnson hadn't returned JB's telephone call the day before. Now JB realized there would be no more telephone calls.

JB took a vial from his coat pocket, removed the red cover from the needle, and injected the contents into the director's arm. "This is the real stuff Mr. Director. Good-bye."

The director's eyes bulged, his heart stopped beating, and his face turned blue. He was dead within seconds.

JB went back into the adjacent office.

Mary was still unconscious on the couch. JB surveyed the room, looked at Mary and thought, *Good-bye Mary, you are a lovely lady; you've done much for your country as well.*

He dialed Security. "Please send a guard to Mr. Simpson's office to escort a guest."

The guard knocked on the door.

JB opened the door, turned, and spoke into the room, "Good-bye, Mary. Thank you for lunch, and I'll see you this evening."

He walked through the doorway, and, putting on his glasses, gestured for the guard to lead the way.

He passed through the security checkpoint and walked away from the FBI building. It would be hours before the director was found. By then JB would be long gone from Washington.

The Chloral anesthetized Mary until mid-afternoon, and she lay in a stupor for some time before she sobered. In her dazed condition, she momentarily misconceived JB's absence, expecting him to appear at any moment. Her mind gradually cleared, and by four o'clock, the reality of the situation penetrated her confusion. She was infuriated and flustered as she dialed Security, and when she heard, "Mister Biloxi left the building at 1240," she procrastinated for only a moment before she summoned Security to her office.

They found the director shortly thereafter. At that moment, JB was leaving St. Louis en route to Dallas. By the time confusion settled into action, it was half past eight in the evening. JB landed in Albuquerque long before agents were in place at the major airports.

He left Albuquerque by bus at midnight and reached Phoenix the following morning. JB took a taxi to the business airport adjacent Phoenix International. He worked his way through the receptionist to Roger's office, where he filled out a job application. JB outlined extensive military fighter pilot experience in his application and convinced the office manager to put the application on Roger's desk.

Later in the day, Roger came into his office, picked up his mail, and went into his private office.

Looking through his mail, he noticed the job application, read through it, and felt a chill run up his spine. He continued reading, realizing he was reading an application that outlined his own personal experience.

Roger reread the application. There was no way the applicant could've flown in the same groups with Roger without his knowing the man. He looked again at the man's name. He had never flown with anyone named Biloxi. He looked at the man's local address. The man was staying at a downtown hotel. He looked up the hotel's telephone number, dialed the number, and asked for Jim Biloxi. As he said the name, it hit him. "Jim Biloxi, JB!!!" After two rings, the call was answered. "Hello."

"Hello, Mr. Biloxi. I'm calling about your job application."

JB recognized Roger's voice. "Well, thanks for calling. I would appreciate a chance to talk to you."

"Sounds good. Why don't you come by tomorrow morning. I would have you come by now, but I have an urgent appointment."

"Tomorrow at 1000 will be fine," JB replied.

They hung up their telephones.

JB left his hotel room, went down the elevator across the hotel lobby, and walked across the street to wait.

Ten minutes later, a car stopped at the curbside. He looked into the car, saw Roger, and got in.

Roger pulled away from the curb, entered traffic, and drove north on Central Avenue.

Neither spoke for a few moments. JB broke the silence, "The doctor is gone."

"I know. I read it in this morning's newspaper. The news article said that he died of a heart attack."

"That's pure bullshit. They found him and murdered him."

"The biggest headlines were for the director of the FBI. Someone got into his office and killed him along with his three bodyguards. Actually the articles said cause of death was a heart attack, but he was being tortured and probably died from stress." Roger looked at JB and continued, "Would you know anything about what happened to the director?"

"I know all about it. I killed the son-of-a-bitch and his three guards! It wasn't a heart attack, it was our red devil vial that put him away. I learned plenty before he died, and we've got a big, big problem."

JB had watched the television news while waiting for Roger to call. All hell had broken loose in Washington because of the FBI director's death.

"What are we going to do?" asked Roger.

"I need to get back to check on the president. Then we need to assemble our group, review what I've uncovered, and plan our attack. I've made a list of names for you. The names on the list work for a Council and are dedicated to gaining international political control. It is our charge to eliminate the people on the list, to identify and locate the Council, and to rid the world of the Council's members.

"When and where do you want to meet?"

"I'll need a few days. Let's plan to meet two weeks from today. Have the others in Phoenix, and I'll let you know where we'll gather. Now, can you get me to San Francisco by 2100 tonight?"

"We can leave anytime you want."

"I'm ready now. I need to make a telephone call before we leave."

CHAPTER SEVENTEEN

JB walked down the hill, past the signora's darkened house, feeling like he was home. He skirted the bistro, not wanting to be seen, and walked up the waterfront to his house. His house was dark, but the adjacent house had a light showing from the kitchen window. He walked to the rear of his house, then across to the house next door. He didn't spot the sergeant, but he knew the sergeant watched.

JB reached for the door handle and heard the sergeant. "Welcome back, JB."

He hesitated, then spoke toward the darkness, "Is everything okay here?"

"Everything is going fine. In fact it has been remarkable. The signora spends many hours each day with the president, bathing him and exercising his muscles. Two days ago the president took a big turn for the better. Go on in; let the doctor tell you about it."

The signora worked at the kitchen sink. She looked up, saw JB, and her face broke into a broad smile, "Oh, JB, welcome home."

He walked quickly over to her, hugged her warmly, and they kissed a hello.

Doctor John walked into the room, saw JB, and hurried over to shake hands. "JB, we've got great news! I had almost given up hope for the president's recovery. Two days ago when I checked him in the morning, his pupils were no longer dilated and his muscles were relaxed. He's no longer catatonic. In fact yesterday, when I tested his vision, his eyes followed my light and he turned his head."

He curiously watched the signora while John was explaining the president's condition.

She resumed cleaning the dishes in the kitchen sink.

JB and John went to the president's room. The room was lighted by a muted night light, and they saw the president sleeping peacefully.

John sat down beside the bed, turned, and whispered, "I want to sit here for awhile, monitor his pulse, and watch for facial expressions that will indicate his mind is working while he sleeps."

JB quietly left the room, closing the door. He went into the kitchen and noticed the signora secretively watching him. "Signora Boronio, you look radiant tonight. Why don't you tell me what's going on?"

"Come over here so we can talk quietly."

JB walked over to the kitchen sink and stood next to her.

"I hope you will understand when I tell you I've been helping Dr. John tend to the president. Each day I bathe the president, change his bed clothes, change the bed linen, and Dr. John taught me the proper ways to exercise the president's legs and arms. Other times I sit and watch the president to give Dr. John a rest. I talk to the president and I sing to him. I've spent many hours alone with the president, and I think he is learning to recognize me. While exercising his legs and arms, I feel the muscles trying to work with me. Last Monday I came here after I finished selling the fish. Guido and Carmine came along with me. We ate lunch with Dr. John, and then Guido and Carmine convinced Dr. John to take a rest from watching the president. The three of them walked down to the fishing beach, and Guido gave Dr. John a ride in a dory. They were gone for almost three hours. Well after they left the house, I went to the president's room to exercise his legs and arms. I worked with him for half an hour. Then I bathed him. While I was bathing him, I could feel his muscles relaxing and vibrating. He no longer was tense. I couldn't believe my eyes! As I washed his body, he . . . , he . . . , began to grow. I watched him grow very hard. I didn't know what to do so, I just watched him. Yesterday he got hard again. Do you think I should tell Dr. John?"

"Yes; what happened today?"

"The same thing."

"Signora, I think we should tell Dr. John. The president is responding to you which indicates his senses are working."

JB went to the president's room, opened the door slightly, and beckoned for John to come out of the room.

John followed JB into the kitchen.

JB nodded to the signora. She shook her head no and turned away.

"John, the signora is embarrassed to tell you what happened with the president. Three days ago, while bathing him, he became erect. Since then, each time she bathes him, he becomes tumescent. Also she noticed a positive response from his muscles whenever she exercises his legs and arms."

John looked at the signora.

She stood with her back towards them, her head slightly bowed.

John stepped over to her, "Signora, please, don't feel that you've done anything wrong. The president has made a rapid recovery this week, and

I'm sure it's because his subconscious started working in a normal way. The president is still a young, virile man, and I'm not surprised he reacted to your touching him. After all you're a lovely and desirable woman."

She turned her head, looked at the doctor and JB, smiled shyly, and said, "Perhaps I touched him a little too lovingly, but then he is a handsome man with a strapping body."

John squeezed her shoulder and patted her. "Signora, your loving touches accomplished more than my modern medicine. Perhaps we have our president back. Now we need to find out how far he's come and how far we have to go."

The signora picked up her shawl, said good night to JB and Dr. John, and left the house.

JB spoke with John for a few moments; then he too left the house and hurried up the hill to catch the signora.

She stood in the shadows, near the corner of her house. He heard her call to him, whisperingly, "JB, over here."

He walked into the shadows to join her.

The signora raised her face to his and they kissed, fiercely, and yet tenderly. Hand in hand, they quietly walked through the shadows to the shed behind her house.

It was almost dawn when JB returned home. He heard the click click signal from the sergeant hidden away in the shadows.

JB fell into his bed, bone tired and drained from the past few hours.

He awakened the next morning with a ray of sun shining through the bedroom window into his eyes. He moved quickly out of bed, shaved and showered, then went next door to see Dr. John.

They sat at the kitchen table sipping coffee.

"His recovery is progressing quickly. I can't tell you if or when he'll regain his speech, but he was awake and alert when I first checked him this morning. He moved his hands and arms, and his eyes followed me around the room, and he ate Signora Boronio's oatmeal. I'm going to get him into a wheelchair today and take him outside. Staying in bed has sapped his stamina. We need to get him moving around."

The doctor was excited and JB was relieved, thinking to himself, *This is as close to a miracle as I've seen in my lifetime.*

He left the doctor and went outside to find the sergeant.

He searched the area and the houses but was unable to locate the sergeant. He sighed and turned to return to the house.

"JB, you looking for me?" The sergeant materialized from behind a tree.

He shook his head. "You amaze me, Sergeant. I tried every trick you taught me; nothing worked."

"Perhaps I held back a few," the sergeant chuckled. "What's up?

164

"It looks like the president will make it. How much he'll recover, we can't tell, but I think we've pushed our luck keeping him here this long. We'll be moving again, soon as Dr. John gives his okay."

"I'm ready anytime."

"By the way, how're you feeling?"

"I've been fine since Dr. Protect did the surgery. No pain and I'm eating okay."

"Sergeant, I think you should know Dr. Johnson is dead."

The sergeant narrowed his eyes but remained silent.

"They finally found him and killed him. Officially it was a heart attack, but I'm sure they tried to extract information from him."

The sergeant remained silent.

"If it's any consolation, the man responsible for the doctor's death is no longer alive. In fact I used the heart stopping drugs exactly as you taught me and was able to learn a great deal before I killed him. With the doctor gone, we must go on alone. I have contact with the rest of my group, and I've arranged for a meeting. We may never clean up this mess, but we've got to try."

JB returned and found the doctor on the front porch. The president sat in a wheelchair, the doctor alongside.

The president's eyes tracked JB.

The signora came out onto the porch carrying a tray with coffee for all, then turned to the president. "Oh, how wonderful! You look fine, Mr. President. I'm going to fix you a treat, my special lemonade."

She turned, leaving the porch, going back into the house. The president adoringly watched her leave and sat looking at the door until she returned with the lemonade drink.

She held the glass, put the straw between his lips, and patiently waited for him to drink.

All eyes were on the president, and JB heard the sigh of relief from Dr. John when they saw the president sucking the lemonade through the straw.

The president looked up at them, then took another pull on the straw, enjoying the sweet drink.

Dr. John explained, "We must not overdo this. Let's take the president back to his bed. We'll get him up again after lunch."

The next two days passed quickly. JB was sitting alone most of the time, consulting the sergeant about the coming move.

The signora watched over the president like a mother hen, and Dr. John stood back and watched the president's progress, amazed at his resilience.

On the third day, JB placed a wooden rocking chair on the front porch.

The signora wheeled the president out onto the porch that morning, and both of them immediately noticed the rocking chair. The president turned his eyes toward the signora, pleading.

The signora smiled and held out her hands.

The president raised his arms, grasped her hands with his hands, and with her help, stood up from the wheelchair.

She helped him turn his body sideways and held his hands tightly as he sank back into the rocking chair.

The president sat quietly for a moment, then he began to slowly rock, back and forth. He smiled and tried to talk, emitting a grunting sound.

The signora reached to her apron pocket for her handkerchief, then wiped away the tears of joy spilling down her face. She clasped her hands and stood, head tilted to one side, adoringly watching the president rock weakly.

JB sat with Dr. John. "Doctor, we need to move. It will be a long drive. When can we leave?"

"I hate to expose the president to an arduous trip, but he should be able to handle it. We can go tomorrow."

JB left the houses and went up the hill to a telephone. Returning home, JB saw Guido and Dr. John walking toward the fishing beach.

JB quietly entered the house and heard the sounds coming from the bedroom.

JB sat at the kitchen table and waited.

Half an hour passed before the signora came into the kitchen. She looked surprised to see him sitting at the kitchen table. She smiled shyly and asked, "How long have you been here?"

"For a while," he answered.

She saw the sadness in JB's eyes as he spoke. "It's been a while since I've heard a mother singing a lullaby, and it was even more beautiful in your language. Don't stop what you're doing; you'll have him walking and talking before the month's out."

"Although he's a young and virile man, he still needs tender loving care. I will do anything to help him, and I feel in my heart and soul that I can instill my love into his soul and help him recover. Right now he's sleeping contentedly as a happy, well-fed baby. I hope you understand."

"Signora, I feel good just looking at your happy face. I must agree, your patient and gentle loving can only help him. I also admit, I feel just a touch of jealousy, wishing it were me you're giving your love. But then again, we've had our times together that I will never forget."

"Thank you, JB. Our togetherness will always have a special place in my heart. I will always remember you as my very best lover, and I must admit, I'll always be comparing our loving to any I find."

"I hadn't intended to tell you the president is leaving tomorrow. I think now it's important for you to know, and perhaps you may choose to come along with us. It would certainly be okay with me."

"Where shall you go?"

"I can't tell you exactly. We'll still be in Italy, about two days away from here by car."

"I will arrange for my young ones to stay with Lucia and Ruby. I want to be with the president. I think I can help him, and I feel he appreciates my love and caring."

"Good. It's settled. We'll be leaving before daylight tomorrow. You should be here by five o'clock. I'll tell Guido we're leaving, and I'll arrange to contact him often, so you'll know all is well with your family."

"Thank you, JB, you always seem to do the right things for me. I hope you realize I would die for you if need be."

JB stood and embraced the signñora, holding her tightly then kissing her softly on her cheeks, eyes, and lips.

He stepped back, held her at arms length, both of them shaken by the electricity of passion passing between them, leaving them breathless. He smiled. "Whew, you are pure dynamite. Get out of here; take care of your household and get back here before five."

She choked back a sob, took a deep breath, and smiled. "You are catastrophic for me. I have no resistance against you, nor would I want any. Your mere touch excites me; your embraces and kisses make me instantly ready for your love. I long for our next time together." She walked past him, out the kitchen door, and across the back yard toward the side street before turning and tossing him a kiss.

Guido helped JB and Dr. John pack and ready the supplies and equipment to be taken on their trip.

The sergeant remained out of sight, constantly on guard against any possible intruders.

JB arranged to communicate with Guido, and Dr. John told the president about the upcoming trip.

The president alertly watched Dr. John's eyes but made no effort to talk. The president seemed relaxed, alert, and nodded his head yes. Doctor John then asked, "Do you wish to have the signñora come along?"

The president smiled wistfully and again nodded his head yes.

John thought to himself, *His recovery is remarkable. At this rate, he'll be walking soon.*

JB slept fitfully, finally gave up trying to sleep, and got out of his bed at 0400. He dressed, went next door, and found Dr. John up and waiting.

Shortly after four, the signñora appeared, carrying a basket of freshly prepared food for their trip. She served them hot coffee and freshly baked bríoche.

He heard the vans arrive and told the group to prepare to leave.

JB went outside and walked over to the first van. Josef stood alongside the van, waiting for JB. "Good morning, Josef. I feel much better about the trip with you driving. Thank you for coming."

"Cosmo told me secrecy is a must. I want to help you as I know the Old Man would've helped you. The other van is driven by the Old Man's valet. Where are we headed?"

"The Anastacio farmhouse where we stopped on our way to see the Old Man, when you picked me up in Zurich. Cosmo has told them to expect us."

They loaded the supplies and equipment into the second van and the president into the first. The signora and Dr. John rode with the president. The sergeant rode with Josef, and JB accompanied the president.

They drove away before 0500, headed down the beach, away from town, circled back, and turned north on the highway, just south of town.

They drove steadily north, skirted Naples, and turned inland toward Rome.

They passed west of Rome during the early afternoon, heading due north.

Hours later they approached Florence, and Josef led the two-van convoy to a deserted farm.

The sergeant immediately disappeared into the darkness. They ate a cold supper from the food prepared by the signora then slept.

They arose before dawn, refueled the vans from the gas drums in the barn, and resumed their trip north.

They reached their destination in the late afternoon.

The old farmer and his wife came out of the house to greet them, and JB saw the young woman standing in the kitchen doorway. Susan did not yet know what was happening, and JB saw the surprised look on her face as he walked toward her.

She flung the door open and ran to him. She ran into his open arms, and he held her tightly, trying to soothe her sobbing."

"Oh, JB, JB, I can't believe you're here. I thought you had forgotten about me."

"No, my dear. I knew you were safe here. I've been busy. We've brought the president here for his safety. I'll be leaving soon, and I want you to come with me. You can become an important part of our plan."

She had a puzzled look on her face as JB continued. "For the moment, though, let's get the president settled and make certain he's comfortable."

They carried the president into the house, settled him into a bedroom, and then unloaded the supplies and equipment from the other van. JB smiled when he saw the Madonna statuette sitting on the fireplace mantel. Josef parked the vans inside the barn, and the valet set about helping unpack the supplies.

Josef and the sergeant discussed the president's security, and the sergeant accepted Josef's offer to help protect the president against intruders.

JB stood in the dark shadows, waiting for the sergeant to appear. He stalked the sergeant through the vineyard and toward the barn. JB assumed the sergeant was headed to the barn loft where he would have an observation point to watch the entire area around the farmhouse.

JB heard a slight rustling noise and immediately knew the sergeant had outfoxed him. Without turning, JB spoke quietly into the darkness, "I needed to talk to you, so I thought I would check your alertness at the same time."

The stern, fatherly voice came back, "I take my job very seriously. I had you from the time you slid out through your window. It was easy to anticipate you. After all, I trained you."

JB chuckled, "Not well enough to take the master."

"What's on your mind, JB?"

"It appears the president is recovering nicely. This farm should be a safe place for awhile. That mess I mentioned to you, it's a long list of names, people we need to eliminate, and I must get started. I'm planning to leave tomorrow, and I'm taking Susan with me. She's a fugitive now, so I'll arrange another identity for her. She's a strong-willed lady and wants to avenge her father's death. She will fit nicely into my plan. The signora, Dr. John, and the valet will stay. They will take care of the president. You and Josef will protect the group from any intruders. I'll be in contact with David soon and arrange for him to visit you to check your condition. From what he tells me, he has probably figured a way out for you. It is important . . . . "

"He's already done more than I had hoped for. Anything further will be a gift from heaven." The sergeant continued, "Josef is quite a man. Never had any formal training, but he's a protector by instinct. I'm glad he's on our side. Between the two of us, the president will be well protected."

"It's been a long road for you, sergeant, but this is where it comes home to roost. All of your experience and training has been for this one exercise, to protect the president. We're both doing what is meant to be. Thanks to you, I feel prepared for the job ahead."

JB extended his hand into the darkness, shook hands with the sergeant, then heard the whisper of movement as the sergeant disappeared. He retraced his steps and returned to his room in the farmhouse. He noticed the scent of Susan's body lotion, undressed quickly, slipped into the bed, and found her waiting. She pulled him hard against her and sighed, her head buried into the crook of his shoulder and neck. He held her tightly and gently stroked her naked back, feeling her tense muscles begin to relax. He heard her muffled whisper, "I'm sorry, JB. I needed to be with you."

He whispered in return, "We're together now, and we'll stay together, at least for awhile. I need your help, and I feel that you want to be a part of what must be done. I'll tell you about it tomorrow when we're on our way back to the United States. For now I want to lose myself in your love."

Susan pushed him over onto his back, and, while holding him with one hand, began kissing her way from his throat down over his body. She kissed his shoulder, then his chest, and began running her hand back and forth over his abdomen. She could feel the chill bumps on his body and the rigidity of his stomach muscles, and when she looked, she saw that his eyes were tightly closed. Tears coursed down his cheeks as he thought of Isabel, and he could not stop the shuddering of his muscular body, so he grasped her shoulders and gently nudged her away from him, and she reluctantly let go. When he opened his eyes, she saw the glistening tears. Then he looked at her for a few moments before he pushed her down onto her back and leaned over her, kissing her deeply on her lips.

Their first love was fast and fierce. Their next was gentle and slow, and he heard her mumbling, over and over, "Never leave me, love me. . . . "

Sometime during the night they finally slept, entwined together.

He awoke at five o'clock, his neck aching from having slept in an odd position. His arm encircling her felt numb, her body weight having slowed the circulation.

JB gently shifted his body to relieve the ache in his neck and lifted her left leg up and over his thigh.

She awoke to his feathery kisses, and she felt his morning hardness. Arousal moved through her loins, whetting her need, and she fervently returned his kisses.

Soon she was ready for him, and they made love in the early morning darkness.

CHAPTER EIGHTEEN

The farmhouse was near Biella, not far from the Swiss border. He needed to contact Cosmo but felt he must be comfortably away from the farmhouse in the event the call was traced. The following morning Josef drove JB and Susan across the countryside to the toll highway leading from Lugano to Milano, sped into Milano, and let them out at the train station. They checked into the hotel and JB placed his call. "Cosmo, I need identification papers and passports for me and Susan. Disguise is a must. I'm staying at the Sforsa in Milano."

"Stay in your room, someone will contact you within the hour. Anything else I can do?"

"Not at the moment. I'll be in San Francisco soon, but until then, I need you available to respond as I call. And Cosmo, thanks."

"See you soon," and Cosmo broke the connection.

Shortly the telephone rang.

"Hello?"

"Do you know the Duomo?"

"Yes."

"Do you know the Galleria?"

"Yes."

"Do you know Restaurante de La Scala?"

"Yes, it's across from the opera house."

"Looking at the restaurant, there's a photo shop about half a block to the left. The name is Florenzo Photos. Can you find it?"

"Yes."

"Come immediately. There's a taxi waiting for you around the corner from your hotel, on Via Dante. You should not expect to return to your hotel." The line went dead.

Susan spoke inquiringly. "JB?"

"Forget your clothes. Bring your valuables, we're leaving!"

They found the taxi waiting. JB inquired, "Taxi?"

The driver eyed him suspiciously and asked, "Where are you going?"

"To have our picture taken," JB responded.

"Get in, quickly!"

The taxi turned down the Via Dante, driving toward the Duomo. He dropped them at Piazza del Duomo and pointed toward the Gallaria. They got out and the taxi sped away.

They walked across the Piazza, past the Galleria, and found the opera house. He noted the Restaurante de La Scala across the street from the opera house, and they proceeded down the street to the photo shop.

As he reached to open the door, it opened, and a young man beckoned them inside and quickly closed and locked the door. "Follow me, please." He led them to the rear of the shop and turned. "I am instructed to change your appearance and prepare papers for you. Please, sit down at the dressing table."

They sat, and the young man proceeded to change their hair style and color, then their facial appearances with pliable plastic devices, and instructed them how to insert and remove the colored contact lens. He took photographs, and while they waited, Susan spoke, "The gray tinge makes you look distinguished!"

He smiled. "Before I thought you were lovely. Now you look exquisite. I love your green eyes!"

She stopped smiling and grasped his hand, "JB, I'm scared!"

He squeezed her hand and replied, "You wouldn't be normal if you didn't feel anxiety. I feel it too. But we've got a job to do, and we need time. Our new appearances will get us that time. Don't lose faith in me!"

"Never, JB. You are my faith!"

He hugged her close, and they sat on the sofa, waiting for the young man to return.

They traveled by train to Zurich. They checked into the Hotel Tivoli, and JB promptly made their reservations for New York. He withdrew 50,000 dollars in U.S. travelers checks from his Swiss bank, and the following morning, they left Zurich, bound for New York.

They arrived late in the afternoon and checked into the Pierre.

The following evening he left Susan at the hotel and traveled alone by train to Washington.

It was a misty, rainy evening, and JB stared out of the rain-streaked window, as the train raced through the darkness toward Washington. He summed it up in his mind. "Ten of the twelve are senate committee members, and five of the eight are house committee members, but five innocents will die." Nine of the charlatan senators were members of the Senate Appropriations Committee, and the four targeted Congressmen were members of the House Appropriations Committee. The Federal Reserve Director would attend the senate committee meeting, and his assistant would attend the House committee meeting.

He rode in the darkness, conscious-stricken about the impending execution of the innocent committee members, but unrepentant about the fifteen who must be eliminated. He thought of the innocents, *If there's a way to spare them, I hope to find it!*

The House and Senate Appropriations committees would meet on Tuesday, the day before Congress would open its final session of the year. The city brimmed with politicians, lobbyists, groupies, call girls, and vacationers in town for the congressional opening. The hotels were full, and JB had to tip the hotel manager $100 to get a small single room. In his hotel room JB assembled two bombs. An ordinary person would refer to the bombs as plastique, simply because they were malleable. To JB they were much more. TNT with added phosphine creates a frightful bomb, and he felt trepidation as he combined the elements. His hands were steady, and he smiled to himself as the trickle of sweat ran down the side of his face. He shaped the bombs to fit inside the small, round shoe polish cans, then he added the electronic detonators. He would need to have the chemicals to assist the bombs in place before the committee meetings in both the House and the senate chambers at the Capitol.

Early Monday morning, JB parked his rented, unmarked van alongside the other janitorial vans, near the service entrance to the Capitol.

Dressed in gray coveralls and looking like the other cleaners, JB carried his furniture polish and box of polish rags into the House chambers. Using what appeared to be a liquid wax, JB wiped every wooden table and chair on the floor of the House. He wiped the railings, the veneered paneling, and doors that surround the floor area. While wiping the tables, JB unobtrusively placed a bomb on the underside of a table near the middle of the room.

JB finished with the House chambers by ten o'clock that morning. Then he moved to the nearby senate chambers and repeated the process.

JB placed his supplies into the van and drove away.

That afternoon JB checked out of his hotel, rode the train to Philadelphia, and purchased a used car for cash.

JB drove back to the train station and waited for Susan.

She left New York City without checking out of the hotel and rode the train to Philadelphia.

Susan arrived approximately on schedule and went outside the front entrance to the train station.

JB parked the car in a nearby public parking lot, walked to the train station, and waited for Susan.

JB spotted her in front of the station; made eye contact; then turned and walked away, toward the parking lot. She followed, and they drove to a roadside motel between Philadelphia and Washington.

They spent the night at the motel. After checking in, JB telephoned Roger in Phoenix.

"Roger?"

JB heard the calm voice respond, "The others have been contacted, and all will be present at our planned meeting."

JB hung up the telephone, breathed deeply, and sat back into his chair. Susan sat quietly, expectantly, waiting for JB to talk to her.

They drove into Washington early Tuesday morning and left the car in a parking garage near the senate office buildings. They walked to the Capitol. Susan went to the senate chambers, and JB went to the House chambers. He joined the few people, waiting to be admitted to the visitor's gallery to witness the House committee meeting. The doors opened at half past eight, and JB entered with the rest of the group.

The session was called to order precisely at nine o'clock, and the official roll call began. The roll call proceeded rapidly. In another fifteen minutes, JB was ready to leave. The ten names on his list were present.

JB left the visitors' section and walked out of the Capitol toward the Capitol Reflecting Pool and waited for Susan.

He saw her walking quickly toward him.

"Bingo," she said, excitedly. "All present and accounted for."

He turned and looked back at the imposing looking Capitol, took the ballpoint pen from his shirt pocket, and pushed the button.

The explosions were noticeable. People walking on the sidewalks stopped and looked toward the Capitol. Smoke was coming out of the doors and windows, and people were starting to run toward the building.

Inside the two chambers the furniture, the people, everything was incinerated. All of the wood inside the meeting halls was coated with an explosive, highly volatile, flammable polish. The bombs ignited the polish, and the inside of the meeting halls suddenly became 1500 degrees Fahrenheit. Nothing remained except charred remains. The humans inside the chambers were turned into ashes. Sirens sounded. . . .

JB and Susan walked away from the Capitol, to their car in the parking garage and drove away.

All hell broke loose in Washington.

JB and Susan drove for eight hours, stopping near Cincinnati.
They slept that night in a roadside motel.

Early the next morning they traveled through Kentucky and eventually found their way to Memphis where they boarded a train for California.

Two days later they left the train at Elko, Nevada, where JB purchased an old used car from a local used car lot.

They drove west on Interstate 80. At Sacramento they turned south on Interstate 5, past Modesto, and west again on Highway 152 over the Pacheco Pass to Highway 101. Just north of Salinas, they turned west and followed the highway to the Monterey Bay and on around to Monterey.

He parked the car in the single garage and led Susan into the small cottage. He was back where it had almost begun, at his private cottage in Pacific Grove, overlooking the Monterey Bay and the Pacific Ocean. Roger and the others would arrive sometime during the next week, and they could then proceed with their plans to eliminate the remaining implanted agents.

Susan stood, looking out of the large bay window, marveling at the beauty of the blue Pacific Ocean and the distant beaches that swept around the bay. She glanced to her right, toward the small front porch, saw JB, and smiled.

JB was sitting in an old fashioned wooden rocking chair, slowly rocking back and forth, eyes closed, lost in deep thought.

Seven thousand miles away, the president sat on the front porch of the Italian farmhouse, in an old fashioned wooden rocking chair, slowly rocking back and forth, a peaceful smile on his face, and the adoring signora was seated near him, watching his every move.